FIRE AND IRON

Enjoy the stories O'haras

Norman

Stories of fidelity, infidelity and daring commitment by

NORMAN FULLERTON

Fire and Iron; Stories of Fidelity, Infidelity and Daring Commitment

ISBN: 978-1-7777623-0-8

DISCLAIMER

These short stories are works of fiction. The characters, names, incidents, dialogue, and locations, except for Winnipeg, are the product of the author's imagination and experiences. Any resemblance to actual persons or events is coincidental.

TABLE OF CONTENTS

ACKNOWLEDGEMENTS

I relied on the help of family and friends while writing these stories. I want to thank my wife, Jean, son, Kendall and his wife, Marie, my daughter Krista, my brother Timothy, who read the manuscript and offered their valuable opinions. A thanks to Dawn Fullerton who helped to create the Reflection Questions and to all my Beta readers.

I truly value the assistants of my editors, Amelia Wiens and Pat Gerbrandt for their help in shaping the stories and polishing the grammar. They made them better stories.

FIRE AND IRON

Two are better than one, because they have a good reward for their toil.
For if they fall, one will lift up his fellow. But woe to him who is alone
when he falls and has not another to lift him up!
Ecclesiastes 4:9-11 NRSV

Pushing back the sheet and blanket, Margaret Brunet urged her long, slender legs over the side of her single bed. Resting at the edge of the bed for a moment, she combed her fingers through her graying hair and waited for her eyes to adjust to the meager November sunlight making its way into the room.

Dressed in a clean, cotton work dress, she fashioned a scarf about her hair. She carried her tall straight figure with aristocratic poise as her mother had prudently schooled her years ago. Now, that graceful carriage belied her social and economic status. Before leaving the room, she paused before the mirror to brush her hair, noting the tiny tension lines etched across her forehead and the delta-like lines fanning out from the corners of her eyes.

The rhythmic pulse of a diesel engine from the nearby grain elevator, and the sporadic clang of hammer striking steel in her husband's blacksmith shop were distant noises behind her thoughts.

She had long ago quit sleeping with her husband. In fact, she had not thought of him as a husband for years. He was one of those figures that remotely moved in and out of one's life during a day, like a person at the bus stop sharing the same space for a moment, or one with whom a rare verbal exchange takes place, but nothing more. Although they occupied the same house, twenty years of determined pride to block out memories of better times had fashioned a routine of indifference which only on occasion brought the two, now strangers, together.

Lingering momentarily at the kitchen table, nursing her morning cup of hot tea while waiting for its stimulation, she ran her thumbnail along the edges of the faded red and white checker-board pattern on the oilcloth.

"I've got you cornered. Mum!" She recalled the triumph her son expressed, years before, announcing the end of a game of checkers they had played on this table. At first, she had let him win sometimes, but eventually his strategy outshone hers and the games ended with her remaining checkers backed into a corner.

Hmmm… that is not unlike my early relationship with André. She had been the initiator in that relationship, much against her mother's wishes, encouraging André's slow awkward efforts at courtship. It had been both an act of rebellion against her mother and a personal challenge to remake this handsome plodder into something refined and polished. But she had lost the challenge and now André had her cornered too.

Finishing her tea, she glanced wistfully at the pattern of the tea leaves in her cup and then washed up the breakfast dishes before setting off for the Claytons.

Most of the women in Kenton hired Mrs. Swenson to do extra or regular cleaning because they felt ill at ease with Margaret socially if she also cleaned their homes. But, because of Margaret's reputation for cleanliness, and because it was general knowledge she could use the money, she had picked up one or two more jobs since her last child had left home.

Mondays she did washing and ironing for the Claytons, the new Anglican priest in town. It would be a long day, but she liked the cheerful interest Mrs. Clayton took in her and the generous payment she always provided.

"When is the baby due, Mrs. Clayton?"

Margaret pushed the iron across the shirt collar and then neatly arranged the shirt sleeve for pressing.

"Doctor says the beginning of February. Margaret, I do wish you would call me Diane. I'd like to think of you as a friend."

It was this kind of easy charm and acceptance that attracted Margaret to Diane Clayton. "You'll have your hands full when you have two little ones."

"Dave loves children. I do too, Margaret. Pearl is old enough now to give a lot of help with the two little ones. We'll make out ok." Diane talked from the stove where she was stirring the makings of soup for their noon meal.

A cry from the bedroom announced that Johnny was awake from a mid-morning nap and Diane scurried to his room.

Margaret hung the ironed shirt on a hanger and proceeded to the next one, her mind sorting through memories untouched in years. It was like turning over pictures in the family album. She hadn't done that in years either. Some showed details completely forgotten, like an item of clothing or friends that had visited, and others revealed feelings staring out through the eyes or facial expressions. She lingered over a couple of distant memories. But she had grown to prefer the safety of indifference and quickly brought her attention back to the pattern of lines on the shirt.

Later Margaret and Diane talked quietly over lunch, savoring the soup that had simmered invitingly on the stove earlier. Diane confided buoyantly Dave's ideas for new programs in the church and shared some of her own ideas for the women. Margaret felt the cheerful optimism of the younger woman push at the wall she had cautiously erected to block out the memories of André's and her early years. Her eventual comment was quiet but pointed. "What about your nursing?"

"Oh, I'll go back to my nursing career when the children are grown. And as circumstances provide."

"Better keep your nursing up. You never know when you'll have to look after yourself." Latent bitterness edged Margaret's statement.

"True, anything can happen. But Dave and I hope and pray for the best." Diane smiled and then in her disarmingly candid way asked, "Margaret, what happened between you and André?"

Margaret was not prepared for the suddenness of the question. In a small town like Kenton, what happened in homes was ferreted out in the coffee shop and the hockey rink, wherever two people met to talk longer than to exchange pleasantries. Stories were shared, versions compared, the details polished until only skeletons of truth remained. What had happened to the once happy relationship between Margaret and André Brunet had similarly been speculated on for hours and details dove-tailed together, but no one had blundered into asking either Margaret or André directly.

Diane was quick to notice the downcast eyes, the awkward moment of silence. "Margaret, I'm sorry. It was rude of me to pry. I think you are a wonderful person. You've been so good to me. I guess I can't imagine what could go so wrong."

The lines radiating from Margaret's eyes deepened into a slight smile. She was thinking of the simplicity of this girl now, rather than the directness of her question. It was a straightforwardness she had known thirty years ago when she, daughter of the prominent Dr. Cameron, had shocked the community by marrying the son of the village blacksmith.

"I'd better get back to work or I won't finish today," Margaret said, directing her thoughts away from that prison of hurt.

When Margaret walked home later that afternoon, the low lines of the blacksmith shop, slightly sunken roof and the pock marked siding, tarnished and rusted in spots as if ravished by a disfiguring disease, registered clearly in her vision. The small window facing west was darkened by years of smoke. A long crack in the glass glinted in the late afternoon sun.

As she walked by the doors, Margaret noticed they were unlocked, slightly ajar. André's truck was not around. Pulling one door open a little, she timidly looked inside. Vague shapes rested in the darkened interior. She pushed the door open further to let in more light and entered for the first time in more than twenty years. She glanced about furtively as if a trespasser. The place looked distantly familiar. Chains of various lengths still hung off to one side from the rafters. The wall by the window was lined with horseshoes of different sizes. Two horseshoes fastened together along a small piece of flat iron on a board formed a B over the door. Margaret remembered them as brightly polished and prominent. Now, one horseshoe hung askew on the bar, and the piece was covered by soot accumulated over the years. "It takes twice as much luck for a Brunet," André had said when he had pointed them out the first time. Margaret mused over the broken B now and wondered about the luck this symbol had brought.

Piled on the floor towards the back of the shop were mounds of angle iron and bars of various lengths and a pile of wood planks used for building wagon and truck boxes. In the center of the building a large anvil rested on a metal frame adjacent to the forge. Behind the forge a rope and chain hung from a pulley attached to a large central steel "I" beam fastened precariously, it seemed to her, to the two central rafters.

Margaret passed her hand over the black pieces of crushed coal mounded in the center of the forge. Sensing a small amount of heat, she reached down and began to turn the crank fastened to the edge of the forge. A low whirring murmur arose as a breath of air entered the forge. A red glow appeared within the heap of crushed coal. Margaret turned the handle a little faster. Tiny sparks sprung up followed by a reddish blue spurt of flame. Watching the flames for a moment, mesmerized by this sudden miracle of heat, Margaret then let the handle go and walked away.

She approached the soot-covered window, picked up a soiled cloth and wiped the four panes of glass. A splash of sunlight marked the dirty floor in four rectangles separated by a narrow cross-like shadow. Splinters of rainbow light burst from the crack running across one of the glass rectangles. A memory struggled to the surface. In a moment of panic Margaret resisted, but nonetheless it flooded her mind. She sat down on the old swivel chair, stared at the small glow of embers in the forge, as fear tightened stomach and chest.

She felt again the fear that had burned itself into the core of her being.

André, exasperated by his long wait, grabbed her. In her efforts to free herself from his grasp she fell against the plate glass mirror hanging on the wall. Splinters of light burst in her head, glass shattered and fell around her in tiny pieces as she slumped to the floor. Then all was silent for a few seconds. She sat stunned, disbelieving. She glimpsed an ashen André surveying the ruin. Then his voice brought back reality.

"Now look what happened! André had turned away. "Never satisfied! The way I look; what I do; what I have to wear. Always a new idea! Always, always keeping me waiting! Get there on your own. I'm gone!"

He'd stormed out, leaving her to watch the small drops of blood fall on the white dress she had so carefully washed and ironed earlier. She touched her face to determine from where the blood was coming. Those prominent cheekbones, getting her in trouble again! It was her cheek. It must have struck the mirror forcefully when she fell. Shock had set her body trembling; remorse fueled tears, and finally desperate loneliness prompted wrenching sobs.

Later, she was not certain how much later, her body exhausted, she'd struggled to stand, managed to drag herself to the wash basin and dabbed at the bruised and swollen cheek. Then she removed the dress and stumbled to the bed where she collapsed.

*****

A shiver rippled down Margaret's body as she sat on the old chair. Darkness deepened. How could it have come to this? She held her face in her hands as if to hide from the memories of that first meeting.

*****

Her first real meeting with André was at the Valley City Fair. Almost every-one in the Valley attended the fair for some part of its three-day stay. The fairground was crammed with the midway, farm machinery, food vendors, prize cattle, pickles and flowers on display and, of course, people. She and her friends walked the circuit. The mingling odors of a variety of frying foods stimulated their hunger.

At such a moment they'd walked by André standing by a wagon with another young fellow. Both looked really good, dressed in clean overalls and shirts open to reveal an abundance of curly black hair on their broad chests. They might have passed right by had Patsy McCormick not stumbled on an electrical cable stretched on the ground from one tent to another. André had bent over her. Although not really physically helping her, he said in a slow deep voice, "You all right?"

Patsy had acknowledged she was fine, but it was Margaret who suggested, "We're just heading for a place to eat; got any suggestions?"

"Nope," André had replied, "but getting a little hungry myself. How about you, Bill?" His attention had gone to Bill as if he had dismissed the girls some time ago.

Margaret was interested in this guy with the body of a weightlifter and a voice that made her think of muddy water and symphonies. She had seen both fellows around before and knew their names but had never talked to either one. She looked at the girls for encouragement and not seeing refusal went ahead. "Well, why not join us in the looking?" Bill and André had looked at each other and appeared about to refuse, when Margaret spoke again. "Come on; don't be afraid. There are three of us."

Perhaps her subtle challenge was what it took. It was Bill. "Might just as well tag along and see what's to be had."

So, it had all begun in a small hot-dog tent on a warm evening in late July. Margaret, schooled as she was in the best etiquette of her mother's knowledge, was conscious of André's large bites and noisy chewing as he attacked the hot dog. But she had been charmed by his forthright speech, slow and colorful, and his beauty. Yes, beauty was the right word. His smooth face, well-shaped nose, between two eyes of dark liquid and an equally well shaped mouth, crowned with a thick head of dark hair on that well-proportioned muscular body added up to beauty. She had fallen for this stranger that very day.

Neither he nor Bill was about to be too forthcoming on this first occasion, but under the playful prodding of the three girls, he had opened up to share in slow modesty his love for the craft of shaping iron. Bill's comment, "No matter whether it's big or small, André can fashion a damn good plowshare, or a pin-sized shaft," had sent Margaret's mind whirling with the potential of this Adonis.

Margaret had gone out of her way to bump into André on a few occasions after that day. She and Patsy found him and Bill in the café one day after school. Patsy was heading toward their usual corner booth when Margaret bumped her arm and headed for the stools beside André and Bill. André lifted his head from staring into his coffee cup and glanced her way as she straddled the stool and spun to face him. "Long time no see!" she greeted.

His reply startled Margaret and encouraged her considerably. "Oh, I see you high steppin' it to school most ev'ry morning; perdy as a picture!"

"Now from where are you spying on me, André Brunet?" Margaret was pleased at André's last comment.

"Have a little bit of a window right over my work bench. So, I keep track of all the comin' and goin' in town." André clutched his coffee mug with both hands and took another deep slurp of the steaming liquid.

"And when do I get to see where you make all your fancy stuff?" Margaret noticed André's dirty hands and black edged fingernails as she spoke.

If André felt the growing web of attachment between the two, his facial expressions and his voice remained detached. "Come by anytime. Don't wear those perdy dresses. The place ain't too clean." He took two more deep gulps from his coffee mug and then turned to face Bill. "Gotta go, Bill, Clem Shanks wants that truck box finished tonight." With that he pushed his coffee cup away, dug out a quarter and slid it beside the cup. Bill followed. Margaret and Patsy moved together to fill the void, to confer and to order coffee.

In the intervening two weeks before seeing André again, Margaret had gone from resolving to forget André to developing the courage to visit him at his shop. Patsy agreed to accompany her to the smithy shop late one Saturday afternoon. Margaret was curious to see what André really did but was not about to go in there alone. She had prepared her opening line but had not been prepared to see André working with another man. She stopped abruptly at the door. The decreased light from their standing in the door caught the attention of both men.

André, sensing Margaret's hesitation, took the lead for the first time. "Margaret, you come to visit!"

Both girls were drawn in by this welcome and the warm smile on the older man's face. Margaret waited for an introduction, but none was forthcoming. She was conscious she probably intimidated men by her height, her intelligence and her forward approach. "So, this is where you work." She looked around to take in the shadowy shapes of equipment and supplies crowded nearby.

"Right here my boy works. Early from morning to late," the older man replied.

If you don't get introduced, introduce yourself. You are a Cameron. You have nothing to be ashamed of. Her mother's voice instructed her even though not present. "Hello, sir. I'm Margaret Cameron and this is my friend Patsy."

"You Doc Cameron's girl then." His speech was flavoured with a strong French accent. The statement was more an affirmation than a question, but he did raise his heavy eyebrows in an interrogative way. Margaret nodded. She concluded he was André's father.

André had put down his large hammer. "Goin' to show the girls some of our work, Pa," and he reached up and turned on a dirty light bulb. Hanging on a rack were chains of assorted sizes all freshly painted black. There were clevises, hooks and an assortment of other objects, but the things that really caught Margaret's eye were the intricate, ornate trellises and an iron bench with similar designs.

"These are beautiful!" Patsy exclaimed.

André waved a deprecating hand. "Too fancy! Not much call for those around these parts."

André then brought the girls to a shelf and pointed out a tiny carriage of iron, no longer than eight inches, the chassis suspended on tiny springs fastened to a frame with beautifully ornate wheels. The hood of the carriage was delicately fringed with precise detailing. The seats were leather and fastened in places with tiny buttons. It was painted black.

Attached to the tongue of the carriage was a team of horses carved from wood. They were fully harnessed and fastened to the carriage with tiny leather traces. Sets of miniature brass rings hung down from the collar, from the hames and across the flanks of each horse. Margaret reached up to touch the horses and feel the carriage. André brought it down so both girls could hold it and spin the wheels as if to prove it was more than a flat carving.

Margaret remembered Bill's comment about plowshares and pin-sized shafts. She mused as she observed the accuracy and detail. This was a gift as noble and honorable as her gift for mathematics or physics.

Margaret was intelligent, attractive, and ambitious. She had just received her final departmental exam marks, the highest the school had ever recorded. Her parents were prepared to send her for further education wherever she wanted to go after graduating from high school next year. If her grades continued as they had this year, she would be honored as an outstanding student. But what about the André Brunets? Where did they get honoured? Oh, she thought, I suppose André could enter something like this at the Fair. There was always an assortment of crafts there with ribbons attached. But somehow it wasn't the same; not written up in the paper or talked about much. Had André even thought to enter this?

And then she wondered if André had gone to school. She could never remember him being part of the older students. He was older; that she knew for sure but maybe only by five or six years. Was this André's work or his father's? She looked at one man then the other.

The question seemed apparent since the older man replied. "My son, he has the gift of his Grandpre. He was a very good carver." She found the French accent charming and felt the father's pride for his son.

"It's beautiful," Patsy whispered as she handed it back to Margaret.

Margaret returned it to André with the care and delicacy of one handling a sacred relic. "It's wonderful work André. I love it."

"You love it! It's yours." He extended it to Margaret.

"No, André, something so beautiful can only go to someone very special or a member in your family. You can't just hand it to a stranger." André returned the carriage and horses to the shelf as if resolving what Margaret spoke was the truth.

Truth. It was truth that challenged Margaret now.

*****

Tears moistened Margaret's cheeks. She became aware of the darkness around her, broken only by the red spark of fire aglow in the forge. The remorse she felt for the loss of all that beauty, that joy of her early relationship with André;

had shaken her into immobility. She knew that André would be returning soon and she did not want to be here when he arrived.

But she lingered, cherishing again the times she had sat in this chair as a younger woman watching André at the forge and anvil, listening to him tell of the quality of iron, its malleability when heated, its strength when cold and how it was cleansed by fire. She could remember watching him twist red hot steel and listening to its sizzle when plunged into the cooling water.

She recalled André's affectionate talk. "Mar,"—he always called her Mar—you're beautiful. Dr. Cameron's daughter lovin' me! Lucky guy!"

How could she allow the gates of these blocked emotions to be opened after so many years? With sudden determination she walked out of the shop leaving the door as it was when she had entered.

But the meticulous management of her emotions had been broken. She spent the evening anxious about André's return, knowing she could not manage the careful indifference, as she had yesterday or last week, to his presence in the same room. He had been very good at detecting her anxieties and her moments of internal bliss.

She retired early and was safe in her bedroom when the truck returned. Sleep would not come. Diane's statement, "I guess I can't imagine what could go so wrong," sent her to sorting old details throughout the night.

Morning brought fatigue and a determination to lock up the specter of lost happiness. She set herself to the demanding goals of cleaning and preparation for winter. Despite the rigor, as the days progressed, she found herself unable to ignore André's activity about the house in the old way and so avoided him more than ever.

"Margaret, you are awfully quiet today." It was the silence in which they sat enjoying their sandwich and tea several Mondays later that prompted Diane's statement.

Margaret sipped her tea. She was all too aware that with Diane she shared more than sometimes intended. Hesitantly, she ventured, "Diane, must one be a prisoner forever to earlier mistakes?"

Diane let the question hang for a minute to see if Margaret would continue. Margaret nibbled on her sandwich and then touching her teacup to her lips, looked across at Diane waiting for a reply. "What kind of mistakes?" The question was voiced softly.

Margaret hesitated. Never since her carefree days of high school had she confided in a female friend. She knew she could stop now, keep the question impersonal. But Diane was looking at her, willing her to talk, it seemed, and she did. "Remember you asked me, what could go wrong between André and me? I've spent a lot of time sorting through the mistakes."

"Want to talk about it?" Diane encouraged. And so, the story unfolded; at first hesitantly, but more confidently as Diane listened, nodding encouragement from time to time.

"From the beginning everything was wrong. My parents were against the relationship as soon as they discovered my interest in André. My mother spelled it all out. The academic opportunities I could have—doctor, dentist, lawyer—with my abilities and my father's influence, although a woman. Those were ideals that had held my interest too, but now I had another dream just as challenging—to bring André along with me.

"From my first glimpse of his creativity, I had wanted to get him away from wagons and truck boxes, from horseshoes and clevises. Those were part of a dying enterprise. Electrical welding was replacing André's forge. But my mind had even higher goals—jewelry. I knew the precision of André's work. With some training he could easily learn to craft fine rings, bracelets, necklaces in gold or silver. Why work with iron?

"My father, ever gentle, had nevertheless been scornful. 'Is that his idea or yours?' he'd questioned. 'If it's his, I admire him for the dream. But that's what it is—just a dream. Does he know that to learn gold-smithing he would have to apprentice himself to a jewelry maker? What chance has he got, living here in Kenton, of finding one that would agree to help him? If it's your idea, and I have half a hunch it is, then you are a poor dreamer. Young men don't take easily to women's ideas for them, Margaret. You had better recognize that right now. Many a young man has been captured by the maternal charms of a young lady, only to find later that those maternal charms have turned out to be maternal demands and all the hate of mother-driven sons takes over.'

"How correct he was, Diane," Margaret sighed and continued. "The church, or was it God, was against the relationship. André was Catholic; I am Anglican. 'Aren't you Christian, don't you believe in God?' I had asked André in alarm."

"'Not much of anything,' André had confessed, 'Got baptized as a baby, I'm told. Gone to Mass Christmas Eve. I reckon there is a God.'

"Well, then we're both Christian," I shouted. "Can't we be Christian and belong to two different Christian churches?"

"The Catholic priest in Valley City had insisted that I become a Catholic. I would have none of that. I had been raised an Anglican and knew nothing of the mysteries of Catholic worship with its Latin lingo, incense and Hail Marys. But it was one more little wedge between me and my parents.

"My father had begun calmly enough suggesting social, academic and religious differences could bring ruin for any relationship. I tried to reply calmly. "Why can't two people in love forge new directions in their lives? Why must it be assumed that success depends upon similarity, upon repetition of the old? Yes, we are two different people; both gifted in different ways, and out of those differences will come the joy of discovery. We can each encourage the other.

"'I have heard of your plans for him,' my father continued in what I felt was a disturbingly patronizing way, 'but what plans does he have for you? Have you heard him speak of your education, perhaps five or seven years of difficult training? Will he wait that long and prepare himself for your visions of him in the meantime? And…' he continued, 'centuries of experience have shown that common backgrounds whether religion, education or money are important to strong healthy unions.'

"And boring unimaginative ones as well!" I'd managed to get in before father went on.

"'Margaret, you are good at physics and math. Listen to this. Relationships are the flywheel of our lives. They provide momentum, stability and rhythm. If you are always working on trying to balance a flywheel, you don't get output from your machine. The more differences there are in a relationship the more effort both parties need to make the relationship work.'

"Father," I had raised my voice; "what about all the great creative men who had terrible relationships with wives?"

"'My point exactly,' was my father's reply. 'None of them was a happy person.'"

During the weeks of that spring André and I met secretly as best we could to hold each other and resist the forces at work pulling us apart. Then the arguing stopped. Three weeks after I graduated with the highest marks in Kenton's history, I knew I was pregnant. My body was behaving differently. And when the first month confirmed it, I told André. His initial look petrified me. It was a mixture of disbelief and shock. But he took me in his arms, held me tightly while I cried and told me they couldn't stop the marriage now.

He was right. My parents had been adamantly against marriage, but the alternative of the Doctor's unmarried daughter walking around pregnant in Kenton, was a greater horror. They talked to me about a home in Winnipeg, how after the baby was born and adopted out, I could continue there in university. But I had fought too long and hard up to this point to give into that. I would run away from any home they tried to place me. So, the simple, small wedding in the Anglican Church, which my Catholic parents-in-law wouldn't attend, set Kenton tongues in motion.

Margaret paused for a moment sorting details in her mind. Diane filled their tea cups again and added a small biscuit on the side of each saucer.

"André had found a small house we rented. The reality of married life was quite different from the dream and my pregnancy was difficult as well. So many adjustments to make! We did try hard to please each other, but so many changes were forced upon us! André's smiling happy father of earlier days had become angry and withdrawn. My parents had an opportunity for a practice in a larger town several hundred miles away. I interpreted their move as disowning me because they seldom wrote, and my mother was too busy with other things to come when the babies arrived. Within six years André and I had four children. Reality finally hit and I had to admit my own goals of an education were gone. I became a fulltime mother."

"And what happened between you and André?" Diane refocused the story.

"Quite simply, when the glow of youthful optimism gave way to a sense of loss, neglect and disrespect crept in." The room grew quiet. Diane was conscious of the simmer of the kettle on the stove and the click of the clock, but she gave Margaret time to continue.

"I guess you could say I was disrespectful of André first. You know...trying to remake him. He took kindly enough to my suggestions at first about his eating and the way he sat at the table, cleaning his fingernails, learning welding, moving to a larger town. The list went on and on. And being busy with the kids and all I didn't realize I was telling him he wasn't good enough. The gentle chatter we once experienced, the laughter in spite of our circumstances, the tenderness in bed, gradually faded to be replaced with silence, resentment and outbursts. All I had to say was, 'Did you wash your hands?' or 'André, don't sit there with those clothes on,' and he would become sullen, withdrawn and uncommunicative.

"We began to distance ourselves. André kept to the shop, and I looked after the kids. The children became my support, my reason to be. But I practiced a subtle revenge, I guess, by controlling what I could control with no flexibility and by taking my time and keeping André waiting. But anger contained, can explode, and that's what happened one night. André grabbed me and was shaking me when I fell. I hurt my cheek and blackened my eye. I never forgave him for that. I have a bit of a stubborn streak.

"That night I moved to another bedroom. I never slept the whole night, so I heard André come home, look for me in our bedroom and then go from room to room until he came to where I was. The door was locked. I told him to go away. Diane, he said he was sorry; said he never wanted to hurt me. Every night for a week he came to the door and asked to come in, but I refused. I took some satisfaction from hearing his pleading.

"One night three weeks later, he came begging, Diane, begging for me to let him in. He said it wasn't right for a man and wife to live the way we were. He promised it would never happen again. I could hear him crying. That's when I thought, now I have him. Now maybe he'll agree to some changes if I return to our bedroom. But I said to myself, "Let him wait one more night." I heard him leave the house. He didn't return for three days and after that he never came to my bedroom again and I never went to his. It was a battle of wills, Diane. That was some years ago. I was twenty-eight years old."

Tears glistened on the cheeks of both women as they sat across from each other. After a moment Margaret said, "That's what went wrong. I could have been a doctor and he could have been a skilled artisan. Instead, two talented and intelligent people destroyed each other's lives."

Diane reached over and placed her hand on Margaret's. "You should have turned Catholic, Margaret. A priest could have offered you absolution." They both smiled.

The touch of humour gave both women a moment's relief. Then Margaret plunged on. "Diane, I was a gifted and privileged person. I had far more opportunities than all the rest of my class. Look what I am now!"

The low splash of the December midday sun had disappeared behind a bank of winter clouds. Diane stood to turn on a nearby light and to adjust the stove. She replied quietly, "Yes, our decisions have consequences, but we can take opportunities to start over. Think of life as a journey, Margaret, each day..."

She was about to continue when Margaret inserted, "I'm an economic prisoner. How can I start over? If I left the house, I couldn't afford…" She left her thought unfinished and, cupping her face in her hands, looked into the empty teacup. "At least, he hasn't driven me from the house."

"Is the relationship dead, Margaret, Diane inquired, "or just neglected? Could a little attention, a little fanning of some sleeping embers ignite the fire of love again?"

Margaret sat for a moment as if considering Diane's thought. "No!" She finally said emphatically. "Do you know what twenty years of calculated indifference does? You don't expect the other person to speak to you and if they do, it is like an offense to the silent rules established."

"You asked the question earlier, Margaret, about being locked into consequences of previous events. But don't you see how you are victimizing yourself? We are free to start again. You were the initiator in the relationship to begin with. Can you forgive; can your love be renewed? What can you do to get his affection again?"

Margaret looked directly at Diane as she sat down in her chair again. "I don't want to." Her words were articulated precisely and spit out with force. "What I saw then, I don't see now. I was in love with physical beauty and grandiose ideas. It was pride, Diane. I was going to remake him and then he would be forever grateful for what I had done. But he was the stronger. I lost and now I hate him for what he's done to me and to himself. Look—he doesn't have a business anymore. Most farmers have their own welders; they don't need him. Horseshoes are antiques and trucks can be bought with metal boxes. He sharpens some cultivator shovels and fixes the odd chain from time to time for farmers who feel sorry for him. I knew it would come to this, but he wouldn't listen. Too stubborn! Remember, I'm stubborn too," she chuckled.

Diane heard Johnny moving in his bed now after his sleep and knew their discussion would soon come to an end. "Margaret don't let hate be your master. If there is nothing left in the relationship, plan for yourself. Go into nursing. In a few years you could have your own career."

"It's not that simple, Diane, and it's thirty years too late."

"Of course it's not simple, Margaret, but look at your painful alternative. I think you are ready for a choice." Johnny's waking prattle had turned into cries for attention. As Diane stood up to leave, she put her hand on Margaret's arm. "Go forward, Margaret. Gather your courage, make your plans. There is a verse from the prophet Isaiah I have found helpful, 'Do not fear, for I am with you; do not be dismayed, for I am your God. I will strengthen you and help you…' I know Dave will see you can get help if you want it." Then she left to care for the baby.

Margaret did something she hadn't done in years. She bowed her head to say a prayer. Oh, she had prayed prayers from the Book of Worship but to utter her own prayer was foreign. "Dear God, I need your strength, your help," and as an afterthought, "your forgiveness." She rose slowly, feeling tired, more tired than if she had been standing on her feet for hours. But she also felt a sense of excitement, something she had not felt in years. "Go forward!" stuck in her mind for the rest of the afternoon.

She walked home through the gentle drift of light snowfall. Large flakes settled on her sleeves and melted off her eyelids. Christmas lights twinkled from the occasional window and an urge to celebrate this season differently sent her mind tingling. She caught herself humming a Christmas carol as she later prepared a simple supper, but when she sat to eat there was no appetite. A nervous knot gripped her stomach. In an impulse, not unlike many of her decisions as a girl, Margaret placed the rest of her supper in a dish at the back of the stove. She left a note on the table.

Some warm food on the back of the stove.
Please finish it up.

The next morning, the empty dish was in the sink. For several nights then, she prepared supper and left a place setting on the table. In the morning, the dishes would be placed in the sink and the food would be gone. *It's like feeding a wild animal. You never see it eat, but you are aware it has come and gone.*

As she did the dishes, one morning a week later, Margaret watched André as he stood, tall and straight, by the door of the shop, talking to a farmer. His hair was mainly gray now; his face held the wrinkles of time and weather. He was still handsome. Shaking off the thought, she reminded herself she was planning to leave André. Dave had arranged for a house in the city his friend would be vacating. She would work part time and the rent was reasonable.

Was it guilt at the thought of leaving André that drove her to decorating the house a little before Christmas, something she hadn't done since the children left? Christmas morning, she found a small parcel on the kitchen table. At first, thinking it was something André had forgotten, she decided to leave it for him to retrieve. Then she looked closer to see thick pencil lines, printed in André's hand.

For you.

Her hands shook while undoing the brown paper. It was the tiny carriage she had admired so many years before. Margaret had expected that gift from André many years ago. What did this mean? She remembered clearly what she had told him then, "Something so beautiful can only go to someone very special." She couldn't take it now, planning as she was to go away. She placed it on the dining room table and not a word was spoken by either of them. Were her meals, his gift sparks of affection? Could a little more fanning of that spark – some communication, additional acts of friendliness – bring about a flame of commitment? Her plans to leave brought feelings of remorse and regret, but a desire to try.

Two nights after Christmas, passing by the shop, she smelled a whiff of smoke unlike the smell from the forge. André's truck was there. About to pass by, she heard a groan. Hesitantly, she peered in the door. Flames were gathering strength on the planks of lumber. It took a moment for her eyes to adjust to the situation and then she saw things were out of place. The low groan came again. The large "I" beam supporting the chain and pulley had finally broken away from the rafter. André lay face down under the beam. Iron pieces of various lengths lay scattered across and under the beam. The forge had been knocked over in the fall, spreading its coals over a small pile of lumber adjacent to the planks.

Margaret threw away as many of the iron bars as she could. Many remained stuck beneath lumber, caging his body. Looking for a strong plank, one she could handle, she willed her trembling hands to obey. When she found one, she placed the end of the plank under the beam and over a short two-foot block of wood which could act as a fulcrum. She leaned over it with all her weight.

André groaned with the release of weight and looking up at Margaret whispered, "Mar, leave it be. You'll not move it. Go for help."

Margaret was still draped over the plank, pushing downward with all the energy she could muster. "André crawl out when the weight is off." Another groan escaped from his prostrate body as a sharp pain coiled through his back. "Mar," his voice was ragged with pain, "I can't! I can't move my legs—Better go, get out."

"André, I've got to get you out. You're going to burn!"

"Mar, for God's sake go!"

Margaret let her feet touch the floor and heard a sharp gasp as the beam settled back onto André. Helplessness threatened to pin her in place. The flames were growing higher now. Thick smoke was filling the space of the shop as her mind raced over different possibilities. Perhaps someone would see the smoke soon. She ran to the door, but there was no one in sight. The throb of the diesel engine at the elevator told her someone was working there. "Help, someone help!" "Help! Help!" She screamed again and darted back into the shop. The smoke was acrid, thickening in the building. André's groans guided her close to his face.

"André, I'm on my way for help." She felt for his hand. Their fingers touched. "André I am so sorry."

André's voice was weak yet intense with pain. "Mar… damn it… get out! Don't get burned!"

Through the smoke she could see flames burning around his legs. Choking, but fumbling blindly for the water trough, she dumped the water across his legs, and then crawled to the door.

Smoke drifted up from amongst crumpled, sheet metal and clumps of iron the following morning. Tearless, Margaret, erect as always, stood between Dave and Diane on the sidewalk, as a group of men and a police officer dug gently in the smoldering ashes. Others from Kenton stood back on the road, respectful of the dry-eyed widow and uncertain what to make of her lament.

Margaret grieved. She remembered the years of silence, the hurts that went unattended, the hapless beginnings and the silent overtures she and André had made during that Christmas season. After all those years, there had been a tiny smolder of affection. Their cruelty of indifference had been far worse than physical blows. Each had destroyed the other; their pride had denied both the joy of love.

The late December sun rose slowly over Stoney Mountain. Particles of falling frost twinkled in the air amidst this sudden shaft of light. Smoke from Kenton homes built high white plumes against the cold cobalt sky. Gently, the sun warmed the faces of the silent group. She could hold the tears back no longer. Margaret wept and wished her fire-cleansed bones were mingled with André's in the ashes.

REFLECTIONS ON FIRE AND IRON

1. Margaret asks Diane, "Must one be a prisoner forever to early mistakes?" How were Margaret and André prisoners to early mistakes? Under what circumstances have you felt you were, too?

2. In Margaret and André's day, religion was a strong separating factor. Is it still today? How is today different?

3. Given Margaret's reflection on guilt before discovering André in the burning building, what will Margaret do and what would healing be for her now?

4. What is the literal and symbolic significance of the title Fire and Iron?

SECRET GARDENS

I had come to this town to avoid the knowing eyes of familiar faces. The town's tall elm trees held back the blast of summer heat, and the caragana and lilac hedges along the narrow sidewalks provided privacy for my frequent walks. I had spotted the small advertisement in the Saturday paper, and on an impulse, born out of anger, applied for the position in this little town beyond the city. I thought that time and solitude could ease the pain of my recent hurt. But it was here at my daily work as a waitress in the small café I was drawn once again into the lives of others.

Through the jokes and comments shared by the town-people over coffee and lunches, I soon learned about Mr. Thoms and gathered that nobody liked him. The adults in the café saw him as cantankerous, a troublemaker. Mr. Kraft, part-time mayor, full time operator of a car dealership, commented boldly to his companion at the counter that if Thoms tried any more of his tricks this summer, he'd have the old goat thrown into jail. The young people saw him as downright crazy. They called him The Troll, and from what I heard, he sounded like a troll. Billy Brewster had reported loudly just last week to his friends, in the corner booth, how Thoms had come running out onto the road swinging a stick at his car. He acted out the scene much to the pleasure of the group. Sally Collins had giggled a little louder than the others, and then reported how once, last summer, Troll had stood on the road waving his arms. She and her mother had to stop or run into him.

It was Mrs. Donovan's comment to her friend, Mrs. Bruce, one day that threw a different light on Mr. Thoms. "It's a pity," she said her voice frail, slightly trembling, "that everybody picks on Mr. Thoms. He used to be such a nice man before his wife…" she hesitated for a moment, "passed away."

I pictured old man Thoms then as short and hunched, with long gray hair, or even a beard. So, I never suspected it was he the day he entered the café, his tall straight figure momentarily silhouetted in the doorway by the bright sunlight behind. But when he sat down on a stool at the counter seats, I noticed the rugged face, deeply etched with wrinkles, a permanent furrow between his eyes, the corners of his mouth turned down and bordered by a full mustache that accentuated a gloom hovering around him.

"You're new here!" he snapped.

"Yes," I said trying to remain pleasant. "Would you like some coffee?"

"Tea!" he replied brusquely, "Black!"

Selecting a small crockery pot, warming it slightly before dropping in a tea bag, I filled the pot with boiling water. I could feel his green eyes upon me and glancing up at the large plate mirror covering much of the wall in front of me, I saw him staring at the curls in my auburn hair where it touched my shoulders. I turned around, a smile fixed on my face, prepared to meet his chilly gaze. "Our butter tarts are fresh; would you like one?" I asked, hoping to break the power of his stare.

"Yes," came the curt reply, and after a brief hesitation, "Please."

I placed the tart and tea in front of him and was about to go when he spoke, his voice a little less stern.

"Not often you find someone in a café who knows how to make tea."

"My English mother," I replied a touch glibly, wanting to remain distant.

"What brings you here?"

It was the question I found most difficult to answer since starting here some weeks before. "Oh…a summer job," I replied evasively. He looked at me for a moment, measured my height, inspecting the freckles on the bridge of my nose before turning his attention to the tart and tea.

Had it not been for the black car, exhaust roaring and then pop, pop, popping as the vehicle slowed to a stop at the corner next to the café, I would not have known this was Mr. Thoms. Then the car zoomed off, tires squealing on the main street asphalt. The tall man had moved to the café door with swiftness that belied old age, swung it open and uttered profanities before coming back muttering that he couldn't read the license number.

"You're Mr. Thoms!" I exclaimed, surprised, but also immediately aware of my blunder.

"Hump, so you've heard about me," he stated matter-of-factly returning to his tea.

I felt my embarrassment and moved quickly to clean up another table. He left a few minutes later without saying another word.

Mr. Thoms did not return for over a week, but I heard a lot about him. Mr. Swail, the milkman, reported to me that Old Man Thoms had started a door-to-door petition to have a reduced speed limit posted on the street running by his place because, he claims, children crossed it on the way to the park. "Damn fool idea!" Swail exclaimed, pausing to bite off a large piece of donut and then gulp some more coffee. "The only piece of decent road in the town," he continued, his mouth full. "There ain't a stop sign every damn block!" He bit off more donut and holding his coffee cup ready to drink, pushed on, determined to illustrate his point, "besides, no small children in this town anymore. Women quit havin' babies, it seems." His eyes slid over my flat stomach as if to verify the point.

The next day, Mr. Kraft had stopped talking about slumping car sales to a salesman just long enough to report Old Thoms had visited him twice demanding the police do their job and crack down on speeding drivers.

I recognized Mr. Thoms' aristocratic stance immediately when he appeared in the door the second time. He came straight to the counter, his stern face remaining expressionless, but he nodded his head when I asked him if it would be tea and tart. I saw his eyes studying my hands carefully as I placed his tea in front of him.

'Your mother was English," he began abruptly. "Was she a Burton?"

I was taken aback by the directness of his question and unnerved a little by the thought that someone in this town might know me. My privacy here had begun to soothe my pain and draw off the poison from the abscess of my anger. During evening walks, I had relived the searing moment of the awareness a hundred times and fought the encroaching bitterness which at times threatened to blanket me. How could he talk to me nightly while I was away and speak of love when he was intimately involved with another woman? And how could those I called friends be so blatantly complimentary of him knowing full well his betrayal to me? Why did I turn out to be the guilty party as if my absence gave reason for his infidelity? I did not want my experience, to become an arena of public comment again. Panic momentarily flushed my cheeks. "No," I replied, hoping to cover my hesitation. "There were no Burtons on her side. Why do you ask?"

He looked down into the darkness of his tea for a moment as if seeing something within the steaming liquid. "You remind me of someone," he replied gravely.

Mr. Thoms returned to the café on several occasions during the next two weeks, usually at the same time when few people were there. I was drawn to this crotchety old man, perhaps, because of the ill-feeling the townspeople held toward him. He always ordered tea and tart which I prepared for him as soon as I saw him enter. He said little, but when he spoke, he seemed a little less gruff. On occasions I noticed him watching me closely as I served others or busied myself wiping up a table. He had pushed his cup away as if prepared to leave and I went to pick it up. This time his question was just as direct.

"Did your mother like gardens?"

"Yes," I replied, remembering the brilliance of red and yellow zinnias softly bordered by white alyssum in my mother's flower garden.

"The English love gardens," he returned, "Come see mine sometime. I'm sure you know where I live by now." Behind the sternness of his eyes, I thought I detected a twinkle.

I didn't see Mr. Thoms again at the café, but the battle between him and the town seemed to increase with the heat of the summer.

Old Man Thoms had put a barricade on his street trying to slow traffic down, Mike Swail reported to me. The Troll had thrown stones at their car, Billy Brewster, now holding Sally Collin's hand, had reported gleefully to the gang in the corner booth. Then they began to plot revenge. They'd cruise up and down the Troll's street between nine and eleven o'clock tonight. I decided right then it was time to visit Mr. Thoms' garden.

The evening sun was casting long shadows when I looked over the gate into Mr. Thoms' backyard to behold a miniature English garden. Trees and grass were meticulously manicured in places. Flowers of different size and color grew as if at random along a brick walk presenting a kaleidoscope of color. An ornate bench was located along the walk and at the opposite end of the yard snuggled back away from the path was a bird bath, its marble white sparkling amidst the deep green of the trees that closed in behind; the foot of the pedestal lost in a purple spray of flowers.

Mr. Thoms sat facing the bath, a flaxen haired girl beside him held his hand. Much of the yard was now in evening shadow, deepening the greens and softening the flowers' hues, but a shaft of sunlight penetrated through the trees highlighting the sitting man and the little girl beside the bath as if an artist's hand had created the scene. I hesitated, my attention drawn to the young girl, my heart touched by the tenderness of the relationship. I tried to picture a ranting troll-like person, but it was incongruous with the scene before me.

"I've come to see your garden, Mr. Thoms," I called to announce my presence. He stood and turned quickly as if uncertain for a moment from where the voice had come. Then spotting my head above the gate, he looked down at the girl and moved towards me. I opened the gate and stepped inside. The girl pressed in close beside Mr. Thoms' leg.

"My granddaughter, Hazel," he said, looking down at the child and then at me. "Miss…?"

"Clayton," I replied. I smiled at the girl.

"She comes to visit me each summer," he continued.

Surveying the garden again, I sensed the fragrance of blossoms, saw for the first time two sparrows washing their beaks at the bath, and heard the robin's evening song. A solid wood fence behind the trees and the flowers blocked out any view of the adjacent world, and only the occasional hum of a car on the near-by street could be heard.

"It's beautiful, Mr. Thoms! It really is!" I looked at the stern, craggy face and caught a glimmer of pride. We walked the brick path slowly while Mr. Thoms named the flowers at my request, pointed out a special shrub and finally stopped by a tree, its branches burdened with the ripening of fruit.

"My wife's tree," he said slowly, the fading light of the sun caressing its leaves. "She and I planted it on her birthday."

We stood together quietly for a moment, an old man, a child and myself, alone in our own thoughts, my eyes seeing the shape of the leaves on the tree, my mind fighting back the bitter memory of my own situation. Our eyes met his looking down to mine, and I thought for a moment he recognized the hurt I felt.

"It's my turn to make tea," he pointed toward the house.

I hesitated, uncertain, but the tranquility and beauty of the garden surrounding the three of us gave me a new sense of confidence and trust. I smiled and nodded my acceptance.

As Mr. Thoms prepared the tea, I chatted with Hazel and observed the order and neatness of the house. A feminine touch lingered in the polished furniture, the attractively arranged ornaments and the lace scarves of the living room, but a male presence was apparent by the two guns cradled on the wooden rack beside the back door.

I noticed a picture of a much younger Mr. Thoms, his forehead smooth, a touch of a smile about his eyes and mouth, standing beside a young woman. Something about the woman caught my attention. I walked over to the picture to observe closely. It was then I recalled Mr. Thoms' comment to me in the café. The woman in the picture looked a lot like me. Self-consciously I turned to see him watching.

"My wife," he said.

The loud throaty roar of a car broke the silence. An immediate anxiety settled upon Mr. Thoms. I remembered the real reason for my calling, Billy Brewster and the others in that group plotting a disturbance tonight. Two more vehicles roared by horns tooting. His previous slow movements now became intense, his face hardened.

"Damn, fools; they're at it again!" He paced rapidly to the door and shouted into the deepening twilight.

"Mr. Thoms, Mr. Thoms!" Rushing to the door I took his arm. He looked down at me momentarily and then at my hand on his arm, and he seemed to relax. "Please, let's drink our tea and talk." How could I explain he created his own problem? I walked him back to the table. Not knowing just how to begin. "Why do you become so angry?" Another car careened by.

"They killed my wife!" He was emphatic.

"They," I queried?"

"Yes, one of those damn fools was drunk; he drove right through a stop sign and hit my wife." His green eyes flashed; his voice was stone. The conversation stopped as we listened to another approaching vehicle.

"They gave him two years in prison." Mr. Thoms' eyes watered as they held mine. "I lost her for the rest of my life."

Then the screech of tires prefaced the sound of horns blaring. Mr. Thoms had moved swiftly to the door. I remember Hazel and looked about the room. She lay fast asleep, hugging a doll, on the couch. Two loud blasts rocked the evening air. Then all grew silent. Mr. Thoms re-entered the house carrying the shotgun.

"That should frighten those little bastards for a while," he barked.

"Mr. Thoms, you didn't…" my voice trembled, "Now you've done it!" I could imagine the conversation in the café tomorrow and the case Mr. Kraft would have against him.

A pathetic sadness etched itself into the lines of Mr. Thoms' face as he stood inside the door, warrior-like, holding the gun in front of him. Despair was evident in his voice and shoulders.

The little girl lay innocently sound asleep, her doll secure in her arms. My eyes focused again on the picture of the young couple, smiling, in love. I recalled the stab of pain upon reading my husband's note; then the dull ache of emptiness, the remembered bitterness, like nausea, robbing me of trust in any relationship. How long before me had the others all known of his deceptions, silent accomplices to his betrayals? Looking now into Mr. Thoms' glazed eyes I saw how anger and hatred had grown out of the shattering of his world. "Mr. Thoms," I begged, "it is so sad your wife was killed, but Hazel here," I nodded to the sleeping child, "needs to learn love not hate."

The distant wail of a siren could be heard. I knew then I had to deal with my own anger and move on from my hurt or grow old and bitter.

Get rid of all bitterness, rage and anger...
Be kind and compassionate to one another,
forgiving each other...Ephesians 4:31

REFLECTIONS ON SECRET GARDENS

1. As the story illustrates bitterness, rage and anger, the composition of ill-will, can be so easily ignited. In what ways can you relate to this story?

2. Forgiveness is more easily spoken about than achieved. What makes forgiveness difficult?

3. Is forgiving a one-time event? Why or why not? Is forgiving the same as forgetting?

4. We all have secret gardens. Some are comforting, some are not. What secret gardens were evident or can be assumed in the lives of the characters in the story? What are your secret gardens (comforting and/or anxiety producing)?

5. What do you conjecture happened that night? What will be the consequences and next steps for Mr. Thom? Pearl? Billy Brewster and the boys? The other townspeople?

A TOUCH OF SALT

"Let me tell you why you are here.
You're here to be salt-seasoning that brings out the God-flavors of this earth.
If you lose your saltiness, how will people taste godliness?
Matthew 5:14 The Message

His blue eyes narrowed skeptically as he stared at the headline tucked on the fifth page of Friday's paper. Scanning the story, touching on the all-too-familiar events, he was arrested by one detail. "I suppose the bastard thinks it's an injustice—two years, four months in prison. My wife lost her freedom for the rest of her life!" He spoke out loud, although alone. Cradling his fingers behind his head, he gazed out at the lake. Breathing deeply, he let his gaze shift to the western sky. Somewhere deep in his consciousness he recorded the beauty of that evening glow, but it was Carol's comment from two summers earlier he was remembering. "We're going to love this place, Rand!"

The newspaper slipped from his knee, his mind sliding back two years just as easily. A hot one it was—the hottest in twenty-five years the weather reporters told them. He smiled as he remembered how he and Carol had compared the darkness of their summer tans while massaging each other to relieve the ache from those hard, hot days of work. They had framed up the summer cottage, starting late in July and working feverishly to have the roof on and windows in before Thanksgiving. His eyes observing the raw studding, focused upon a cobweb suspended between one of the roof rafters and the wall. A large ant hung in the delicate threads. "I guess we didn't get it entirely ant proof after all, honey." He spoke as if Carol was with him in the room.

Over a number of years, they had rescued a deteriorating marriage, and finally, it seemed, had come to respect individuality and togetherness and to appreciate the other in both work and play. "Let's go for a quick swim!" she'd say after a long work period and off they'd run to the dock to cool themselves in the lake.

Immersing himself now in the memory, he recalled how after the swim, they'd strip off their wet bathing suits, hang them on the makeshift clothesline and dart naked into the cottage to towel. "You look and feel great, Forty-Year-Old," he told her more than once. A deep bond of trust and affection was present in that, their fifteenth year of marriage.

A ragged piece of building wrap, torn loose by the fingering wind, now flapped across the window. He stared at the faded paper, remembering the bright white it had been when first rolled out against the wall. Time, he realized, recoiling from the thought, had equally changed his feelings and passion for Carol.

His eyes refocused on the small newspaper headline on the floor.

Driver Jailed for Twenty-eight Months.

The headline blurred as Rand's gaze shifted to the adjacent pock marked face of Ernest Mason. It prompted a memory, that sensation, of Carol being wrenched from his arm that cool October morning. A shudder rippled through his body. A prayer thought passed quickly, Please God, help me to forgive, and to handle these feelings of loss.

The lake darkened as the western horizon deepened its shade of orange. His buttocks felt the sharp, unforgiving hardness of the old sawhorse. He stood, stretching his six-foot two-inch body and surveyed once again the rib-like features of the unfinished building. The structural lines were bold and daring. A small piece of cutting lay on the floor with numbers scribbled on it in thick carpenter's pencil. The calculation of minute fractions gave evidence of a careful measurement made to ensure a perfect fit. Everything had been done to construct a building of beauty and lasting endurance; a place for him to write, for Carol to paint during summer months and in retirement. Picking up the scrap sheeting, he turned it over. In ballpoint pen in a smooth feminine script was written,

"My Beloved is mine and I am his."

He had not returned to this place since that summer, but the memory of Carol handing him that note after they had eaten lunch flooded his mind. Practical, intelligent, artistic, a person of faith, and ever the romantic, that had been his Carol!

Evening darkened the lake. Those summer's dreams, that summer's love had vanished. The persistent ache of loneliness, of restlessness pushed against those happy memories. A breeze ruffled the twilight water, tearing the faded building paper a little more and slapping it against the window. An ant scurried across the floor. He bent to crumple the newspaper when his eyes focused upon:

Add a Touch of Salt
See Sally Salt for all your Real Estate Needs.

Impulsively, he had called the real estate woman after reading her advertisement. Expecting a matronly, well-dressed, middle-aged woman, driving an expensive foreign car, he was surprised to see a well-used Jeep Cherokee nosing its way down the declining lane. Clad in his usual blue jeans, white tee shirt and sandals, he walked out to meet her. She certainly wasn't what he had expected! The thirty-something female, five foot six, with shoulder length, copper coloured hair, dressed in jeans, hiking boots and a plaid shirt, bounced from the vehicle and with an extended hand announced, "Hi, I'm Sally!"

"Rand Gavell." He noted Sally's firm handshake.

"You have a beautiful location, Rand! Sure like the way the property is laid out! Great view of the lake! Sally's eyes finally rested on the unfinished building. "Interesting structure! Moving?"

Her vehicle, her energy, the clothing, but above all her voice had caught Rand off guard. "No! No! My wife's...well, it's a long story...too many memories."

Sally stopped her perusal of the property, looked closely at the lines that creased Rand's cheeks, the fatigue pockets under his eyes. Had she detected bitterness or loneliness? "I'm sorry," and for a moment both, ensconced in personal moments, watched a morning breeze ruffle the placid water near the dock. Sally continued. "Show me around, Rand."

He listened to her assessment and comments, watched her measure distances, touch this, and examine that. Her knack to see little details as a selling feature, her aggressiveness, the aura of her energy, gave Rand confidence in her ability.

"I'd love to list your property, Rand."

Rand did no more thinking. His split-second decision last night to be rid of this place and its many "ghosts" was final. Sally prepared the papers.

Her call, a week later, sent Rand driving out to her office to finalize a deal. With the papers signed, Sally didn't lose a beat. "I have another place I think you'd like, Rand. I'd be glad to show it to you now." She tapped her pencil on the desk, waiting, her smile warming the offer.

Rand hesitated. He did not have an atom of energy or motivation to begin another project. Could he enjoy any place without Carol? Miffed by Sally's attempt to sell him another place, he declined, but, fascinated at the speed with which she had sold his property, he questioned her technique.

"Oh, relocating people to new places really only involves a few things," she explained, as if it were a simple equation. "Determine the client's needs, match the buyer to a property and help the client visualize the new property's potential. In this case I had a fellow looking for unusual property who is a do-it-yourself type. I knew as soon as he saw your property, finishing off the building would be no problem."

"And since you have a property you want me to see, what's your read on me?"

Still working that one out to some extent," Sally replied, her eyes suggesting a smile. "Right now, I'm thinking you would like some place private, different, newer, but with the opportunity for you to put your mark on it." Coming out from behind her desk, she sat beside him.

Rand moved his chair and turned to face her. "Why not finished? I've lost motivation." *You didn't detect that?*

"No offense, just thought…Rand, you're single?" The question hung for a moment as Rand appeared to ponder. He was unprepared for such directness.

"Separated…at the moment."

"So…under the circumstances you might appreciate a work project, perhaps involving someone else, more than a hide-a-way. Am I wrong?" Her smile was direct, her voice smooth, the tone challenging.

"Perhaps," he was piqued by her probing. "If I need anything right now, I need expanse, view, a need to look out, as well as in." Rand was annoyed at himself for being drawn in where he really didn't want to go.

"Think I know better now what you might want," Sally commented, rising and moving to a cabinet.

The distance between them now allowed him to observe her carefully. The burnished glow of her hair, a touch unruly, framed an oval face. Alert, dark brown eyes, well positioned between a lightly freckled, slender nose, revealed intensity and intelligence. Her body appeared athletic, but well proportioned. For just a moment, as Rand observed, neither her unpainted lips nor slightly tanned cheeks shaped a smile – silence developed.

Upset by her attempts to interest him in another property, he nevertheless was drawn to prolong her company. "So, that fellow who bought my place is keen to finish it?" Rand broke the silence. "Did I tell you my wife and I tried to make it ant proof? Our old place was overrun by ants; Carol detested them. In building our new place, we carefully sealed cracks, used treated lumber where appropriate, secured the windows and painted all areas touching the ground with a sticky paste. But…I noticed there were ants in it now."

"Nothing goes unattended for two years and improves." Sally turned to face him, "unless it's wine. Everything takes maintenance. Do you know how many people sell and buy another property just because they don't want to renovate or repair? Fortunately, I make a good living from those people."

"I'm sure you do." Rand stood up, prepared to leave. "Thanks Sally. I'm not ready for another place."

"Not to worry. Can I be in touch if something interesting comes up?"

"I'm not interested, Sally, in any more property."

Despite that assertion, Rand's thoughts were on Sally, not cottages, as he made the drive back into the city. He recognized for just a few hours he had been drawn out of his gloom. The energy, decisiveness, leadership were so much like Carol's. Physically, Sally was much more petite, but certainly she was just as attractive. Rand recalled the unique voice—a mixture of velvet and Velcro™. He had been surprised by the vulnerability of his emotions, having looked at her today. Although aggravated by her, these feelings of attraction now reproved him for his disloyalty.

He drove on, unaware of the tabletop farmland bursting with the tiny shoots of spring; stretching out infinitely it seemed on both sides of the highway. Loneliness, the ache of loss, remorse, fatigue, had all returned.

"Rand, I have a darling of a place I'd like to show you." Sally called two weeks later. "Priced right too. I thought of you just as soon as I viewed it. Can you come out tomorrow or Sunday?"

Rand hesitated. Having put Sally and cottage property out of his mind, he hesitated to open that chapter again. "Sally, I'm not interested in another property, but thank you for thinking of me."

"Rand, this one won't be on the market long. You owe it to yourself to see it before saying no," her voice persisted, a soothing contralto, vibrating energy and excitement.

I owe it to myself. Rand smiled.

"Rand, are you there?"

Was it the voice or the thought of one day possibly free from…what was the feeling …malaise, depression? That word evoked repulse. He remembered her energy, the vibrancy which seemed to bring him alive… I'm like a moth drawn to an open flame. "OK…Sunday, two o'clock at the office?"

"What makes you think this one's for me?" Rand asked, once they were on their way two days later.

"It's unique, Rand, private, but not confined; not big, but completely adequate; attractive, with appealing lines in the structure. It's well-built and very well maintained."

Rand smiled at "maintained." The richness of her voice never failed to stir him. The profiles of her face were captivating. "You're sure big on maintenance, aren't you?"

"A building lasts a long time when properly built, and then cared for. Like everything else, wind, rain, sun, ants," she smiled over at Rand, "just keep working away at a building and if it's not repaired it's gradually destroyed."

"What else?" Rand attempted to keep it lighthearted, enjoying her conversation.

"Well, your vehicle for one thing; your body, for another."

A flashback gripped Rand, revisiting the moment Carol was torn from his arm, her body sent twirling into the air. Then there was that horrible thud as she dropped to the pavement to crumple, her legs and arms twisted like those of an old rag doll. Quiet hung in the car. He struggled with lungs and heart to regain their natural rhythm.

Sally glanced across, "Rand, something wrong?"

"Forgive me," he choked out, struggling to regain his composure, "memories—that bastard!" He clenched his fists and gritted his teeth as he muttered, "Some things are not repairable!"

"Like marriages!" Sally voiced emphatically; her composure broken momentarily by the effect of Rand's emotions. An unspoken bond of experience seemed to form between them.

"Your marriage?" Rand ventured to probe.

"Rand, I don't know what happened between you and your wife," Sally began, and then asked abruptly, "How long were you married?"

"Fifteen years." *She's taking control again.* Rand worked hard to regain his composure; unaware he'd miscalculated the years. I don't want to become too personal.

"And at the end of fifteen years?" She glanced over at Rand before pressing on. "Fifteen years ago you started out very much in love, you were hard workers, compatible, had common goals. 'A marriage made in heaven,' they called it. Then within months little things began to interfere, differences, work schedules." She dared a quick glance again at Rand to judge his attention. "No time to stop and adjust or tweak; just carry on and hope it goes away and of course it doesn't. Then add children to that, sometimes without much planning or unexpectedly." Sally's voice projected an increasing resentment. "Now there are more of you and the lopsided relationship like a wheel out of alignment only aggravates and creates more problems. Now we have irreconcilable differences."

Rand sensed the bitterness in the monologue. "That...wasn't exactly my experience...was it yours?"

Sally ignored Rand's question. "How far wrong am I?"

Rand reflected on his years with Carol. What is a 'marriage made in heaven?'

They had both been twenty-five the year they married. Both had successfully completed university and had jobs. They had decided to postpone marriage although many of their friends had married while still in school. "Birth control covers all," friends had chirped as they met for one of those Friday night parties after a long term of intense studies. Occasionally the monthly stories of "The Shakes," they called them, had sent them into a panic. One couple or another recalled how menstrual periods, out of whack from stress, had triggered great apprehension.

Carol and he had not experienced those tremors. Later, they discovered they couldn't have children. Carol wanted to adopt but he was hesitant. He regretted that now. Perhaps children would have given him focus, companionship, purpose. There had been tension between them over that issue. Carol, then, had thrown herself into her job and had done well. Company relocation options for her meant resignation and finding another teaching position for him— leading to more disagreement and tension.

"How far wrong?" Sally repeated bringing Rand back to the question.

"Good marriages don't come ready-made," he stated reflectively. "They're the results of years of learning how to trust, forgive, communicate, develop honesty, respect self, and resolve difficulties...create a relationship."

Sally glanced over to note Rand's serious face. "What happened?"

"We learned how to resolve difficulties over the years."

"I'd like to hear about that!" her voice, raised slightly, one eyebrow arched.

Rand bristled. *Knows it all or at least thinks so.* "A bad experience, Sally?"

"Two years away from an ugly divorce and a man who thought only of himself."

"I'm sorry about that."

"From what I've observed," Sally continued, having said more about herself than she intended, "Men and women just come from different planets. The concept of marriage needs some reworking." Her left hand held the steering wheel, and her right hand punctuated her points. "Deep down, honestly, is there such a thing as a deeply happy marriage?" Again, she shot a quick glance at Rand. "Isn't it common to call the wedding day 'the happiest day of our life?' And isn't that the truth! Then reality sets in and two people have to deal with the fact that one person or both has just given up being herself or himself; from that day on happiness fades."

Sally exited the narrow-paved road to enter a well-maintained, grass edged, gravel road sheltered by large conifers and birch trees. The border grass was dotted with white daisies. "Rand, sometimes we're ready for something new." She had switched topics as quickly as roads. I think this place could give you a new vision, a touch of excitement, new friendships. The neighbours are great. I loved it when I first saw it. I think you will too." A smile directed at Rand radiated her enthusiasm.

The road widened to be met by a broad carpet of mowed grass, encircling rock outcroppings. Soaring red pines lifted one's gaze heavenward. Nestled in this beautiful context of grass, tree and rock stood a uniquely designed building. Angular windows, high and low, accentuated the elevations of the roof. A calm cove off the lake, transitioned by smooth gently sloping bedrock met with grass in front of the building.

Rand sat intrigued, studying the beauty of the property, noting its isolation, yet the scope of its view in all directions. Touches of neighbouring cottages, at respectful distances, could be glimpsed through bordering hedges. Sally, silent beside him, observed his reaction.

"Is it a chapel or a cathedral?" Rand mused aloud.

"Come! I'll take you inside." The velvet in her voice reflected awe.

The soft glow of pine lumber, the roughness of rock facing, the smoothness of tile and the strength of timber frame, highlighted by the uniquely shaped windows, blended into a work of art. It was a building letting the outside in but allowing those in to look out, a beautiful coming together of human and divine creativity.

"And you thought this one was for me?" Rand's eyebrow lifted as he spoke.

Sally had been quiet while watching Rand study the building. She would never express this openly, but she was attracted to this man. There was a quality of vulnerability, of tenderness, yet also of mystery and strength she had not previously associated with maleness – companionable without taking control.

"Don't you think so?" Sally refocused her thoughts. "The building incorporates a sense of masculinity, sensitively graced with a feminine touch. Look at the location; private but not insular. One can look out and much comes in. Are you impressed?"

"Sally, it is a magnificent structure and setting!"

"It's a consummation of so many things! Come over here." Sally's previous silence gave way to exuberance and spontaneity. She beckoned Rand to join her in an area of vaulting ceiling and spacious windows. A rock outcropping just feet away, on the exterior side of the window, touched here and there on its face by clusters of wildflowers and sprays of grasses was backed with clumps of shrubs, then the soaring pine. This canvas of nature filled the window frame like a beautiful work of art. "One can stand, or sit for that matter, here and not be sure whether he or she is inside or out. That's a consummation of the interior and the exterior."

Walking to another area she touched several light switches. Lighting directed from several points caused the polished pine to glow with warmth. A native stone, free standing fireplace highlighted the central area of the room. Its chimney flue soared into the ceiling above. "The collaboration of strength and beauty, Yin and Yang," Sally uttered quietly, her smile expressing a genuine regard of approval for all she had said.

"Do you see what I meant when I called this place unique? It stimulates thought but promotes rest. It provides cover but allows exposure." Sally was animated, her hands and arms sweeping to emphasis. "Look at the beauty we see all around us inside and outside. Imagine what this would be like on a cold December day, sitting right here in the warmth and beauty of this room, but watching the wind drift the snow and rabbits hop from place to place just on the other side of that glass! It's all this variety accompanied with harmony that gives quality."

Sally sat on one of the chairs. Rand sat across from her; one arm slung over the back of the chair; his long legs lapped one over the other. "Sally, this is the most beautiful place I've seen. It's all you said. But…what would I do in a place like this…alone?"

"Everything you might do with someone – read, think, write, watch television; the fishing's good. Whatever you like, Rand. I know. I know. When you've lived fifteen years with someone, it's hard to think of yourself. But this is the perfect place to get in touch with you again. We are so used to being 'married' that we think there is no life apart from being with someone. If you need occasional company, invite someone out for a weekend. It doesn't have to be marriage."

Contrasts in harmony, richness in diversity wasn't that what he and Carol had struggled to attain in their relationship? Interesting phrases to express the joy and frustration of commitment, Rand thought.

"Sally," he, purposefully digressed, "you haven't even told me the price."

"That's the best part of it. This is a bargain!"

Having heard the price, he untangled his legs and walked over to the window. As he gazed toward the lake, his mind took him back to another time.

The house had been magnificent and located in the older part of the city. Carol had fallen in love with it immediately. He had envisioned something newer, already finished and in the suburbs, but she was inspired. For two weeks she sketched plans and found pictures to help present her vision of what they could achieve. With her artistic skills and his ability to build, she argued, they could restore its splendor. He questioned his ability, his energy. Carol was not deterred; she knew he could do it. If they got stuck, they'd look for help. Finally, a commitment.

At first, it was a project, and not all harmonious, but as his confidence grew with the beauty that developed, it became his vision too. They had developed something together that neither could have done alone.

Turning to face Sally, Rand declined the offer.

In the weeks that followed, he cycled through periods of regret for having turned the offer down; failure for not seizing a bargain and simply reselling it; relief that he didn't rush out and commit himself; anger that Sally had put him through the emotional turmoil of decision, and a touch of sorrow he had no reason to see Sally. Her outgoing energy, her smile, her voice, beckoned more than he wanted to admit. He found himself looking obsessively through the classifieds to find, **"Add a Touch of Salt."**

His visits to Carol provoked horror and frustration. Hers was a broken body, kept alive it seemed by mechanics.

Three weeks later he found it.

> *Add a Touch of Salt.*
> *Handyman special. Excellent location. Beautiful beach.*
> *Priced right for the one who can complete a job already begun...*

Rand read no further. I'll bury myself in work. He called Sally.

The sun was already warm when he left the city early Saturday morning to meet Sally by eight. "Why the Zodiac?" Rand asked, seeing the inflatable boat strapped to the top of her jeep when she emerged from the office carrying a small lunch cooler and her satchel.

"Didn't you read the full ad, Rand? This is island property! You had better be serious about this one. It's costing me a whole day. Did you bring a bathing suit?"

"In the car."

"Get it. We may have to swim part of the way."

If Sally felt apprehension it might be a worthless trip, she didn't show it. Today she seemed content to chatter about her children, her place and how busy she has been; apparently stimulated by Rand's occasional encouraging response. She told him about the older couple who had purchased the first place she had shown him but made no comment about his not buying it. When they arrived at the boat launch area, she directed Rand in helping her unload the Zodiac, but without appealing for help pulled the twenty-five horse Yamaha motor from the back of the jeep and fastened it onto the Zodiac. It was developing into a hot, late June day. "Want to change before we leave? It's a half hour or more ride to the island," Sally informed him.

When Rand returned from the men's washroom in bathing suit and shirt, Sally was waiting, clad in an attractive short, sleeveless dress and water sandals. Still professional, Rand thought, but classy. Sally and he pushed out the boat and they were away, a beautiful, wedged wake of water feathering out behind.

They said little in the next half hour. Rand, sitting in the prow, watched the shorelines, the islands, the pelicans, and he observed Sally at the tiller. Without reference to a map, she found the way through channels, around islands and across the big water. Her hair was swept back from her face with a bandana, sunglasses covered her eyes, and her bare legs stretched out in the sun. She could have been a movie star on a yacht. She was beautiful Rand admitted and felt his breathing deepen, but his joy was blunted like a schoolboy's guilt when playing hooky. Are we two individuals engaged in buying and selling or a couple on a clandestine summer weekend rendezvous? Is virtue more a matter of circumstance than character? Rand's mental musings battled his physical stirrings.

Sally pulled up easily to the dock that fingered out from a narrow ledge running along a steep rock face. Rand helped her tie up and reached for the lunch cooler.

"You'll need your walking shoes here," she said, kicking off her sandals and pulling sneakers from her bag.

The climb up to the cottage area was arduous. As Sally guided him around the five-acre island site, Rand mused on the failure of someone's dream. The poetic lines surfaced in his memory; 'Between the idea/And the reality… Between the emotion/And the response/ Falls the shadow.' What isn't touched by the inevitable shadow? Rand pondered the question.

Sally was thorough as usual in her presentation of the property and finally, returned to the incomplete cottage. "Rand," her look was disarmingly direct. "Is this what you want?"

Rand knew from her tone she knew his answer. "Sally, why did you bring me out here knowing I wouldn't want it?" He held her gaze, studying her brown eyes for clues.

She walked away, swung her legs over the edge of the sun-weathered deck to sit, and motioned Rand to do likewise. Methodically, she opened the lunch cooler, unfolded a small tablecloth and arranged an assortment of food and cold drinks. "I brought us a picnic lunch." Rand, recognizing this as not a quickly tossed together creation, reached for a carrot stick, caught her eyes again attempting to read emotions.

"When you called about this property, I knew you either had not read the ad completely, or you were looking for an opportunity to be with me again. I decided on the latter." Sally looked away.

From this high point on the island, Rand looked out across the miles of blue in the distance, flecked by white curls of rolling water. Her directness, although refreshing, was challenging an openness and disclosure he was not prepared to give. His thoughts returned to Carol.

The wait had been endless. He watched the medics work meticulously as if attempting to piece together a broken vase. Finally, with her neck, arms

and legs in somewhat of a straight line, bound to a gurney, they had carried
Carol to the waiting ambulance. One nurse after another came and went into
the operating room. Several hours later a doctor emerged with the non-committal face of a press secretary. Her situation was critical. Touch and go he
put it. They could find no response in her lower body. She lay unconscious;
life supports keeping her alive for weeks. The evening she opened her eyes
he was overwhelmed. They were much bluer than he had remembered. Her
smile of recognition was a gift, a reward, unlike any he had ever received; her
helplessness was devastating. He had wished then it was he and not she who
was injured, and so pledged silently to do everything he could to make it up
to her. He was beside her daily massaging her body hoping for a twinge of
response. Then she slipped back into a coma —no more smiles, no more teary
blue eyes, no response. He was at her bedside every day, talking to her, holding
the limp hand, kissing the dry lips. Weeks passed, then months. It was as if a
switch had been turned off. It pained him to see the body of the woman who
once was so lovely, now trapped in a body that was wasting away. The bright,
alert person he had known was so different from this one with sunken cheeks
and an aging face. His daily visits turned into weekly ones, sometimes less, and
even that took more effort.

"Sally," Rand broke the silence, "Will you tell me what went wrong with
your marriage?"

Sally cradled a cold drink between both hands, her eyes also tracing the
horizon of water as she struggled to maintain emotional distance, her mind
retracing years of hurt which she desperately wanted to share.

"Gord and I grew up together amongst lakes and boats and fishing camps,"
she began quietly. "We knew the ins and outs of camp life before we were teenagers and by the time we were teenagers we were a part of it. Our parents owned
a successful lodge together. Both our fathers were guides and our mothers were
the cooks, housekeepers, receptionists, booking agents, whatever it took to keep
the business running, and mothers. Our fathers came home once a week, maybe
once every two weeks or a month, depending on the length of the outing. They
fixed an engine or two, repaired a boat, made love to our mothers, I presume,
and readied themselves for the next guided trip.

As children, Gord and I were friends. As teens we became lovers. I liked
Gord, probably even loved him, whatever that means. We had ideas to run an
upscale lodge and let others do the guiding, cooking, whatever." She stopped

to reach for a veggie, nibbled on it slowly for a moment then resumed her story. "For a couple of years after marriage it worked, but when the funds weren't there, we found ourselves falling into the same pattern as our parents. After our second child and a lot of lonely nights I wanted out. 'Let's do real estate.' I told Gord. 'We know the area, the properties. With a little training we could be good.'" Another pause and a nibble. "No, he wouldn't even discuss it. He had fallen in love with guiding, being away, with little responsibilities for the kids, I presumed. A third child came unplanned. I couldn't manage it all."

Sally had her legs up on the deck now with both arms wrapped around her knees facing the open water. "I had seen it with our parents and then with Gord. Men probably can be somewhat romantic during courtship and that's even a given, but once the relationship is formalized, they're into their own little or big world, come home occasionally to eat and copulate and return to their sanctuary of work." She paused again, her gaze still on the distant water. "Finally, I resolved to do what I wanted to do. I took my Real Estate training through correspondence and a short stint down East to become a broker. Gord didn't want a divorce, but couldn't see it necessary to make changes, so I had to make the move. We had a fight over the kids. I won."

Swinging herself to face Rand, Sally picked up a pepper slice, and chewing slowly continued, her voice confirming determination. "I love my work and am successful. Except for my children, I'm independent. I don't have to deal with a husband."

If Rand's silence had confirmed his listening, now his gentle eye contact conveyed an acceptance, an understanding. Both shared the agony of separation and the fear of experiencing it again. He hesitated to say, "I understand," lest it appear to trivialize her story. Instead, he thanked her for sharing and complimented her on the lunch. They ate in silence.

Sally felt foolishly vulnerable having revealed so much so easily to a man she liked but was just getting to know. Observing Rand as he sat looking out over the lake below, she took stock. She decided his large hands were the hands of a carpenter, and that his face was that of a thinker with its forehead, traced with thought lines, and the bushy eyebrows merging above his strong straight nose. His silent attention to her story, his passive acceptance of her reason for this trip made her feel safe.

A gentle breeze swept the deck, moderating the noonday heat. Sally gathered the remains of the lunch and packed them into the cooler. "I haven't shown you the beach yet. Maybe after you see it, you'll decide to buy it." A smile brightened her face. She took Rand down a winding path on the south side of the island leading to a large smooth rock outcropping that gently sloped into the water. It was a perfect place to sunbathe and swim. "Want that swim?" Sally proposed, her eyebrows arched.

"Got my trunks on," Rand replied. "What about you?"

Reaching down to the hem of her dress, she drew it up over her head exposing her bikini. Sally's look at Rand held a touch of shyness and uncertainty. "I'm ready."

Oh my God, what beauty! Rand remained motionless. Like a bright light being turned on in a dark room revealing all, Rand realized Sally was also attracted to him. He knew now his moral struggle had just intensified. He unbuttoned and removed his shirt. Sally, noting his hesitation, turned from him, carefully folded her dress and laid it on the rock. Then she kicked off her shoes and with a shout as if to break the awkwardness called, "Last one in the water buys the property." She ran down the rock slope and did a clean shallow dive into the water. With a strong front crawl, she headed out into the lake.

Rand observed Sally's graceful departure and clean dive. The sight of her bikini clad body had revealed a moment of truth and awakened a memory.

The white sand, the warm sun, the gentle ocean breeze, made the southern Mexican beach a tropical paradise. His attention had been focused on the strong and confident front crawl of the female swimmer. When she stood waist deep and began her walk out of the water, the fullness of her breasts, scarcely covered by the tiny top, the narrowness of her waist, confirmed how physically beautiful she really was. Then the huge rogue wave came in from behind, knocking her down. Glimpses of legs and arms protruded from the water as she tumbled, the undertow sucking her back. He had watched her frantic struggle and disappearance. Finally, she emerged, stripped of her bikini top and her breasts exposed. A movie scene could not have been more dramatic or erotic. A spatter of applause, his included, rippled across the beach. Other admirers had obviously also witnessed the event. Recognizing her situation, the woman screamed and with arms crossed attempted to hide herself. It was Carol who ran to her with a towel to wrap her body and assisted her to shore. "What that woman experienced was akin to a physical assault! And what do people do...applaud as if she were part of a stripper's act in a sleazy bar!" Carol had been indignant.

Remembering that moment of shame, he walked down the rock and plunged into the water. Sally continued to swim straight out, her strong front crawl challenging Rand to follow. He went as far as he thought prudent and began his return. Before reaching the shore, he could hear the beat of her strokes behind him. Climbing up onto the rock, he laid face down to dry in the sun sensing that Sally did the same. After fifteen minutes, feeling dry, he put on his shoes, and shirt, picked up the lunch cooler and waited discreetly while Sally put on her dress. They headed for the Zodiac.

The boat trip back was made in silence, both were absorbed in their own thoughts. Once in the jeep, Rand broke the silence. "Sally, I'm sorry…I felt uncomfortable back there and I made you feel that way too. You are spontaneous, and without guile. I carry baggage. Really, Sally, the outing and picnic, everything, was delightful." He glanced over at her after the last comment, but her eyes never left the road and her expression remained the same.

He continued cautiously, watching her as she drove. "Sally, You're wonderful in vacation real estate. You know property. Do you know that so much of what you say about property, applies to relationships: design, maintenance, fighting off the ants?" A smile flickered momentarily on Sally's face. "It took Carol and me quite a while to figure out the maintenance part of relationships and we didn't have children to complicate the situation. At first, of course there is the thrill of newness; then, a contest to see who got his or her way. That means keeping track of the score – winners, losers. From there, we were into compromise, but compromise can mean no one wins, breeding disappointment and hurt. We hadn't learned the art of good communication. Finally, we bottomed out."

Sally glanced at Rand. "What do you mean?"

"It means we began to ask if we wouldn't be better off single – on our own."

Rand had touched a resonating note with Sally. She glanced at him again. "And…?"

"Carol had another business trip. Her company wanted her in Montreal for six months to do some buying and to improve her French. She was keen to do it. I took it as a personal rejection at first and had refused to consider it. How could she even consider leaving her husband for that length of time unless she didn't care? Carol was adamant she was going. We couldn't get beyond the impasse. We agreed to a 'time out' to consider our next move upon her return, including the possibilities of separation."

"After three weeks, the bed felt cold at night, and you were horny. You wanted her back. Is that it?" Sally's pretty face etched with cynicism, her voice brittle.

"Well…somewhat true, but much more," Rand continued nonplused. Yes, I missed Carol and she reported missing me. But to get us back together and talking, she had saved her meal stipends and with that and extra money her company provided for expenses, she flew me down for a weekend after four weeks. This little act of sacrifice, her reassurance and suggestion for me to come visit on a monthly basis, helped me get beyond my own selfishness. It was a great growing period in our lives. The roots of trust were pushed deeper with the separation. The monthly visits were anticipated and treasured.

"It wasn't the separation that pushed the roots of trust deeper," Sally countered adroitly. "The deepening had something to do with what occurred on either side of the separation. Gord and I had lots of separations; we just didn't have much to return to after the periods apart." She looked his way and then refocused on the road, her expression stoic.

"May I be personal now, Sally?"

She raised an eyebrow with a non-committal nod Rand took as permission.

"You are a physically beautiful woman, and you have wonderful qualities of aggressiveness, mechanical aptitude, physical strength, all traditional male attributes. Those qualities, I think, enhance your beauty. Carol helped me realize I was no less a man if she made important decisions about her work, and she was no less a woman for making those hard decisions. We weren't appendages of each other, but individuals who chose to share the journey of our lives together. The many things we did together, we agreed required mutual consent. That's what I believe happens in relationships where two people come together in love. Contrasts in harmony, you called it. It's complex. It takes work - maintenance. But for Carol and me the struggles brought us together and coming together was better than the two separates. I think many people divorce and remarry because it appears easier than renovating a marriage. The renovation requires communication and commitment. When that fails…" he left the sentence dangling.

They had reached Sally's office. Before leaving the jeep, Sally looked at Rand, "Good speech!" Then added, "Actually, I liked it. You're different." And with that she jumped down from the cab and began telling Rand how to unload the Zodiac.

Rand thanked Sally for the picnic lunch again and expressed pleasure for the day. They shook hands and parted, like two people who had chatted most of an afternoon at an airport but were leaving in opposite flights never expecting to see each other again.

For two weeks Rand found himself thinking about Sally. Finally, he decided to take a page from her book and concentrated on himself. He reorganized the furniture in the house, arranging it his way. He adjusted his meals to match his biorhythms, his reading and writing schedule; got rid of things Carol had hung onto for years. He started exercising again. He was going to move forward.

It was later in the evening three weeks later when the phone rang. "Rand, Sally here. That first place I showed you…, it's on the market again."

Rand's heartbeat became erratic when he heard that velvet voice. He didn't want to let it go. "Sally, how are you?"

In characteristic fashion, she ignored his question. "Had some property listed, that I expected you might call about, Rand. Two more island pieces."

Rand was working frantically to decode the message. "No, island property I'm not interested in, but the trips out there would have been fun. Now, what's the scoop on this property?"

"Well, the older couple who bought it…she passed away suddenly. He's not interested anymore."

"I know the feeling," Rand replied quietly.

"The place has not been maintained now for a while, probably ants in it; you might get it for less."

"I'd like to check out those ants, Sally."

"Sunday afternoon, ok?"

The first Sunday in September arrived hot. Sally had given up her jeans and hiking boots for a short skirt, summer blouse and sandals. Rand noticed she wore lipstick, a subtle pastel shade that accented colours in her blouse. He was dressed in light, pleated cotton trousers with coordinating shirt and light canvas shoes. They looked more like a couple dressed for an evening barbecue than a business trip.

Rand listened contentedly as Sally talked about properties, her children at summer camp, about…then, as if suddenly aware that she was monopolizing, abruptly asked about him.

"I've been taking steps to get in touch with myself, Sally. I've decided it is time in my life for something new."

They turned off the paved road onto the lane leading into the property. The tall grass on both sides showed the signs of a summer's neglect. The previous manicured look was gone.

"He mailed me the key," Sally informed, "so I know there has been no preparation for this visit." The beauty of the house had been only slightly compromised by a few dead moths on the floor; a spider web dangling from light to ceiling anticipated a catch of something. A light film of dust covered everything. "Things deteriorate quickly when not looked after," Sally agitated.

"I haven't seen any ants," Rand chuckled. They strolled down to the dock after their perusal of the house. In spite of it being afternoon, the lake was placid, soaking up that September sun. Rand bent over to look down into the still water. He watched a crab inch itself backward into the sand at the bottom. Sally had stopped further down the dock quietly observing the water. "What can you see?" Rand asked casually.

"Myself!"

Rand moved beside her and looked into the water. The supporting crib under the dock formed a dark shadow on the water creating a mirror effect. Two faces looked up at them.

Rand took off his shoes, sat on the edge, his feet dangling in the water. The reflections distorted, in the rippled water, then disappeared. Sally sat down beside him.

Her presence so close stirred him deeply. Her hair, threads of bronze, fluttered lightly about her shoulders. The urge to put his arm around her to draw her even closer almost overwhelmed him. He was fighting a losing battle. Why didn't the two of them admit what was happening? Their pretext of meeting was business, but their purpose seemed to be something other. The circles of the mating dance brought them closer and closer. Yet, each remained silent as if in denial.

We look into mirrors to see what we look like, but we only see how others see us, a certain image which in some ways defines me. It is less often we investigate ourselves past that image to see what else lives there, lurks there. My friends think me honourable…faithful, when I am dishonourable, unfaithful, clinging to ideals, trumpeting concepts for me already dead.

It was Sally who placed her hand lightly on the back of his. "Rand, what are you thinking?" Rand smiled. I'm seeing something about relationships here in this water," Rand hedged. "Sometimes…we look into the water, but we don't see the water; we see a reflection of ourselves. And then again, we look into the water and we see through the water to what's in it. But, when a wind comes along and ripples the water, we can't see our reflection or what's in it. We see the rippling water, really, just the surface; that's how we most often see water. Similarly, in relationships what do we see – a reflection of us, all that makes up the relationship, or just the surface?

"You make water and relationships sound horribly complex; Sally chuckled and inched a little closer."

"I believe both are."

"So why complicate it more by marriage?"

"Maybe that differs from marriage to marriage. Possibly, one upside is that out of this tension, one becomes a stronger, better person; two people energizing each other beyond what one could produce."

"Gord didn't make me a better person, Rand. He made me just the opposite." Sally stood up and began to pace the dock. All I got from him was anger, neglect, numbness, and… well, of course my children.

Rand swung his legs up on the dock to look at her. "But, Sally, the children are a perfect physical example. A product of two people, not one, just as trust, understanding, compassion, and insights are generated from the interactions of two people. I believe after a while you and Gord didn't have a relationship. Gord felt his role was to be a provider. You, Sally, expected more out of a marriage—romance, communication, equal roles, nurture. In that style of relationship both persons must provide and nurture – reciprocation – and that takes communication, maintenance. If the relationship isn't maintained, well you know the cottage crumbles."

Rand turned to view the smooth water again. Sally returned to stand beside him, to look into the water at the reflection of his broad hunched shoulders, the mat of unruly hair and her face beside his. She recognized how in his quiet unassuming way he had allowed her to be herself, while he had become an interesting companion.

"Rand," she began, unwilling to concede too much too quickly. "I've never talked to a man about ideas like this. I ended my marriage because it provided me with nothing. This marriage thing, it was such a prison!"

"Sally." Rand utilized the hesitancy, "I theorize better than I behave. Marriage is a commitment of two people, each to the other. Don't our vows tell us when that commitment ends?"

"Those vows are romance. Reality is different. The commitment ends when it's all give and no get."

"I've come a long way in the past months exploring myself again, moving beyond my dependency on another," Rand continued. "You helped me see there can be joy and strength in looking out for oneself. I realize now I let Carol set the tone in our relationship. Maybe I'm ready to move on."

"That's really good, Rand!" Sally interjected.

Rand put on his shoes and stood up to face a smiling Sally. Her smile expressed warmth; her eyes an invitation Rand recognized. For a moment they stood face to face, silent, two adults, toe to toe, on the threshold of something new, uncertain of the consequences. *I'm going to cross the line between commitment and gratification.*

Sally suddenly looked serious. "There is one question." Her voice broke through his thoughts.

"Yes?" and what is that...?" Rand studied her face.

"What happened to you and Carol?"

Rand was quiet a moment. The question was inevitable given Sally's direct-ness, her lack of dissimulation. Suddenly, all that he had lost two years ago he sensed he was about to lose again. Rand's fists clenched and unclenched; his voice strained with emotion. "Carol was hit by a drunken, unlicensed, uninsured driver. She's a quadriplegic and has been comatose for the past eighteen months. I'm sorry...I didn't mean to deceive..." He dropped his head into his hands.

"Rand, stop! You're too hard on yourself, too hung up on ideals. You go on and on about the virtues of marriage when it's obvious you're a hurting, lonely person. Your situation makes this place perfect for us. I don't want mar-riage and you don't really have one. Can't two people live independently but share harmony?" We have both improved each other's life. Isn't that what you said relationships were all about, energizing the other? Rising on her toes she drew his head down and kissed him. Rand hesitated for a moment, and then swept her up in his arms, their kisses intensifying, their need urgent.

Then just as quickly, Sally pushed Rand gently away. "Rand, I'm not going any further until you decide whether your wife is dead or alive. Let's get back to my office and write up an offer."

Rand experienced a turmoil of emotions on the trip back to the city – a sense of excitement and new life, but mindful of Sally's question, "Is Carol dead or alive?"

The blinking red light on the home telephone seemed to flash a message of alarm as soon as Rand returned that evening. He touched the button. "You have two messages," the machine informed in a soft female voice.

"Message one: Rand, Loretta here at the home. Carol opened her eyes today. She spoke your name. Call or come as soon as you get in. Bye."

"Message two: Rand, Sally here. Congratulations! I phoned and your offer has been accepted. You have just acquired a new location with exciting possibilities! Come out Friday and I'll help you take possession. See you then."

Rand stood motionless. His giant of a body tensed as if inadequate for this epic battle. He squeezed his eyes tightly. He could see Sally, her face coloured by sun and wind, her copper hair, her lips softly pink as they were this afternoon. He could feel her energy; hear her invitation and sense again the tug of companionship and passion. Then, Carol's pallid face appeared, her eyes shut, her cheeks sunken, her head with tousled graying hair resting on the pillow. Slowly the eyes opened, and the blue circles smiled.

Rand paced the distance of the hallway in thought. He picked up the picture of Carol from the hallway table. Only in memory could she now match the attraction, the allure of Sally. Both physically and mentally she was but a shadow of her former self. It was she who had helped shape his very self, his confidence, his integrity, his knowledge of trust, his understanding of the word love.

He sat down in the hallway chair. For the first time in months, he wept. His tears were for loss, for separation, for loneliness and hurt, and for his betrayal. He remained motionless, breathing deeply, Carol's picture balanced on his knee. Her eyes looked directly at him. "My beloved is mine and I am his." He knew that with the same need he had to fit a perfect corner cut, to find the exact word or image to match an idea in writing, or the perfect illustration in teaching, he would honour the commitment and bond he and Carol had worked so hard to forge.

Holding Carol's picture at arm's length he muttered, "Sorry, Sally." Rand picked up his keys and touched the speed dial of the telephone. "Loretta! It's Rand. Tell Carol I'll be right over."

REFLECTIONS ON A TOUCH OF SALT

1. Sally and Rand hold two different views about marriage. What is the position of each?

2. Sally and Rand also had different outlooks on how to navigate the "death" of their marriages. What do the concepts of "move forward" and "move on" imply?

3. Salt has positive and negative aspects. Discuss the adage "pouring salt on wounds." How might Rand and Sally's relationship add flavor to their lives? How might it be described as pouring salt on each other's wounds?

4. Under the circumstance, in your opinion, is Rand's fidelity to Carol the right or only response? Does Sally's option have merit?

SEWER RAT

"Are not five sparrows sold for two copper coins?
And not one of them is forgotten before God...
Do not fear therefore; you are of more value than many sparrows.
Luke 12: 6-7

I took that picture at work, not realizing how important it would become to me. Having just graduated from high school, I planned to go to university in the fall, but found myself on the university campus a few months before classes started. I began working for a company trenching in an eight-inch water line. Louie was down in the trench when I arrived on the job. Steve, the foreman, quickly explained what was expected of me: to remove the lumps that might fall into the trench, pass planks and jacks down as called for, and throw down the sand used for a base for the pipe. He introduced me to no one. I learned my co-workers' names by listening. Johnny, Louie, Mike, and the trencher operator, Boris, were already hard at work.

At 9:30 a.m. the canteen truck stopped by. The whole operation ceased for fifteen minutes while everyone bought something to eat or drink. Louie and Johnny crawled up out of the trench. Johnny always chose to climb up the sloping back-filled earth leading up to the trencher, but Louis, monkey-like, climbed up the jacks that held the support planks with an agility that belied his 50 years. The wiry energetic style which most often saw him down on hands and knees grappling with a pipe on the trench floor, together with his dishev-eled appearance won him the title "Sewer Rat."

Louie drank his coffee quickly, crumpled the cup in his hands and tossed it into the partially refilled trench. Then lighting a cigarette, he walked along the road and gazed off at the western horizon. I soon recognized this stroll and gaze as a standard daily procedure. I thought then it was to gain a sense of distant perspective because so much of his time was spent in the confines of a narrow ditch. Strolling back, he seemed to see me for the first time. "You new here, kid." His voice was raspy, the tone challenging. It wasn't really a question, but a statement of sudden recognition. He observed me briefly, giving me the feeling either he didn't approve, or I didn't belong.

"Yes, I started work this morning."

"You want to be a sewer rat all your life, Kid?" His voice was rough, his style demanding. I felt it was a put down. He never called me anything else but Kid all summer. I didn't know what to make of this man. His dark eyes, peering out from underneath the long peak of a greasy cap, bored into mine.

"No, it's a summer job; I'm planning on going to university this fall." At the word, "university" I sensed Louie thought I was attempting to distance myself from him and the rest of the crew.

"I'm at university now," he gestured to the campus just south of us and laughed. "If you're smart, Kid, and want to go to university, stay out of the trench." It sounded like a command. With that he climbed back down to the trench floor.

Initially, I resented Louie, but as the summer progressed, I learned he had an uncanny ability to detect things that were not readily apparent. Out of the trench, one morning, for coffee break, Louie unexpectedly announced, "You didn't grow up here," his hand sweeping the north horizon indicating the city.

"No, I'm from Valley City."

Louie rarely smiled, but now a smile worked its way into the wrinkles around his eyes. "I lived in le paw."

Louie spoke so quickly in his French accent that I couldn't figure out the "Le Paw." "Where?"

"Le Paw, nort' of Valley City."

Oh, The Pas!" I exclaimed in recognition. Louie's French pronunciation of The Pas as Le Paw was new to me. I interpreted his smirk as berating me for my ignorance.

Two days later when the canteen truck arrived, Louie and Johnny were in the trench fitting an obstinate joint. Steve, who generally called a halt when the truck arrived, was away. Boris climbed off his machine and ambled to the canteen truck. I had noticed Louie always ordered coffee double sugar, which probably accounted for his badly decayed front teeth. Before the truck pulled away, I bought coffees for Louie and Johnny and put their cups on a plank beside the ditch. I knew they'd be disappointed when they got out of the trench to realize they had missed the truck.

Moments later, I pointed to the cups indicating the one with double sugar. Louie's eyes communicated his appreciation better than his slight smile.

The day Johnny hurt his hip when a jack gave way and hit his leg; I joined Louie in the trench.

"Why you down here, Kid?" Louie demanded.

I didn't feel welcome. I doubt he saw me as capable. "No, I volunteered." I had found the work above quite monotonous and was looking for a change.

"No good you down here," Louie continued. "You want to go to university; you stay on top. Too dangerous down here.

Louie quickly showed me how to tamp down the sand on which the pipe was laid, grade the pipe using a level and finally push the pipe into place with the crowbar once we had greased the "O" ring. "You did ok Kid," he said when the day was over.

When our trenching had moved into the campus area, we were digging in front of the library. Summer school students walked around the machinery to get to and from the building. There were no tapes to mark off the construction zone. At that time there was no steel cage that surrounded and protected the workers. Workplace safety was minimal as I remember.

After I'd eaten my lunch in the shade of a tree, I had stretched out to rest and soak up a little sun. Coming back to the work site, I noticed Louie, watching a group of female students pass by' "You got a woman," he asked?

"No."

"To lie beside soft woman is beautiful. You need a good woman." His comments seemed to spring more from pleasant memories than lustful desires.

Later that day, someone disturbed the earth lying beside the trench. A shower of soil and lumps rained down on Louie and me. We both jumped suddenly and began scrambling out of the trench. When Louie realized what happened, he unloaded a string of vulgarities – a mixture of French and English. Resuming work again he said, "You no swear?"

"Sometimes," I replied feeling sheepish as if I had to justify. "I just didn't develop the habit." We worked quietly together for a while.

Louie finally spoke. "You mad at Louie for swearing?"

"No." I was suddenly aware this man felt he had offended a younger person. I was beginning to feel a kinship.

Outwardly Louie appeared unkempt; usually unshaven, his clothing wrinkled and soiled, and although he was short, his gruffness projected a hard image that made him loom taller than he was.

One hot day about noon, Louie opened his top shirt button, something he rarely did in spite of the weather. I glimpsed a small gold chain and a tiny crucifix nestled among his graying chest hairs. The delicacy and obvious quality of the piece seemed strangely incongruous with his image. As we prepared to go back to work, I said, "I like your chain!" Quickly he buttoned up his shirt but said nothing. It was now my turn to feel I had offended him.

"I'm sorry." We walked toward the trencher in silence.

Before descending into the trench Louie said, "Chain belonged to my wife. She died five years ago."

"I'm sorry," Louie, "I didn't mean to…"

"It's ok, Kid." Louie said brusquely. After a short silence during which he looked out toward the horizon, he added, "She was a good woman."

Just two weeks before I was to quit work, the trench caved in on Louie. We were digging near the river then. The soil was soft and the trench deep. Steve had never let me go back into the trench after a cave-in that sent Louie and me scrambling. I suspect Louie had something to do with that. We had used extra bracing and longer planks, but when the earth begins to move, one jack slightly misplaced can give way weakening the whole support. Steve saw the plank begin to bend and shouted. Johnny, who always worked at the end nearest the trencher, scrambled up, but Louie had been bent over greasing the "O" ring just below the plank. Once the earth started moving it couldn't be stopped. The motion snapped the planks and twisted the jacks out of effective position.

The extra jacks, like bars in a prison cell, trapped him. When we finally dug to Louie, we found him pinned chest down, his lungs crushed against the lowest jack. His right hand clutched at the neck of his shirt as if trying to clasp the crucifix.

I had taken a picture of Louie during coffee break the week before the accident. Louie, as usual, stood looking out to the horizon after finishing his coffee. He was unaware that I snapped the photo. I now saw a longing in that gaze, which earlier I attributed to the need for perspective.

There was so much of interest in that picture, his clothing, his pose and even the cigarette. Something about Louie had stuck with me. The picture remained on my dresser top for some time before I placed it in a drawer.

It was after I met Victor that I looked for the picture again.

My Auntie had asked me to help at the Main Street Mission on Saturday mornings. At first, I agreed out of a sense of obligation to Auntie. After all, she had provided me with free board and room while I was at university. But spending my Saturday mornings making coffee and cleaning up tables opened my eyes to a different world.

Some of the clients came for warmth, a bite to eat and a cup of coffee but many for the sense of community. Some were friendly, others private, closed and perhaps a bit defensive.

Victor seemed out of place there. He stood head and shoulders above others. Thick-waisted, his bulk and his square face, full head of thick greying hair and a three-day beard also helped set him apart. Unlike the others who arrived dressed in shirts and jeans, with coats only when necessary, Victor wore a brown sports jacket over a dress shirt and a pair of cords. He had large hands with short chubby fingers, a signet ring on the finger of one hand and a plain gold wedding band on the other.

Victor preferred tea to coffee and was careful to make it just right, warming his cup first under the hot water spigot before putting in the tea bag and then covering it with hot water. He would submerge the tea bag and draw it up in yoyo-like fashion. Adding the sugar and whitener was a deliberately fastidious operation.

He was a friendly giant, chatting with many including me as I manned the coffee urn. He was interested in knowing what I did outside of volunteering, my age and if I was married. I felt at ease then to ask him some questions. "What brings you to the Mission, Victor?" It was not the kind of question I would ask most or any of the other clientele. I felt the circumstances that brought them there were private and perhaps embarrassing. But Victor seemed out of place.

"Broke," was his one-word reply.

"What happened?"

"My wife."

I waited for an explanation.

"In a divorce settlement. The judge froze my assets until this thing is settled." He motioned me to his table. We sat and he continued. "I own a trucking firm, Northern Lights Transfer."

"You mean big trucks, eighteen wheelers? How many trucks?" I was fascinated. An owner of a trucking firm here at the Mission!

Victor settled in to tell me his story. "I have eighteen wheelers, twenty-four wheelers, pups, the whole lot; trucks all over western Canada and into

Ontario." When the Judge froze my assets, I had trucks stuck in every province from Alberta to Ontario. Couldn't get a lot of those trucks back to base. My bank accounts and credit cards were frozen. Drivers were not able to buy fuel. I'm as good as penniless."

I spoke without thinking. "Wow, from riches to rags just like that!"

Victor seemed to take no offence to my comment. He went on. "The Bitch, she did nothing to help my business and now she wants half of everything! I don't think so! That's why I'm in court."

"When's the court date?"

"Next week."

I had to get back to my post; the coffee urn was empty and clients were waving cups in the air. But when Victor came in the next Saturday for breakfast, I asked him how the court event went.

"Didn't happen," he muttered. "Judge put it off for another two weeks. Wife's lawyer making more demands; wants more time."

"So, your trucks are still stuck all over western Canada?"

"Judge released ten thousand dollars, so I was able to bring most of them back and deliver the goods."

I didn't know much about business. My father had died when I was quite young and my mother was a teacher. Not having trucks on the road, losing contracts to other trucking firms while you waited for issues to be resolved; I could imagine how expensive and difficult that could be. Then there must be a lawyer and court fees. "That's costing you a lot of money! Can't you work something out between the wife and you?"

Victor's blue eyes seemed to drill into mine. "You can't imagine what this is costing me and her. Every day we are not on the road, there's less money; less money to be divided. She doesn't seem to get that. There's still license fees and insurance. I'm losing contracts and good drivers."

The intensity of the words, the steely gaze, even the spittle on his lips conveyed the bitterness he felt. "There's no way I'm working something out with **her**!" I could feel the contempt in the way he said "her." I never did learn his wife's name. It was always, "the Bitch" or "Her." I left Victor then to continue wiping tables pondering how a relationship declined from the Sweetheart or Honey stage to Bitch.

The following Saturday, Victor was at The Mission wearing a black leather jacket. Printed on the back in red letters were the words, The Pas Trucking.

That's when I remembered Louie. "Do you come from The Pas, Victor?" We were standing at the coffee station, Victor methodically stirring little bits of creamer into his tea.

"Yeah, I grew up in The Pas. That's where the business started. That's what I first named the company." He slapped his hand over a shoulder in reference to the name on his back. "We still have an office there."

I was wiping up coffee spills around the urn. "I worked with a man from The Pas a number of years back. His name was Louie. He was tragically killed on the job when a trench caved in." Victor's demeanor changed in a flash. I had never seen him smile but now his face was radiant. It was like an electric light bulb had just turned on.

"You knew, Louie?"

"Yeah, we worked on the same crew."

Victor motioned me to a table. I knew then I was in for a story.

"Louie and I married sisters." He got the good one."

"Louie spoke highly of his wife."

"Did he tell you about her then?"

When Victor started telling this story the narrative was so different from the details of his troubles. His own story was told with gutturals, invectives and sneers. Now this storyline was touched with admiration and pleasantry.

"Emily was the older of the two sisters. She was sickly; had been all her life. She and Louie met each other at a dance. Still kids really. But he loved her. Old Louie stuck with her. They didn't have an easy life."

"How so?"

"Her health mainly. TB is what the doctors said was wrong with her. She wasted away. Louie did the housework eventually making the meals, pushing her everywhere in a wheelchair. Doctoring and drugs cost them lots of money.

"But you know she always had a smile on her face. I don't think I ever heard her complain; maybe when no one but Louie was around. She was a religious woman. Maybe that helped her. When she passed away, Louie took it hard. You'd think it would have been a relief – days to yourself again, more money in your pocket. But something died in Louie the day she died. He was never the same. Pulled up stakes from The Pas and moved down to the city."

My admiration of Louie, despite his gruffness, was growing. He had kept all those details to himself just saying "She was a good woman."

Victor wasn't homeless just as most who frequented the Mission were not. But he had made the Mission his place for breakfast. Another week passed. I greeted Victor while he was preparing his tea. "Court case this week?"

He took his time in replying. I think he was counting the number of times he dunked his tea bag. "Should be all over Wednesday. Then I can get back to my life."

"Will you win?"

"Of course; no doubt about that."

"Why so sure? You got the better lawyer?"

"My wife's an Indian."

The shock on my face was transparent. I was taken aback that his wife was Indigenous. I was pretty ignorant about Indigenous people then, and my confined, white experiences didn't include mixed marriages although I knew they happened. There were no reserves close to Valley City. It wasn't until I came to the city that I saw an Indigenous person.

"That's right. My wife is an Indian. Louie and I married Indian sisters. He got the good one even though sickly. I got the pretty one who turned out Bitch."

"How does this guarantee you a win in court?"

Do you think a judge is going to award an Indian half of my possessions? Lawyer says there has never been a precedent. Maybe even laws against it."

"So why does she try then?"

"She wants to set a precedent."

I was about to say "good luck" but didn't. Did I really wish him the right to win?

Different laws for the Indigenous people were common then – laws about possessions or inheritance. I looked out at many of those men and women sitting around the tables in the Mission. Yes, the majority were of Indigenous background. Their lives were lived out on a different playing field than mine.

On my way home from the Mission that Saturday, I stopped at a Kresge store and purchased a picture frame. Louis's picture, now framed, sat on my desk until I moved. It became an icon of sorts reminding me, not only of his death, but that what appears slovenly may actually be saintly.

That picture now hangs with my other prize-winning photos. As a photo-journalist, I portrayed Mela from India carrying her load of firewood on her head and Fabiola from Haiti filling her water jug at a spigot surrounded by three small children. These pictures are icons and hallmarks of my growing awareness of cultural inequities and the depth and beauty that lies in the complexity of a human being.

REFLECTIONS ON SEWER RAT

1. Identify the differences of appearance and the differences of heart in the story.

2. What were your immediate reactions and attitudes toward the characters based on their appearance?

3. From your own experiences, trace the progression of change when initial appearances, and your reactions, gave way to heart knowledge.

4. How have you benefited, or not, from white entitlement and privilege or lack thereof?

5. Are there different laws for different people of which you are aware, and have these differences benefited or harmed you?

6. The last paragraph speaks to a growth of understanding for the storyteller. What experience might you have had that has given insight into injustice, inequity or misunderstanding not previously recognized?

THREE WISHES

Hanna stretched languidly beneath her bed sheets. Through half open eyelids she identified daylight above the heavy linen drapes. Groping for the remote on the bedside table, she pressed a button and watched the bedroom brighten as sunlight washed into the room filtered through the white sheers. The drapes, like trained sentinels, quietly retreated to stand vigil at the corner of each wall.

Picking up a second remote, she scanned selections and decided it was a Leonard Cohen morning. She liked the ambiguity of his lyrics and the minor cadence of his songs. Cohen's voice filled the room singing about a bird on a wire, a drunk, both wanting to be free. Yawning she retreated beneath the sheets and blankets to listen to the plaintive call for freedom.

It was her birthday. At her birth, when a neighbourhood midwife assisted her into this world, she entered a world of poverty. *Such a long journey from the small country home of my birth.* Her natal home was without running water or an indoor toilet. Water for washing came from a large crockery pitcher stationed on a small table with a basin in the bedroom area her parents used. The kitchen table, dining area, a couch and the kitchen stove had all competed for the same floor space. Her two older sisters and she had slept in a small garret above the main floor.

This bedroom is twice the floor space of that entire house. Materially she had done well; emotionally and spiritually, her outcome was quite different. For the past several weeks, months really, she had been rethinking her life. Life-long regrets crept in.

Today I will celebrate my birthday with my two closest friends.

That thought energized her. Throwing back the covers, she tucked her feet into soft padded slippers, and moved toward the ensuite. Reaching into the large walk-in shower, she turned the handles to start the spray, moved back for a moment, selected a tube of scented soap and stepped into the jets of warm water spilling from three different nozzles. After a quick soaping and

rinsing, she turned off the side jets and for several minutes stood under the
rain shower nozzle. She relished the soft tactual touch of warm water

A memory interrupted this pleasant moment – thoughts of the many times
she had dipped her fingers into the baptismal font at the rear of the church
and touched her forehead in an act of penitence and baptismal renewal. She
visualized the Hindu brothers, as she had seen them, submerging and rising
from the waters of the Ganges River while murmuring prayers in acts of absolution. Of late, she too entertained the need for forgiveness and renewal. She
turned off the refreshing warm water and stepped out of the shower.

Cohen's sultry voice now intoned his wonderful "Hallelujah." Wrapped
in a large towel she rubbed her hair and body and hummed along hearing of
Bathsheba bathing on her roof and David watching her in the moonlight. Guilt
etched her thoughts as she recalled her own sexual indiscretions prompted by
jealousy.

But this was her birthday; she had wonderful plans for the day. Selecting
and laying aside slacks and blouse for the morning, slipping on a gown, she
hurried to the door to receive her breakfast from Carmen.

Seated at the small glass-topped table in the sitting area of her bedroom,
Hanna looked over the beautiful gardens of her back yard. Visitors called it
Eden; she knew it was lovely. She also knew it would not be so beautiful without consistent hard work to remove the unwanted elements. Just now Jose was
busy pruning back rose bushes for the spring growth. The daffodils, tulips
and narcissus were all in colourful bloom. She loved spring and always had – a
great season in which to be born. The pungent aroma of her coffee and its
warm stimulation encouraged her to enjoy this moment a little longer.

A large portrait of her husband, Einar, hung on the wall across from her
bedroom sitting area just as paintings of great men have hung in homes for
centuries. *He was a good man. I have not been a good woman.*

Her portrait of equal size hung next to the entrance of Einar's personal
walk-in closet. They had posed for the pictures forty years ago. She would have
been thirty.

Einar loved that picture. Einar had loved her totally, unabashedly. His
death two years ago left her a wealthy widow with endless possessions.

Her coffee was cooling, her toast almost eaten. Her two long-time friends,
Rebecca and Ruth, were also celebrating birthdays this week. It was a remarkable thing that they had initially met years ago and now after a long period of

separation found themselves living in the same city. She had volunteered to host today's birthday party and planned to share a well-kept secret.

*****

Rebecca stood at a distance from the small table, arms crossed, examining each of the pottery figurines. Then picking up King Balthazar, she examined him closely. He knelt on one leg. His opulent white robe, trimmed with a narrow gold border draped gracefully in smooth folds. A white turban highlighted the dark skin of his face, hands and feet. Turning him over, she looked carefully for any flaw or imperfection.

For each of Hanna and Ruth's birthdays during the past four years, she created pieces of the nativity scene – Mary and Joseph, the baby Jesus, a shepherd, and an angel. This year each would receive wise men — Balthazar and Melchior.

Holding Melchior now she perused his standing figure, the blue robe tucked at the waist with a braided yellow rope belt. A white cloth, carefully molded to cover cheeks and neck, covered his head. The intricacies of his sandals had been a challenge, but she loved the results. Both men reached out extending gifts. They were perfect. She could wrap them now in tissue and place them in the boxes. Her skill in pottery had come a long way in the past decade. She loved her studio and her house from here she had been able to paint and sculpt, but above all, where she could be herself.

As she wrapped the gifts, she reflected on her choice of characters. They were wise men, not kings as so commonly held, but powerful eastern bureaucrats—influential policy makers— choosing subsequent leaders. They were in fact not kings but king makers; powerful males who called the shots. Not unlike her husband, Ike, she realized, who was a powerful man familiar with making important decisions. He would no longer call the shots on her life.

The Wise Men were remembered as seekers, astute in reading the signs of sky and political times. Her husband, on the other hand, had been easily deceived for years. The Wise Men were humble, willing to bow before a little child born in obscurity but having the potential, they thought, to greatness. Her husband was a conceited taker – a user.

She had allowed him to use her as his pawn for too many years. Yesterday, forty years to the day after they married, she had walked out on him. She chuckled with delight at the irony. He would have arrived at home last evening anticipating a meal like the ones she prepared faithfully, only to find an empty house, an unset table and a note which read:

You're on your own. Don't bother looking for me.
We'll see each other with our lawyers.
Call one of your mistresses to cook your supper.

Rebecca

Twenty-five years ago she first became aware Ike was cheating on her. Her first thought had been confrontation; her choice was to delay. Today, on the threshold of a new beginning she felt a twinge of regret for that decision.

The wrapping was finished; the bows, artistic in detail and attachment, were in place and the name cards attached. She would take these gifts to her friends today.

*****

Ruth adjusted the rubber mat on which she had been kneeling. She was relocating some perennials and weeding before planting this year's annuals in her flower beds, this morning. As usual, she'd begun her work at seven. The early start gave her an hour or more in the garden before stopping to prepare her breakfast. It was her period for meditation and reflection on the coming day and a moment to give thanks. For me, Ruth mused, God has been good.

On rainy days and in the colder months she would be at her sewing machine. Her mother had taught her to sew as a child. Her high school Home Economics teacher had seen her talent and pushed her to try new and imaginative things, but it was her mother-in-law who had insisted she enter competitions.

Her favorite was the sunrise bed quilt. Edged by a dark border, the top pillow area was designed as hills with a spray of orange sun peeking out. Done in a semi pinwheel design, the brightening colours of orange and yellow then stretched out over the remainder of the quilt in graduated blocks, with the larger ones anchoring the foot end. The quilt was an artistic metaphor of that day when the sun broke through the dark clouds of her life.

The morning sun provided Ruth a warmth of happiness – glad she could garden. Working with the soil and plants reminded her of another Ruth who had worked in the field. She had found the Bible in the small attic suite where she and Bo had first lived at her parents-in-law's home. An old family Bible it was. As she ran her thumb over the pages, she noticed this section called *Ruth*. Intrigued, she read all four chapters about Ruth and Boaz. She had identified with Ruth the Moabite's feelings of rejection and disdain.

Glancing at her watch, she noted it was past nine o'clock. It was time to pack up the gardening stuff, cut some fresh flowers for a bouquet, prepare a light breakfast and get herself ready for lunch with Hanna and Rebecca.

Ruth missed Bo. *It has been six months since he left me. We always did this spring gardening together.* They had done almost everything together and for that reason she missed him grievously. What a remarkable couple they had been. Brought to marriage by problematic circumstances, they had forged out a loving relationship and an equitable partnership. They had agreed some fifty years ago that only they would know that secret. But now, after Bo's death, she felt at liberty to share her story.

*****

Hanna was ready for her quests. She'd chosen a comfortable off-white knit outfit. The grey high-heeled shoes complimented the grey of her suit's cloth-covered buttons. As she surveyed her table, light from the window picked up the white highlights in her dark-dyed hair.

Her Amherst Wedgwood china, elegant against the pale gray tablecloth, surrounded by spotlessly polished silver was enhanced by Carmen's artistic touch. The placement of crystal wine glasses and embossed napkins made the table a work of art. Together they had prepared a gourmet lunch and a small platter of fresh shrimp to go with a cool white chardonnay to enjoy before their meal. The table needed one more thing – a center piece, but she was sure Ruth would bring a lovely bouquet of flowers. Hanna looked at the sophisticated and extravagant display. It was the kind of thing she had grown to love. Now, she realized, it had become a necessary part of her identity.

The soft chime of the doorbell announced Ruth's arrival. They hugged briefly at the door before Hanna relieved her of the beautiful fresh cut tulips, surrounded by yellow daffodils with sprigs of white hyacinths as accents. "They're beautiful," Hanna exclaimed, taking Ruth's light coat.

"Happy Birthday, Hanna!" Ruth rose on her toes and kissed Hanna lightly on the cheek. At sixty-eight years of age, Ruth was striking. Her pure white hair without a touch of tint or colour, framing her oval face, contrasted nicely with the short black jacket she wore over a white knee length dress. Her attire complimented the relaxed and friendly bearing she possessed.

Hanna handed the coat to Carmen and then stood back to admire Ruth from head to toe. "You are lovely, as always. How do you keep away from those extra pounds and a double chin?" touching her own chin as if to illustrate.

Ruth smiled at the compliment. "Pure genetics, I'll assure you."

The doorbell tones sent Hanna scurrying to the door to welcome Rebecca and relieve her of the two beautifully wrapped gifts. Rebecca was the tallest of the three women. Carmen took Rebecca's coat while Hanna stood back admiring Rebecca's attire. Her salt and pepper hair in a pixie cut with a somewhat disheveled twist suited her artistic flair. She wore a three-quarter length knit topper with smocking extending from shoulder to waist, providing a shapely fit to her tall body. Below was a white cotton top that hung loosely over blue pants.

"I marvel at your ability to look so striking," exclaimed Hanna reaching up to hug her and kiss her cheek. Ruth joined them and the three came together in a communal hug of affection.

The meal was delightful: excellent food, light conversation, reminiscing about birthdays past, lots of laughter prompted by good wine and light hearts. If each carried with her an emotional story, it was not evident.

"Let's take our dessert and coffee in the sunroom," Hanna suggested. There amidst potted tropical plants and soft green coloured furniture they settled facing each other in comfortable chairs. Carmen entered carrying three pieces of chocolate cake with a single lit candle in each. Spontaneously they broke out in singing Happy Birthday followed by a good laugh. As the candles flickered, Hanna commented, "Let's each make a wish before blowing out the candles. I have a wish and a story I'd like to share."

Rebecca and Ruth both nodded affirmatively; they paused for a moment in reflection before blowing out their candles.

Hanna took a small bite of her cake, chewed quietly, and looked at both women for a moment. In the pause, Ruth interjected. "We're curious, Hanna. What could you possibly wish for?"

"I'm sure this is more a confession than a wish." After a pause Hanna continued. "Today I want to tell you some things about my past." Pausing again for a moment, she took another small bite of cake before proceeding.

"I'm sure I appear a sniveling Ahab here amidst my abundance; but in spite of that abundance, I have struggled to find satisfaction." Her well-modulated soft voice made it easy to listen to her tale. "I respected Einar, but deep down I resented him."

Rebecca and Ruth cast brief glances at each other. "Why would you resent him?" Rebecca questioned incredulously while arranging a small piece of her cake on her fork.

"But you and Einar appeared so compatible," Ruth commented.

"We were not the soul partners you might have imagined." Hanna continued. "Einar felt and thought so much differently than I." Again, a pause, as Hanna took a sip of her coffee and a small bite of her cake. "When we met, he had a university degree, managed his own business and I was just a couple of years out of high school. I didn't feel his equal. When he asked me for that first date, I was the envy of the office. I liked him; he was attractive, decisive, thoughtful – always considerate. When he asked me to marry him a year later, I considered myself the luckiest woman in the office.

Hanna busied herself with her cake for a moment, put down her plate and sipped her coffee before continuing. Ruth ate quietly giving Hanna her time; Rebecca added, "You've got our interest, Hanna."

"There was another woman in the office, Honor, who liked, perhaps I should say, loved Einar too. She had a head for business and worked closely with him. At first I was uneasy." Hanna sat erect, her legs crossed, the toe of her right foot tucked behind her left leg. "He had ideas he shared with me which I either didn't understand or didn't care enough to understand, but I knew he shared those ideas with Honor who capably understood and assisted him in his decisions."

"You sensed Einar gave Honor too much attention, placing her ahead of you?" Rebecca was curious.

"I had little reason to think that. Einar lavished me with gifts. At first it was a bit overwhelming. I came from humble beginnings. Einar had money and he made money. Our first home was nice, our second nicer and this one palatial."

"It certainly is beautiful!" Ruth commented, her eyes doing a quick sweep of the room.

"Einar was gentle and generous. Thinking I deserved better, he encouraged me to furnish, to lavish. It was one of his ways of showering love, I guess."

"It's very obvious then that he loved you," Rebecca interjected, her eyes scanning the room. "So why the resentment?"

Hanna smiled an acknowledgement to the compliment and proceeded to the question. "Yes, something was missing. I wanted to be more than the mistress of a beautiful home, the host to his business friends, including Honor."

"She did bother you more than you're telling," Rebecca said.

"With Einar's coaching, Honor started a business of her own. She owns Honor's Fashions, the women's accessories line of stores.

"Oh, I love all the things in that place. It's a favorite stop for me, exclaimed Rebecca."

"So, Honor worked for Einar, then began her own business…" Ruth prompted.

"Yes, and Einar provided her with start-up money, an investment in her idea, which really paid off. She went ahead and made it a success."

"So, you had difficulty with all this obviously." Rebecca was nibbling at the cake in front of her.

Hanna set aside her cup on the small table beside her. "It wasn't easy to be the passive hostess while the real interest and activity was the business talk going on around the table. I had no voice." Hanna reached for her cup, noticed it was empty and set it back. "Honor could keep up with the men, with the business jargon, the jokes. With her smiles and gentle hand touches to those beside her, she was a warm and welcomed participant at any gathering." Hanna had been sitting primly but now planted her feet firmly apart and leaned forward. "I felt I was totally ignored. I was nothing but the pretty icon, the good wife, sitting at the end of the table."

"But I never knew Einar to be scornful of you, Hanna," Ruth interjected. "He always seemed appreciative and considerate of you."

"Oh, don't get me wrong. He was." Hanna's carefully manicured, slender long fingers encircled the cup Carmen had replenished. "Einar was always very complimentary to me. It was me. I was jealous. You know Shakespeare's 'green-eyed monster.' I looked at Honor; she was pretty, intelligent, and admired by my husband. Why did he marry me? Jealousy makes you paranoid. I was sure he thought more of her than of me.

Ruth reached over to take Hanna's hand.

"Somehow, I had become swamped by Einar, by Honor, their success. I continued to lose self-confidence and a little more of my soul – who I was."

For a moment she stared into the dark liquid in her cup. "I lost my voice – my ability to say what I wanted. I was nobody."

"Did you express that to Einar?" Ruth voiced the question both she and Rebecca had.

"Not emphatically enough. I suppose I was intimidated in those first years, being a decade younger than Einar."

"Are you painting too glowing a picture of Einar, Hanna?" Rebecca's pointed evaluation indicated she had some awareness. "The older man marries the young, uninformed country girl just so he can exercise all the decisions. That's men, Hanna!" Her voice was emphatic, and she plunked her plate down on a side table as if to reinforce her point.

Hanna weighed Rebecca's comment for a moment.

Carmen stood in the doorway. She asked quietly if she could pick up the plates. As Carmen reached down to retrieve a plate, Ruth touched her arm. "The cake was delicious."

"Thanks, Ruth. Can I refresh your coffee cups?"

"No, Carmen, we'll have some tea later." Hanna directed.

Hanna picked up her story. "When I turned thirty, I decided I wasn't going to be the pretty, passive little wife anymore. I was going to take things into my own hands, make something of myself."

"Ah, so what did you do?" Rebecca asked eagerly.

Hanna looked at both women as if unsure about proceeding. "Well, first I had an affair."

Ruth was visually shocked. "Oh, Hanna, how did that happen? That comes with risk and betrayal."

"I know you're disappointed in me, Ruth, but I was lonely, angry and frustrated.

"Yes, it wasn't without some anxiety. It wasn't planned; it happened. I was angry and upset enough with Einar to create a fertile moment for it to occur." Hanna's answering smile bordered on a smirk. She freed the toe which she had tucked behind her leg again, placed her feet together and began speaking in a confidential tone. "A single fellow my age at Einar's office liked me. I knew that from attention Hans had shown me at office parties. When I got sidelined in the group by business talk, he would come to my rescue by joining me to chat. He was blonde, blue eyed just like Einar, not quite as tall. Einar was in Europe on business for a month. It was St. Patrick's Day. Several from the office were going out for drinks after work, and ironically, Honor called to ask me to join them. 'You can't sit at home all by yourself; join us,' she pleaded.

Sitting back again in a more relaxed position Hanna continued. "Hans agreed to pick me up and drive me home."

Both Ruth and Rebecca's faces reflected expressions of astonishment, but they chose not to interrupt.

"The following week, I was called again and asked to join them for their Friday evening snack and drink. Before Einar's return, it happened."

"Did he find out about this tryst?" Rebecca asked.

"He did. The conqueror, as he probably thought of himself, may have bragged to his male friends."

With hands raised in a helpless gesture, Hanna continued. "Einar never said a word to me, but Hans was transferred to the Europe office within the month. Einar took me out for supper after Hans had left and asked how things were going. In the course of our discussion, he must have sensed loneliness or better described emptiness." Hanna sighed deeply. "He never asked a thing about Hans, but suggested I get involved with some charities or go to college. So, I went to the community college and got my business diploma."

Rebecca shifted uneasily in her chair. "Well, that was good."

"I had resolved while at college I could be as good as Honor at business. By this time she had left Einar's business and was operating her own."

"Did you have regrets about your affair?" Ruth asked quietly.

Hanna nodded her head in agreement, "Einar's response to that affair should have taught me something about forgiveness and the enduring quality of love. Instead," she threw out her hands in an expression of exasperation, "I became more resentful than ever. I felt guilty. Had Einar asked some questions, gotten angry, scolded me or prompted a confession on my part, perhaps I could have felt some relief." Her voice became soft, sorrowful.

"You were overwhelmed by his forgiving attitude. I know the feeling exactly." Ruth ventured.

Hanna hesitated, "Yes, definitely but more! I felt trivialized, unvalued, dishonoured and confused." Hanna reached into the pocket of her carefully tailored suit jacket, took out a tissue and touched her eyes.

"I thought about confessing…but to admit to adultery?" Her voice rose slightly, and she looked directly at both women. "I thought I would lose everything!"

Hanna' voice took on a reflective tone. "Before college days, I fell in love with possessions. It became an endless want list. A new carpet prompted the need for new sofas and chairs and then new end-tables or a coffee table, art for the walls and then all the little curio pieces to be talked about and admired by the guests."

"I would have longed for that addiction," Rebecca joked.

Hanna became animated and expressive, pointing out furniture and pictures as she spoke. I began a frantic search for more and I realized then if I was like that, there must be hundreds of women in my position just as frantic for that special little piece. Again, she chuckled and shrugged her shoulders. "So, I set up a business providing unique one-of-a-kind things for people looking for a little more. I traded companionship for curios."

"You have a wonderfully successful business. Now don't feel guilty and beat yourself up about being successful!" exclaimed Rebecca, a strident tone to her voice.

"No and yes," Hanna replied. "I am good at business; partly, I have to admit, from Einar's mentoring. But I did lose some perspective. It was a rush not only to build the business, to gather more "enviables" for myself but to prove something to Einar. I could do just as well as Honor. But, in the doing, I lost touch with him."

"But did Einar find time for you?" Rebecca challenged placing her feet back on the floor and sitting up straight.

"I know he tried, but I was involved with a business." Hanna looked directly at both her friends as if to ensure their loyalty.

Rebecca reached over to take the hand of her troubled friend. "Hanna, your efforts at revenge were child's play in comparison to mine."

Hanna took Ruth's hand too. "It's not my wish to compare my love, or better still lack of it for Einar, to other women's love for their husbands. In retrospect, I now recognize that my efforts to strike back became so obsessive I lost the opportunity for a great relationship. Jealousy had prompted contempt." All three sat quietly for a moment.

"That obelisk symbolizes my passion," Hanna rose to pick up a finely tapered bluish obelisk about twelve inches in height, sitting on a table near Ruth. "While in Hong Kong, I took the best part of two days to locate the stone carver in a small village near the China border." Hanna caressed the smooth side of the lapis lazuli. "I had seen that lazuli stone obelisk," she handed it to Ruth to feel its weight, "in a Hong Kong shop and wanted several more. I just knew they would sell well."

Rebecca scratched her head thoughtfully and then palms facing upward she reached out her hands toward Hanna. "Hanna, are we to feel guilty for what we have achieved? You have been creative and industrious."

"Yes, I have worked hard. But since Einar's death, I have come to realize what I have is also because of him." Hanna rose from her chair to face out toward the pool. Turning back to the women, "My wish is that I had learned to truly love the way Einar loved me rather than try to prove myself as good as he or Honor. But…" she hesitated for a moment, "I feel as if I rode through life in the same vehicle as this man, but not beside him as he would have liked. Jealousy and ambition held me back."

Hanna returned to her chair. "I'm sharing this with you today because I am contemplating doing something different. Like a drug addict who wants to go clean but can't bring herself to give up the opiate, I waffle.

"You're looking for some sort of redemption, then, are you?" asked Ruth.

"I want to sell my business and this place."

"But Hanna, it's very beautiful," Rebecca chided. "I can see your touch in every room."

"Exactly, it's not easy. I love all of this." Hanna sat down, crossed her legs and folded her hands on her lap, her expression suggesting uncertainty.

Rebecca interlaced her fingers and rubbed her thumbs along the side of her hands as if somewhat agitated. "Hanna, are you off to the convent then? What's happening?"

"No, Rebecca, that's a bit too severe. Anyway, I'm not Catholic. It's too late for Einar's forgiveness but… I need to do something redemptive. What I wish I could do now is to appreciate each remaining moment of my life and to become a giver." Hanna paused again, interlaced her fingers on her lap and looked at these two trusted friends. "I've never had children. God alone knows how I have wanted and prayed for them…"

Ruth jumped in, her smile suggesting inspiration. "God also knows, Hanna, how many orphaned children there are in the world. Thousands of women here and in developing countries could use your expertise to set up small businesses to support those children. You have the resources, the connections and the business experience to help. It could give you purpose and satisfaction." Ruth's voice rose in that gentle reflective tone but full of excitement.

"But do I have the courage to dare? Could I after all these years now truly learn to give and be forgiven?"

"Ruth leaned forward, "I believe you are already on your way. Forgiveness starts, does it not, with repentance. I hear that in your story."

As if that were her entrance cue, Carmen entered carrying a tray with teapot, cups, the condiments and some chocolates. She poured the tea. Rebecca called for a toast; "To Hanna and a new resolution!"

Cups in hand, they touched the rims and took their first sip.

*****

Rebecca fumbled in the pocket of her topper and pulled out a small packet of cigarettes. "I have a story I planned to share with you today. I also have a wish." Holding her cigarette between two fingers, she raised it toward Hanna. "Do you mind?"

"Yes, I do, Rebecca. Carmen is quite allergic to smoke. It's warm enough, so let's move out onto the patio."

Carmen immediately gathered the teapot and accessories and carried them out. The women followed through the double French doors onto the field-stone patio.

The patio faced a small kidney-shaped pool. Vines, freshly clothed in light green, spring leaves, grew upward all around the patio and across the lattice roof. Shrubs and potted tropical plants added to the tropical atmosphere. In one corner three smaller lounging chairs, set in a circle, invited conversation. Hanna and Ruth sat; Rebecca remained standing, lit the cigarette and inhaled deeply. She blew out two lines of smoke before she began speaking. "Well, my story is one of regret, deceit and revenge." She paced slowly in a small elliptical pattern behind her chair.

"Is it that bad with you and Ike?" Ruth asked in a note of quiet sympathy.

"Not any longer! I left him yesterday. It was our fortieth wedding anniversary. As far as I know he is either still looking for me, or was so relieved I'm gone, he never bothered. I'm free at last."

"Oh, my goodness! Where are you staying?" Hanna asked.

"I'm in my own home. I bought it some years ago unbeknownst to Ike or anyone except my brother. But wait, I need to start at the beginning." Rebecca took another drag on her cigarette and blew another pencil thin projectile into the air.

"At age thirty-three I knew our marriage had gone flat. Ike showed little interest in my art studies and even less in my teaching. We lived in two different worlds. It was as if I didn't exist. Our only common interest was our boys.

Rebecca had been pacing behind her chair, looking out toward the garden. "Similar stories from colleagues at school convinced me this state of marriage was common. I was prepared to resign myself to what it was." She stopped her pacing, looked directly at her friends. "One of my fellow teachers had the courage to inform me Ike was cheating – with his secretary of course. My friend's husband had connections to a private investigator. He confirmed the report.

"I'm so sorry, Rebecca. That must have been devastating." Ruth consoled.

"Oh, I wish I had known. Perhaps I could have helped you, Rebecca," Hanna offered quietly.

Rebecca dragged on her cigarette, felt the refreshing calm as the smoke coursed through her lungs. Then she ground out the butt in the ashtray Carmen had provided. She indicated the ashtray. "I'm going to quit this dirty habit now too." Finally settling herself in her chair she kicked off her shoes, tucked her feet up under her crossed legs, and then refreshed her mouth with a sip of tea.

"I had prepared my confrontation with Ike. I was angry and was determined to get out of this marriage immediately and take the boys with me. But Ike was away for a couple of days. That gave me pause for thought.

"I had seen firsthand how children are affected when parents split. A friend of mine at work is still resentful towards her mother over her parents' divorce years ago."

"Divorces can be so messy and difficult, especially when children are involved. I understand your hesitation," Hanna sympathized.

Rebecca looked out toward the pool before continuing. "I began to understand what marginalized meant. Over and over, I asked, why was I being cheated on? Was I not pretty enough, intelligent enough, sexy enough or outgoing enough?" She looked first to Hanna, then Ruth. "Suddenly I questioned my worth, my competency, my capacity as a spouse. So much of who I was, seemed tied up in my relationship with Ike." Her hands now went up in an expression of exasperation.

Moving from her chair to where Rebecca sat, Ruth put her arm around her. "Rebecca I'm so sorry for you. I knew those lonely feelings. It's scary!"

Rebecca reached up to touch Ruth's hand on her shoulder. "Thank you, Ruth. Ike loved his boys. He did give them time even if he cared less about me. He got them into hockey, swimming, fishing, skiing, and Tai Chi. Ike made good money. She punctuated her points with quick hand movements.

"What were you planning?" Hanna asked.

"So, after two days of thinking, I decided against the divorce. A divorce would negatively affect the boys' sports and education as my salary was a pittance in comparison to his. I wanted my boys to have the best. I had worked out this plan of revenge." A sinister smile crossed her face as she took in the inquiring faces of her friends.

Ruth had remained standing beside Rebecca with a hand on her shoulder but now returned to her chair.

"When Ike returned, I suggested we start education funds for the boys. He agreed. I channeled my salary into savings and let him carry most of the household expenses. I turned on the charm without being too obvious."

Hanna and Ruth exchanged raised eyebrows but remained silent.

"I know, I know. But I was determined my sons would have everything they deserved; it became my mission. I kept my PI friend on him. His secretary got pregnant. By all accounts he was the father.

"Oh, Rebecca," Hanna leaned forward and took Rebecca's hand. "That kind of news is so devastating. It just confirms the degree of betrayal that's taking place."

Rebecca held Hanna's hand as she continued, "Yes, I felt violated and totally betrayed. At that point Ike wanted to review our expenses." Withdrawing her hand from Hanna's she sat back in her chair. "I had been meticulous. His money was only spent on household items and education. He already looked after the sports. My personal items and clothing came from my salary." Rebecca reached into her pocket and pulled out the cigarette pack, had second thoughts and put it away again.

"The secretary was obviously demanding money and probably more commitment." Rebecca stood, gesturing with her hands as if to indicate she was justified in what she did, "Hey, I was giving him the best of both worlds. He had a home, the dignity of marriage, his sons were looked after, and he got sex from me occasionally and the thrill of a younger woman also, until she was pregnant. That's when his stress and unhappiness began to show."

"But why would you provide all that?" Ruth asked, her forehead furrowed in perplexity. "It must have been worrisome and stressful. What if Ike suspected your deception and became angry?"

Rebecca relaxed in her chair again. "I was being very careful and getting some pleasure seeing him squirm. This was costing him financially. Besides, what fun are pregnant secretaries?"

"My brother helped me find a house across town. For a number of years we rented it out. Five years ago I remodeled it and built an art studio with a kiln. The boys had left home by this time, so whenever Ike was out of town, I'd be there. It is my sanctuary."

Rebecca chuckled seditiously. "Ike abandoned the first secretary and her child for another younger woman at his office. My PI informed me he had to make a financial agreement for childcare with the first secretary. His infidelity was becoming costly."

Rebecca rose from her chair, circled behind it and holding onto the back of the chair with both hands leaned in toward Hanna and Ruth. "Ike has been postponing retirement for a while and I know why." Her voice rose slightly. "Like Hanna's Einar, he's a few years older than I. Now I'm filing for divorce and demanding half. It's legally mine. He may never be able to retire."

A gust of wind rattled the leaves of the potted plants.

"Could this plot backfire on you?" Hanna queried. "You don't know how he's going to react to your note?"

"But can't Ike claim half of your possessions, including your house?" asked Ruth astutely.

"Yes, but one-half my retirement salary is pittance in comparison to one-half his total worth. The house I bought is in my brother's name just for that reason. Ike can't touch that. Rebecca beamed broadly and took her seat.

"Rebecca, I hate seeing you so malicious." It was Ruth's cautious comment. "I hope you don't become bitter toward life."

A stronger gust toppled a plant. Hanna jumped to right it, but the wind steadily blew more strongly and toppled three more. The sky was ominously black. Ruth and Rebecca jumped up to help. Hanna stopped them. "Thanks. I'll have Jose look after things here. Let's move back indoors."

Standing side by side in the sunroom, they watched the storm swirling dirt into the air, bending the trees and dropping the temperature dramatically. "There goes our perfect day," lamented Hanna.

"Your story's so sad," Ruth uttered demurely. "I never realized it was that bad with you and Ike."

"I wanted to confide in both of you," Rebecca added, "but I couldn't take the chance Ike would get wind of it. Now I wonder what you must think of me for my behaviour."

Oh, Rebecca, we've all had our personal struggles. We don't condemn you," Hanna sympathized. "I just hope you are safe."

They seated themselves facing each other again. "And your wish?" enquired Hanna.

"Well, first, I wish I had left Ike years ago." Suddenly Rebecca's mirthful attitude changed to sadness. She unwound her legs from beneath her, stood up and resumed her elliptical pacing. Stopping, she looked at both women. "I have spent thirty-two years of my life, no doubt the best part of my life, in a loveless marriage scheming and deceiving. I feel hostility at the loss in my life.

"Yes, we would have suffered economically, and the boys would have been upset." She paused, staring at the floor in front of her. "But what have my boys learned about marital love, companionship or relationships from me? Nothing!" She paced again; stopped, looked at her two friends, her hands spread out in an expression of exasperation. "What have I gained from deceit and revenge: some security, freedom? For every bit of satisfaction I obtained, I gained bitterness; I've become more pessimistic, more guarded. What have my boys learned about trust or fidelity from either of us?" Her voice took on a pleading expression. Rebecca paused to ponder her next thought.

"Ike and I did love each other once." She returned to sit in her chair; sat quietly reflecting. "Maybe, if I had confronted Ike earlier, we could have worked something out. I had a good job. The boys and I could have managed. Perhaps I would have met someone who really cared for me." Looking off beyond to the storm filled sky, she sighed wistfully. "That would have been nice."

All three sat silently for several minutes processing the impact of Rebecca's story.

"I also wish," Rebecca continued, "to tell my sons and grandchildren men and women enter marriage as equals. Each party must recognize that from day one. My marriage was ruined when Ike decided I was a plaything, a person of no significance. I prolonged the agony by enacting revenge." Rebecca covered her face with her hands. Quiet sobs shook her shoulders.

They could have been the subject for a beautiful painting; Hanna and Ruth kneeling down by Rebecca's chair holding her tightly. Then suddenly Rebecca pushed both Hanna and Ruth aside and stood up. Speaking with a new sense of determination she exclaimed, "I've done what I've done and nothing, nothing will make me regret that."

A burst of thunder could be heard in the distance. All three women stood up to watch the plants in the gardens bend and twist in the wind as if fighting to remain upright. "You want to leave all this, Hanna?" Rebecca asked, her arm sweeping out toward the garden.

"I'd like to… if I have the courage," Hanna added. "Your ideas are wonderful, Ruth. It's just so hard to leave this and pick up anew! Rebecca, I'm just so sorry for the heartache you've experienced."

Ruth took Rebecca's hand. "Thanks for telling us. I think sharing helps with healing." They remained silent watching the storm punish the plants outdoors.

"Ruth, do you have a story or wish?" Hanna ventured, breaking their silence.

*****

Ruth, poised on a threshold of indecision, looked at each of her friends. It had remained a secret for so long, the thought of exposing herself even to her friends was frightening. But the occasion seemed right; each of the others had candidly shared her life. They returned to their seats. Ruth shut her eyes, her hands folded on her lap, as if in an attitude of prayer. "I have a wonderful story;" her voice just above a whisper. "Bo and I have kept a secret for fifty years. With his recent death and the death of our son, Otto, some years ago, I know it's ok to share this with you today." Both Hanna and Rebecca waited expectantly.

"Bo and I were special friends from as early as elementary school days," she began, her musical voice growing more confident, the cadence resembling the telling of a children's story. She sat upright in her chair; her legs crossed demurely at her ankles. "I knew I was special to Bo by his Valentine and birthday cards, and his looking out for me. In high school we chummed around. It was generally known that Bo and I were a pair." Ruth picked up a chocolate to place on her napkin and smiled as she remembered details.

"A new guy came to our school in our final year." The smile left her face and her beautifully smooth forehead wrinkled. "He took a liking to me and asked me out to a movie."

"I see a conflict developing here," giggled Rebecca.

"I really didn't know what to do," Ruth's glance acknowledged Rebecca's interruption. She gestured now with her hands as if weighing a decision. "Bo and I were friends and we just did things together. It was more like 'let's go to the movie tonight' rather than some formal invitation."

"Did Bo see it that way, I mean being 'just friends?'" Hanna asked.

Ruth raised a hand but smiled to soften her gesture. "I'm getting there. This new guy wanted a date and he persisted until I said OK." Ruth took the first nibble of her chocolate. "That was just the beginning. Then every weekend it was one thing or another. He waited for me at the school door, and we walked in together and met between classes. You know, it was kind of exciting. Mel was a handsome guy. All the girls thought he was hot. I felt very special."

"Whatever happened to Bo?" Concern wrinkled Hanna's forehead.

"I had hurt Bo – badly. I could see that in his eyes whenever we met each other in the school hallways. He never confronted me or asked me out – just avoided me. It was as if he disappeared." Ruth pauses to nibble on her chocolate. "I did think about Bo from time to time and I rationalized we had been friends, but we never declared we were going steady or anything and I guess I was just enjoying something new."

Rebecca wanted more details. "Bo never talked to you again?"

"Yes, one day we met. We were both out on our bicycles. He came up behind me and he asked me right out, 'Is Melvin your boyfriend?'

"'Well, yeah, I guess. He calls me his girl.' I said rather flippantly but nervously too.

"And he shot back, 'And is he your boy?'

"I didn't answer that question; I just got upset and challenged, 'We were childhood friends, Bo. Did we ever really date? Melvin takes me out on dates. He makes me feel very special.?' I was getting upset and I stopped pedaling and hopped down off the bike.

"Bo did too. We stood facing each other. 'You were special to me since grade two.'

"'Why didn't you do something when you saw Mel dating me? Why did you disappear?'

'I was hurt, Ruth! I was hurt!'

"He was nearly yelling at me. Then he continued, 'I thought we both understood that we were more than "just friends" as you put it. I thought if that's what you want then I'll disappear.'

"I was upset too; partly because I liked Bo and didn't like to see him upset but also because I was confused. I yelled right back at him, 'It's a bit late now to tell me all this. Mel and I are going steady.' I showed him Mel's ring on my finger." Ruth held up her left hand and pointed to her wedding band as if to illustrate.

"Wow, that must have hurt Bo," Rebecca twisted uneasily in her chair.

"Of course, it did, and I didn't feel good about having done it," Ruth continued. "He just jumped on his bike and took off." Ruth nibbled on her chocolate again and took another sip of tea.

"Well, there has to be more to this story than a high school tiff," Hanna added.

"There is, I'll assure you," Ruth continued. "That happened in the fall. I saw Bo occasionally, but we never spoke again until late spring."

"What happened?" Rebecca held her teacup poised to sip.

"I got pregnant. When I found out I just cried and cried. Well. you know – the thought of telling your parents. Your whole life suddenly changes. All the girls are talking about what they are doing after graduation and I'm just a bundle of nerves, crying secretly in my room, my life on hold. You can't imagine how devastating and life changing that is!"

"Oh, Ruth I can imagine! My best friend in high school got pregnant in her final year too and I lived through her agony," Hanna added.

"I wanted to run away but I hadn't worked out where. Finally, I got up enough courage to tell Mel. I thought he would know what to do."

"Did he?" Hanna quizzed her contralto voice low.

The scene came back to Ruth as if it were happening again. She held the tea cup tightly with both hands. "It was Saturday afternoon. The doorbell rang. It was Mel.

"'I got the old man's car. Want to go for a drive?' "Mel was bouncing with excitement.

"'Where are we going?

"'Some place private' He was all big mischievous smiles, so I knew he was up to something."

"I already don't like this guy, Ruth," Rebecca interjected.

"With good reason, let me tell you," Ruth retorted. "We drove out to the swimming hole at the river, walked a short way until we came to a fallen log and a beautiful grassy area and sat down. Mel took my hand. The look in his eyes was inviting. It's now or never, I thought. 'Mel, I have something to tell you,' I began.

"'Make it good, honey, cause there's something I want.' I could see he was getting impatient.

"'It could be good… I'm pregnant,' I said more bravely than I felt.

"Mel released my hand so abruptly it made me think it was dirty. He sat so still, immobile; I knew this was not going to be a happy moment. Finally, it seemed like forever, Mel stood up and set his hands on his hips, stared at me, kicked the log so hard his foot glanced off and struck my ankle."

Both Hanna and Rebecca jumped as if feeling the impact themselves. "Ouch," Rebecca exclaimed.

"I clutched my ankle and cried out in pain – pain from the kick and pain from his reaction. I don't think he even heard my cry or saw my pain. He swore, walked away cursing and swinging his arms like a mad person. I was so intent on my own pain I wasn't aware he had come back. He grabbed me by the shoulders and hoisted me to my feet. 'Get in the car!' he ordered."

Ruth looked up to see both the ladies frozen in place.

"Nice guy," Rebecca uttered sarcastically.

"I was limping, but he kept pushing me along to the car and into the front seat. Then he peeled off onto the road driving way too fast.

"'Mel, what are we going to do?'" I reached over to take his arm and he shrugged my hand away.

"'It's not what are *we* going to do. It's your problem, baby, not mine. I didn't ask for this.'

"'No, you didn't, but you pushed for sex over and over until you got your way. Now it's my problem, is it?' I was so angry at his indifference. My ankle hurt, my heart was broken, and I knew I was alone. I started yelling, 'Slow down or you'll kill all three of us.'

"'Maybe a good thing,' he pouted.

"We reached my home; he told me to get out and he disappeared. I thought he would go away, cool down and come back reasonable. He didn't speak to me again at school. In fact, he never spoke to me again."

"You mean to this day," questioned Rebecca in a tone of disbelief.

"To this day."

"The bastard!" Rebecca was furious. "They're all bloody alike." She raised her cup to her lips and took a deep drink. She drew her feet up under her legs on the chair crisscross again. A chocolate went down in a single bite.

"That has got to be terrible, Ruth. But where does Bo come in?" asked Hanna, her voice a quiet contrast to Rebecca's.

"Well, it was common knowledge Mel and I had broken up. At first, I didn't have a date for the prom. Bo did. I didn't want to go but my parents insisted. I agreed to go with Lonnie. Later in the evening, not feeling well, I came out of the dance floor to the sitting area alone. Bo came out then too. I don't know if he saw me go out and followed me or just came out and saw me sitting by myself. I expected him to say something about Mel and me breaking up. He sat down beside me and very quietly said, 'You ok? Is everything alright?'"

"That was nice of him," Hanna reassured.

"I felt his question was deeper than a simple query about my physical health. I turned to look at him and tears came to my eyes. I could hardly breathe. So desperately alone the past three weeks, I just ached to tell somebody...but Bo?"

"'Are you with somebody tonight?' he asked quietly.

"'I came with Lonnie.' He took my hand and very quietly said, 'Janet, my date, has to be home early. Can I come over later so we can talk?'"

"He's a winner!" exclaimed Rebecca.

"I was happy and fearful. Lonnie came out soon and I told him I wasn't feeling well, could he take me home." Ruth's facial expressions changed. "The wait seemed like an eternity, but I realized as I waited, I never doubted Bo would come. It hit me then! Maybe I could trust Bo." Ruth's voice took on more volume and intensity. "He arrived at my door still dressed in his tux, he approached hands in pockets. He didn't seem to have a care in the world and my world was falling apart. He took my hand as he led me to his car, opened the car door for me, saw that I was in and shut it gently. We stopped at the park."

Neither Hanna nor Rebecca interrupted Ruth and she continued.

"When the car was shut off, he spoke, not looking my way. His hands were fixed firmly on the steering wheel as if he were driving a hazardous road.

'What's wrong, Ruth?'"

The intensity of that moment fifty years ago was starkly present. Ruth's voice had become even softer. Rebecca and Hanna listened attentively, sensing the intimacy of the moment. Hanna held her teacup tightly, hardly daring to breathe, as if any movement might interrupt the story. There had been a pause in the telling. They waited for the answer.

"'Bo, I'm pregnant. Other than Mel, you are the only one to know.' I struggled to contain my fear and emotions. I was not about to cry on Bo's shoulder, but I needed so badly to talk to someone I trusted; I was trembling waiting for his reaction.

"'And Mel?' Bo asked. The pregnancy bit didn't seem to faze him.

"'When I told Mel, he went berserk. Drove me home and hasn't spoken to me since.'"

"'Figures,' Bo commented, 'and your parents?'

"'I haven't told them,' I whispered. 'I'm so ashamed and well I guess I'll be shipped off out of sight for the duration. Isn't that the common practice?'

"'How far along?' Bo was sounding so clinical, hadn't changed his position, still staring straight out the windshield his hands fixed tightly on that wheel.

"'Two months,' I murmured. Bo absorbed this information philosophically for a moment.

"'Do you love him?' Now he looked over at me, I think to see my face when I answered.

"'Who, Mel?'

"Bo nodded.

"'I hate him. He's a cad, a jerk! I hate myself for getting involved with him. For what we did.'

"That's when I began to cry.

Bo was quiet for the longest time; just staring straight ahead again. 'Ruth,' he turned and looked at me; he reached over and touched my arm, 'Everything will work out all right.'

"He started the car and drove me home."

"That's it," exclaimed Rebecca! "Well, that was sure a comforting scene!" She was up out of her chair, walked to the side table and returned. "I was expecting a little more than that."

Ruth touched her lips to the teacup, seemingly ignoring Rebecca's outburst, took a sip and continued in a slightly stronger voice once Rebecca was sitting. "Bo arrived at our house early afternoon the following day. I was up in my room when I heard my mother say,

"'Bo! Come in! We've missed seeing you.'

"I heard Bo asking if I was home.

"'She's in her room. I'll call her.'

"I took a minute to look at myself in the mirror. I had slept poorly at night but had determined I would tell my parents that day. I quickly brushed my hair, touched my lips with some colour and went down. Bo and I looked at each other as strangers might assess each other on a first meeting. Mother hovered about, obviously pleased by Bo's call. She was all instructions. 'Ruth, take Bo to the living room. I have work in the kitchen.'

"But Bo had different ideas. 'I thought Ruth and I might take a walk this beautiful afternoon, Mrs. Booth,' he replied."

"'Oh, of course! Do enjoy!' My mother encouraged us to go.

"We walked down the street casually, neither of us speaking. It appeared to be just that – a walk; two former friends getting reacquainted. Finally, I broke the silence. 'Is this to be another interrogation?'

"But Bo had a purpose, a direction. He led me out of town on a path along the railway tracks, around a bend and to a large boulder. There he sat down. His silence and this location were mysterious, but I didn't feel anxious. I was remarkably calm.

"'Ruth, we haven't talked to each other in months,' Bo began. 'I don't know where you're at except you're pregnant and scared. Last night I had to get the facts.'

"I continued to stand there.

"'I did a lot of thinking last night.' Now he reached up to pull me down on the rock beside him. My heart was suddenly pounding wildly. I didn't know which way this was going but I could only think of condemnation. Bo looked down at the ground. He had pulled a grass stem up and had it in his mouth. 'I have loved you since you had pigtails,' he continued, not looking at me. 'I have a plan. Please hear me out. Let's say this is our baby.'"

"Wow, this is a lovely story," Hanna inserted.

"'But you just said we haven't been together in months!' I reminded Bo.

"'Hear me out, Ruth.' Bo was taking his time. 'That doesn't mean we didn't get together sometime and got carried away. We had been a pair for years. It's not unbelievable.'

"'But I was having sex with Mel. How is he going to think it was someone else?' I reminded Bo. But he just smiled.

"'Listen to my thinking. You told Mel right, and he blew his top. Don't you think he'll be only too glad to have someone else take the blame?' Then he put his arm around me, 'First, we are going to tell your mum and dad we got together a couple of months ago and things went too far. They'll be upset but judging from your mother's welcome today, they'll want us to do the right thing and get married.'

"'Are you proposing to marry me?' I studied his face in shock. 'But the story will get out that we have to get married and all. When Mel hears the story is he going to contradict it?'

"Bo looked at me, his eyes squinting in disbelief. 'Not a chance. He'll be so relieved he's off the hook. He would have denied it was his baby if your dad had gone after him.'

"What Bo was saying was so wonderful, but I just couldn't accept it and stated emphatically, 'Bo, I can't help but be grateful to you. You can't do this. It's not your baby or your problem. I could never do that to you.'

"Bo was becoming much more tender. Now he was looking right at my eyes. 'Ruth, let me say it again. I love you. I will accept this child as my child without regret. I've thought further. My dad and I have been talking about expanding our plant nursery business. We need a bigger location. I'll work for him. After the baby's born, you can help too in the busy season. I know my parents will be upset when we tell them, but they will help us. They've always thought a lot of you. Ruth…I love you. My question is, do you think enough of me to accept my proposal?'

"I sat there stunned. Here was Bo offering me the best exit for my dilemma, but I knew I just couldn't let Bo take the blame. 'Oh, Bo,' I was shaking my head negatively with each word: 'No! No! No!'

"He was so tender; put his hand on each side of my head to stop the negative motion and tilted my face up to look at him, bent over and kissed my lips. 'Sure, our parents are going to hit the roof. Your dad may even hit me, but they'll calm down.'"

Neither Hanna nor Rebecca wanted to interrupt this story. They sat motionless but Hanna couldn't resist. "We know you married Bo but how did it all work out?"

Ruth smiled. "By then I was crying. Huge explosive sobs shook my body. It was my body's reaction to weeks of pent-up tension. Bo put an arm around my shoulder, pulled out his handkerchief and said nothing until I finally got control."

"'We'd better be getting back,' Bo said. 'Someone may have seen us wander out of town and they'll think we're up to hanky-panky.'

"I smiled for the first time in weeks.

'You think about it tonight. I'll call on you tomorrow.' We walked back into town hand in hand."

"Ruth, what a beautiful love story! It turned out you married; now give us the details." Rebecca asked again.

"We were married in August. We lived in the upstairs area of Bo's parents' place. Our son, Otto, was born in January. He has always been *our* son. Our daughter Jessica and son David made our family complete."

"Wow, what a love story," Hanna exclaimed.

"It's obvious Bo loved you," Rebecca ventured; "but what about you? You're now in a marriage of convenience and beholden to Bo's magnanimity. How did that work?"

"That night after Bo's proposal I took a walk of my own. I kept saying to myself "I can't do this to Bo. This is my problem. I'm going to tell my folks tomorrow morning before Bo comes over." But again, that night I didn't sleep much. I thought about Bo and me before Mel came along; how comfortable we were together. I thought about the concern and courage shown by his proposal. Then it struck me! For several years I had held a beautiful gem and then I threw it away. Now I was being offered a chance to reclaim it.

"Bo told me later how he thought he had lost me when Mel came on the scene. When he heard that I didn't love Mel, he knew he had a chance to get back the girl he lost. We told our parents together. The story stuck. We told Otto when he was eighteen; no one else knew until I told you today.

"Because of Bo's gift to me, I felt only joy in giving back to him and others, Rebecca. I think love nourishes love. Hanna, I'm sorry you recognized that so late. One kindness prompts another. It may sound corny to some, but Bo and I developed a beautiful, loving relationship and a partnership in a company besides.

The three women sat quietly for a moment lost in the paradox of the three stories.

"And what's your wish?" Hanna asked quietly.

"I wish…" she hesitated…

A loud knock on the front door startled the women and sent Carmen hurrying to the front door from the kitchen. "Is my wife here?"

"Please wait here, I'll bring Hanna. But an irate Ike pushed through the door following her into the hallway. The strong odor of whiskey assaulted Carmen's nose. "Let me get Hanna," Carmen replied and started off to the sunroom, but Ike followed a step behind.

When they entered the room, Ike planted his hands on his hips. "Here you are! Nice anniversary surprise after I'd been planning to take you out for supper and all. You planning to take me to the cleaners? Like hell!" Ike's voice rose to a yell on the last two words.

All three women were stunned by his sudden loud entrance. Hanna rose quickly to her feet and rushed over to him. "Please, Ike, let's talk reasonably."

Ike moved Hanna aside and focused directly on Rebecca. "Now come along home with me and don't make a scene."

Rebecca remained seated. "I'll not be going with you, Ike. Now leave us alone. You and I will work out our differences in court."

Hanna had returned to stand in front of Ike. With a sweep of his hand, he pushed her aside again and grabbed Rebecca by the front of her clothing. With one hand he lifted her up to within inches of his face. "You are not running out on me at this point in our lives you scheming bitch. Not after all I've done for you," he snarled.

Rebecca grabbed his hand to pull away and the lightning struck. Released from Ike's hand at the boom of thunder, Rebecca went reeling across the room as if struck by lightning. Landing beside her chair, she sprang up like a panther after prey. "You low down creep. You're damned right I'm leaving you, you adulterous fraud. Don't think I don't know about your affairs and children with another woman." She side-stepped Ike's second attempt to grab her.

Catching hold of her hand, he pulled her toward him and then pushed her back sending her sprawling across the floor again. "Don't you ever think you can best me! Now pick yourself up. I'm taking you home."

Rebecca scrambled to her feet prepared to meet Ike's threats and blows. "Just keep pushing me a round in front of these witnesses and you'll make my case against you all the easier."

Ruth had sat stunned in her chair while this scene played out in front of her, but Hanna had silently moved out of the room and dialed 911.

Ike was moving towards Rebecca again when Ruth sprang into action, planting herself between the two. Ike hesitated for a moment as if perplexed by this tiny woman's audacity. His hesitation was momentary. He pushed her aside. "You stay out of this. This is between her and me." At that he staggered forward, grabbed Rebecca's arm and twisted it high behind her back. Rebecca uttered a gasp as pain shot through her arm. Ike pushed her toward the door but again Ruth stepped in front of them blocking the doorway.

"I said stay out of this!" Ike bellowed. But he had to stop or push Ruth over.

"I won't stay out of it as long as you are hurting my friend." Ruth stood firmly in front of them. She saw Rebecca's face contorted in pain, tears rolling down her cheeks but remaining silent.

And then in one swift move Rebecca reached up with her free hand, grabbed Ike's hair and pulled his head down against her shoulder. Ike let out a squeal of pain. As he released Rebecca, she tumbled into Ruth who was sent sprawling onto the floor. Ike grasped his jaw between both hands. He could taste the blood in his mouth from his punctured tongue.

In this pause of conflict, Rebecca scrambled behind the sofa. Ruth was slowly picking herself up from off the floor. Then with a warrior's bellow, Ike grasped the ornate lapis lazuli obelisk from the side table, brought it up above his head in a menacing position as he advanced toward Rebecca. Ruth had circled behind Ike and with a hop reached up to grasp the obelisk. His grip was firm. Her tug did not disarm him but diverted him from his advance on Rebecca. He pulled the obelisk free of her clutch, but it tumbled to the floor. Rebecca was out from behind the couch and threw herself at Ike's legs. Taken by surprise and unstable due to inebriation, Ike collapsed onto Ruth.

Between the bellow and the receding rolls of thunder, none had heard the knock on the door or seen Hanna's movements. Two police officers rushed in. Their assessment of the situation was instantaneous. Catching Ike from behind, they snapped cuffs on his wrists and hoisted him off Ruth. Ruth lay motionless.

Police took a bewildered Ike out of the room. Medics worked to strap Ruth onto a board before carrying her out to the waiting ambulance.

Rebecca could not be consoled. The impact of the events of the past few minutes and the thought that she might be responsible for the injury of her beautiful friend were emotionally overwhelming. Struggling to maintain some composure, she and Hanna made their way to the hospital where Ruth lay sedated waiting to be operated on for a broken hip.

*****

The wind was warm as it swept off the mountains and into the Valley. Hanna, Rebecca and Ruth made their way slowly towards Ruth's house. Ruth walked with a cane, her injury having left her with a limp and much less flexibility.

"Ruth, what is this plan you are so excited about?" questioned Rebecca.

"Let me tell you over a cup of tea."

Sitting around Ruth's kitchen table, the women settled comfortably into conversation again. Hanna began. "Ruth, our birthday party was interrupted, and we never did hear your wish. What was your wish?"

"I don't rightly remember what I had planned to wish for that day, but I do have a wish."

"Please tell us." Hanna reached over to touch Ruth's hand.

"I've had plenty of time to think about your stories you shared at the birthday event and the incident with Ike that followed. I'm so sorry, Rebecca."

"Oh, Ruth each time I see you walk with your cane, I am humbled by the grace you have shown, and I'm hurt by my complicity in that accident."

"Rebecca, that was unfortunate, but it's what follows a tragedy that can make the event a moment of turning. I thought a lot while lying on my bed those following days – Hanna, your regrets, Rebecca, your anger, and Bo's snatching me from dark days of despair."

"Come I want to show you through my house."

Rebecca perused the quilted art – some large, some small – on the walls of each room and experienced a sense of calm. These were more than pieces of cloth sewn together. Like great pieces of art, they embodied stories, moods or an emotion, refreshing the viewer. Each bed, too, was covered with a different hand stitched quilt, expressing quality and care.

Hanna joined Rebecca as she studied a framed piece of quilted art, a picture of a young woman holding stalks of grain in her arm. Textured, sand coloured material behind the figure represented a field of grain; beyond the grain, blue fabrics shaped distant hills and sky.

"I took inspiration for that quilting from Charles Landelle's painting of *Ruth the Gleaner*. It's a presentation of the biblical figure of Ruth gleaning," Ruth explained. As they studied the intricacy of the cut materials, the textures and the stitching amazed at the proficiency, Ruth quietly added, "This is my masterpiece. Ruth, the Moabite, was an outcast. But through the help of her mother-in-law and a relative, Boaz, Ruth was made part of the family and an important person in the history of that nation. My Bo rescued me from shame and gave me a new opportunity in life."

"I'm going to make this house a refuge for abused women. I can no longer tend the gardens and look after all this."

"What a perfect place to seek refuge—within the fenced garden space and these art covered walls," Rebecca concurred, thinking of her court injunction against Ike. Twenty-some years of plotting revenge and spewing bitterness had yielded injury and remorse. As bitter as she was over years of his cruel indifference and infidelities, as angry as she was over his role in Ruth's injury, it had never been her vengeful goal to have a friend hurt in the process to gain a little money. Now, she had no desire for any of Ike's pension. She could manage well enough without that.

"This is my wish." Ruth's voice broke into Rebecca's thoughts. "Hanna, I would like you to act as director of this place—be my CEO. You can assist these women in all kinds of ways. You have all the business skills for that."

A thoughtful smile followed Hanna's initial look of shock.

"Rebecca, would you be willing to provide classes in art, pottery, whatever you like? I can teach sewing and quilting.

Rebecca looked at the quilted artwork on the wall pondering Ruth's suggestion. Haunted by memories of that fateful afternoon, her little home and kiln – longed for acquisitions – had become her own prison of late. She now saw a new vision. She too turned to look at Ruth and smiled.

Ruth added, "I'd like to call it Ruth's House."

Hatred stirs up conflict, but love covers over all wrongs.
Proverbs 10:12 NIV

REFLECTIONS ON THREE WISHES

1. Can you relate to the marriage situations of Hanna and Rebecca? Are they too out of the ordinary?

2. Is Ruth's story hard to believe? Why or why not?

3. Compare and contrast Ruth's story to that of her biblical counterpart (The Book of Ruth).

4. Hanna said, "[S]he knew there was nothing beautiful without consistent hard work to remove the unwanted." How is this statement illustrated in each woman's story?

5. "They remained silent watching the storm punish the plants outdoors." How did the storms of life punish each of the three women? How have storms of life punished you?

6. How did Ruth's experience ultimately change Hanna and Rebecca? Has there been an incident or person which has changed the course of your life?

THE DANCE

Jim stood behind the giant spruce, his mind a turmoil of indecision and despair. He had been honored that June afternoon of 1957 with the highest academic award – the Governor General's Medal. It was the culmination of a four-year struggle to gain a moment of recognition from a town that loved to honour its own – an honour Jim and his family had never achieved.

Jim contemplated his next move, oblivious to the sensuous beauty of the evening. Sunset painted the sky in flaming oranges and reds then softened into twilight pink before merging into darkness. The midsummer-night air was heavy with the scent of lilac and crab-apple blossoms.

The doors of the dance hall opened; a flood of light spilled onto the street and a burst of music beckoned. Glimpses of flashing red and blue in the hall's cavernous interior evoked a memory from a child's storybook of King Nebuchadnezzar pictured peering through the door of a great furnace to see three men alive and walking about inside. *Those young men refused to deny God. What am I doing here lurking behind this spruce hoping for an opportunity to enter the dance hall?*

"You know, Jim," his mother informed earlier, "We don't agree with dancing."

"Is music evil? Is moving to music evil?" His voice had become strident and impatient. "King David danced!"

"Satan often comes as an angel of light; things seeming to be innocent are inherently evil."

"Like what?"

"Drinking and… other things take place outside the dance hall. You know this."

"How am I ever going to have friends if I can't enjoy being with them?"

"You have friends at church."

"Yes, in a different town!" He had looked at his mother closely for any sign of weakening.

"Choose your friends carefully. Christians are to be set apart from the ways of the corrupt world." The phone rang interrupting the argument, but when his mother returned saying she would be going to the Mission Church that evening for a committee meeting, Jim resolved to be at the dance.

In his fantasies, he had wanted to invite Pearl. They had been study buddies for the past two years. He recalled her quick wit and insights and valued her encouragement. Working feverishly together preparing for the June finals, they had then each gone their own way during the last hectic days of exams and grad preparations.

But it was Cheri Metcalf who had touched his arm that afternoon. "Jim, come to the dance tonight. It's lots of fun." He was thrilled by Cheri's invitation. He secretly admired Cheri. His attraction to her went back to his first day of school at Kenton four years before. She had reached out to help him after he had been publicly embarrassed. Now he wondered whether he had missed her going into the Hall. Entering alone was too overwhelming.

A burst of familiar female laughter and a giggle rippled across the air. It was Cheri. Jim could never mistake the lightness and beauty of her laughter. Three people moved into the yellow cone of the streetlight. Jim recognized Susan Clark, Ray Ferguson and Cheri. *Is Cheri alone?* He sauntered out from behind the tree.

"Well look who's here!" Cheri took his arm and pulled him next to her. "So, you decided to join me after all," her infectious smile inviting.

"Well…" Jim began, "Where's Jeb?"

Cheri shrugged. "He chose his male buddies rather than me."

Ray opened the Hall door. Felicity Winters, the town gossip, was in the ticket booth.

"Well, well," Felicity's voice seemed to boom across the hall. "Look who we have here—the Gordon boy! Good to see you at the dance!" Jim's face reddened, his ears burned; he thought to bolt down the stairs and get home to safety. *It will be all over town before morning.*

Cheri's smile beckoned. Her off-white dress showed off her beautiful shoulder-length, raven black hair. A red belt emphasized her narrow waist, the curve of her hips. He loved the easy grace with which she moved.

"You're not thinking of running? Come."

The dance floor throbbed as bodies moved to the beat of a boogie-woogie. Students sitting out this dance observed Cheri and Jim. *Are they admiring Cheri or talking about my appearance at the dance?*

"Nice speech, Cheri!" "Congratulations, Jim!" A couple of students shouted as they walked by.

Cheri Metcalfe had been the class valedictorian in the afternoon ceremonies. Traditionally, the student with the highest average was valedictorian. Although Jim had earned that right, Principal Ferris told Cheri she was the school's choice. Jim complained to his mother, but she was not willing to talk to Mr. Ferris and Jim resigned himself to the situation knowing he would not be able to change Ferris' mind.

Once seated, he observed his classmates and others, their faces glowing, bodies gyrating in time to *Jailhouse Rock*. He never imagined dancing was so intense, so invigorating, so much fun, yet so intimidating for him. The band began playing *Wake up Little Susie* and Ray said, "That's your song, Susan. Let's dance!"

Left alone with Cheri, Jim felt at a loss. She sat quiet, pensive, observing the dancers. *Is she waiting for me to ask her to dance or is she thinking about Jeb?*

Saul Ferris entered the hall and stopped to speak with Felicity for a moment. Then they both looked over at him and Cheri. They seemed to be sharing something as they kept glancing his way.

Jim and his brother, Todd, had been called "farm boys" and "Jesus freaks" and bullied by a group of students on their first day of school in Kenton. Jim, in a burst of anger, had lost it and, using curse words learned from their farmhands, condemned the lot to hell. Unfortunately, Ferris heard his vile language and, seeking to teach the newcomer a lesson, gave him a real strapping.

Without a tear, Jim had taken each hit of the strap stoically although his hands burned. It seemed Ferris was frustrated and angry his discipline had not achieved Jim's tears. Ferris took every opportunity after that to manifest his grudge.

"Cheri…"

"Yes?"

"That was a good speech you gave." Jim attempted to break the awkwardness.

"Thanks."

"It was so funny."

"You think?" Cheri giggled.

"Didn't you hear us laughing?"

Cheri's smile spoke her pleasure.

Jim combed his hair with his fingers. "I don't know how to dance."

"It's ok. You're a fast learner. Come." Cheri was animated; she stood, took his hand and led him back to a darker, less congested corner.

Is she aware of my discomfort, or being considerate? She doesn't want others to notice?

She turned to face him. "Look at the dancers. The moves aren't complicated. Watch me and do what I do…"

Jim watched; she made the moves look so easy.

"Ok let's try a few steps." For the next few minutes he self-consciously watched their feet. Then the music stopped. The band picked up a new beat and the floor rocked again. Cheri made a few different moves and he followed; not well, but he caught on and began to enjoy himself. One dance led to another. *The Stroll* was a group thing. Cheri guided him through it. Others encouraged, "Way to go, Jim." Soon he was dancing with other partners. For a moment he was partnered with Pearl.

"I'm real proud of you Jim," Pearl said as they held hands briefly and moved with the crowd.

Time flew. Cheri made her way back to Jim. "You're doing great!" The band moved into *Love Me Tender*. "This one's easy, Jim." She took his hand and placed her other on his shoulder. "Put your hand on my back and let your feet move to the music." He was nervous, aware of Cheri's closeness. He caught the scent of her perfume and the cleanness of her hair. Red lipstick defined the beauty of her mouth, the white gleam of her teeth.

Her twinkling eyes met his. "You ok?"

He nodded and she rested her head on his shoulder. How he wished he could thoroughly enjoy these moments without guilt. Jim looked down into the cleavage, trying hard not to focus on her white mounded breasts. All the sensuality of the moment sent his heart racing. His arm tightened around her back.

"They're lovely, aren't they?" Cheri whispered.

Was this what his mother meant by dancing leading to other things?

Cheri's eyes were focused elsewhere scanning the dance floor; then, bringing her attention back to him, she whispered, "The band…they play beautifully don't you think?"

Jim relaxed. "Yes, they're lovely!"

Was it an hour or more during which he forgot about where he was or who he was? He was having fun; had dreamt about this kind of approval many times. He was flattered by Cheri's attention. Why would Cheri Metcalfe, belle of Kenton, be interested in Jim Gordon? Was she just flirting? Was it because he had finally proven to himself and the town of Kenton he was their best student? It had come with hard work and with no favors from Ferris.

He had done well in his first rural school and enjoyed the competition for the highest marks. Sports, such as they were in a rural location, were his delight: soccer in the winter and softball in the summer; then came the upheaval – his father's death and moving to Kenton to become nobody and begin a four-year pilgrimage?

I always think negatively about myself… Why shouldn't Cheri Metcalfe feel lucky to have Jim Gordon as a partner? But no, I can never bring myself to assume that.

It was Pearl Clayton who said to him one day a long time ago, "Jim, you have such an inferiority complex!" She was right. He didn't belong. Neither he nor his family belonged to Kenton. It wasn't because he hadn't tried.

"We hold different values," his mother explained.

"Yes, I know we hold different values." His reply defiant, "But why are our values necessarily the right ones?"

The answer was always the same; "Our values are based on the Bible, Jim. You can't go wrong with those."

At that moment, the luster of Cheri's black hair, the subtle sweetness of fragrance, the motion of her body, the movement of her lips, bombarded Jim's senses. Yes indeed, an angel of light.

Then he saw Jeb talking to Felicity who was pointing toward Cheri and him. Jeb closed the distance between them in rapid strides. Cheri, looking the other way, did not see him coming. Without a comment Jeb pushed Jim aside.

"You little tramp!" He grabbed Cheri by the shoulders. Shaking her, he growled, "Don't you ever walk out on me again!"

"Jeb, let go! You're hurting me!" Struggling to be free from his tight hold she gasped, "What did you expect me to do? Wait endlessly while you got yourself piss-drunk with your friends? I wanted to dance."

"All you had to do was wait! Is that so hard? So, you take off and I find you snuggled up against Gordon here."

Cheri's face revealed the pain from Jeb's hands pinching her shoulders. "Jeb, let go! You're hurting me."

Jim had stood by but now he moved to take Cheri's arm. "Jeb, you're hurting her. Leave her be."

Jeb turned on Jim. "You shut up, you lily-white, too-good-for-everyone, sweet little Jesus boy! Who taught you how to dance? Does your mother know you're here? I suppose you've had your hands all over Cheri. She's my girl. You…"

Cheri's hand hit Jeb's face. Jeb, stunned for a second, covered his cheek with a hand and then reached out to grab her again. Jim's arm intervened. Jeb turned and with a punch hit Jim's shoulder. Jim stepped back; then Jeb's fist hit his jaw. Shaking his head, he felt a surge of anger. Did he know how to fight properly? No, but here he clearly knew the enemy and his anger gave him energy if not form. Jeb was taken aback by the sudden fury.

"Fight! Fight!" The cry went through the hall and instantly an arena of urging spectators circled them.

Cries of, "Hit him, Jeb!" "Clean his clock, Jeb!" "He took your girl, Jeb!" came from the circled spectators.

Jim knew he was on his own again. The group that just moments ago seemed to embrace and welcome him now were on Jeb's side. Nothing had changed.

Jeb came back fast, his fists flying at Jim's face. Jim ducked a couple and took another one on his mouth. Then he delivered a hard one on Jeb's jaw, driving him back. He saw his opportunity and was about to move in when strong hands from behind bound his rage. Other hands took Jeb's arms.

Saul Ferris appeared planting himself solidly in the middle. Cursing quietly to himself, Jeb held his face. Cheri was in tears and Jim, red-faced, blood on his lip, stood by. Ferris looked at all three and finally focused on Jeb. "Jeb what is going on here?"

"I was talking to Cheri and Gordon was suddenly all over me; jealous or something."

Ferris turned on Jim, his eyes flashing anger. "You are trouble! Wherever you go, you are in the middle of it!"

A thousand condemnations crowded Jim's mind; he barely heard Mr. Ferris. What had he been doing here in the first place, dancing and now in the middle of a fight? The story would be all over the Valley by dawn. And his mother…he could see the disappointment in her eyes and hear her reprimands. She was right; that's why he was in trouble again.

"You have nothing to say?"

It was Ferris. Jim had obviously missed something. He looked at Cheri. She was crying in Susan's arms. If Jim had learned anything in the past four years, the lesson was he would have to defend himself in Kenton. "Mr. Ferris…"

But Ferris either didn't hear or didn't want to hear because he started barking commands. "Albert, see that Jeb gets taken home; he's in no condition to drive. Then facing Jim, he ordered, "You get out! Go home!"

A quiet, clear, female voice broke into the commands. "Mr. Ferris! Mr. Ferris!" Ferris turned. There was Pearl Clayton, confidently facing Ferris. Every bit as tall, but only a portion of Ferris's size, she stood resolute, a Davida against Goliath. "Jim didn't start the fight. He only stepped in when Jeb was mistreating Cheri. Then Jeb turned on him. Jeb gave the first punch."

Jim's eyes focused on Pearl's level gaze, those captivating green eyes, her straight and commanding posture, and his mind raced back to the way she had saved him from the water that June day so many years ago. She had confessed once she had felt sorry for him in another one of his confrontations with Mr. Ferris but stood silently by. Not this time.

"Pearl," Ferris' voice entered the stunned silence, "no matter who is to blame, we don't allow fighting at a school dance." Turning to Jim he ordered, "Go!"

Jim, head bowed, felt as if he were running a gauntlet as students backed away to make a pathway for him as he headed to the door.

Jim started the long walk home. The distance wasn't great, in fact only a few blocks, but he didn't intend to go straight home…maybe he'd not go home at all. His body trembled with anger, his mouth hurt from swollen lips; he tasted blood and salt from tears.

From among the thousand crowded thoughts filling his mind one idea slowly emerged. Cheri's attention to him this evening was nothing more than a ruse. Was that why she danced with him so often, hoping Jeb would arrive to find her attention elsewhere? Why him? She could have danced with anybody. The agony of this treachery! In his desperate need, he had fallen victim. Despair overwhelmed him. His hope for acceptance in Kenton, in spite of proving himself over and over physically with the guys in sports, or academically in school, was never realized. He didn't belong.

He had passed the last streetlight and was now far beyond light's reach. He pounded his fist into his hand. Death-beckoning thoughts pushed into his mind as midsummer-darkness, as brief as it was, surrounded him.

Jim observed the moonless sky flooded with star points of light; the Milky Way washed its center. A faint line of yellow caressed the northern horizon;

late June's promised dawn wasn't far away. But celestial beauty did not lessen his despair. His ignominious exit from the Hall in front of strangers, adults and peers, who had applauded him earlier in the day, provoked a crushing shame. But the hurt of being used as a pawn by Cheri was far more severe. The darkness of night matched the despair of his soul.

The bridge at Diamond Creek was an old one. The narrow structure was bordered by trapezoidal sides reaching six feet in height to their top. The twelve-inch timbers could easily be climbed. This night Jim scaled the sloping edge to the short parallel beam to the road and sat, feet dangling over the water twenty feet below. Hearing its rush, he remembered clinging desperately for life some years ago. He had been accidentally swept down a fast-moving flow of ditch water following a torrential rain and dragged toward a waterfall plunging into the current of this river.

He leaned out recklessly over the edge. *Who would care?* He listened to the rush of the water, heard its somber melody and saw within its dark surface his father's kindly smiling face. The face faded, but then his mother's face took shape, her lips moving. "Sometimes there is a way that seems to be right, but in the end, it is the way to death." Jim shook his head; the face faded.

Whom could he call a friend? I always thought in some way Cheri cared. In some ways she seemed to be watching out for me. But after tonight, can I ever trust her again? The lines of Keats' poem eased into his thoughts.

> *When I have fears that I may cease to be…*
> *When I behold, upon the night's starr'd face,*
> *Huge cloudy symbols of a high romance*
> *And think that I may never live to trace*
> *Their shadows…*

Subsequent lines failed to come as Jim sat, eyes pinched shut.

Car lights turned at the corner near town and approached slowly. Jim turned, gazing deeply into the darkened waters.

Jim heard the car, swung around to jump to the floor of the bridge, positioning himself behind an upright timber. The car's approach was cautious. Light flooded the bridge; the planks rattled under the wheels; then halfway across the car stopped. *Someone's looking for me? Is it mother? Does she know already?* The car door opened; someone stepped out—remained motionless, listening.

"Jim…? Jim…? Are you here?"

It was Pearl.

The uneven murmur of the idling car and the more distant rush of the water below intruded on the silence. *Car sounds as if it's giggling; even the water is laughing.* Jim's resentment rose.

"Jim…? Jim…?" Her voice was cautious. He could picture her there on the bridge listening carefully; intuitively aware, like a hunter, the prey was close. In a strange way Jim felt like a frightened animal, trapped, cowering in the shadows.

Then, the image of her speaking to Ferris just a short time ago surfaced. Pearl, the advocate! He could not forget how strong she had been. *Who would miss Jim Gordon?*

Jim was overcome by emotion and exhaustion. Tears pooled. Pearl Clayton would miss him! It was she who had appeared as an angel as he had hung over the falls right here four years previously. It was she who had challenged him to resist Ferris' provocations and prove himself the student he could be. She had become his study mate, indeed his friend the past two years. So wrapped up in his own delusions about Cheri, he had forgotten Pearl.

"Jim…?"

He could hear her moving slowly, quietly toward the pillar, her shadow, from the headlights, was phantom-like in proportions, distorting her height and exaggerating her movements.

"Jim…?"

He could see her now beside him. Inch by inch she scanned the head-light-flooded bridge until, with caution she reached out to touch his arm lightly. The lights from the car glistened on her damp cheeks. Silently she moved forward and slowly wrapped her arms about him. Jim remained rigid, the warmth of her arms slowly thawing his resentment.

Carefully she began drawing him away from the edge of the bridge. Awkwardly he allowed his arms to go about her. Framed in the glare of the headlights, they clung to each other. The purr of the car, the murmur of the water below now seemed a quiet symphony serenading this sacred embrace.

"Jim." Pearl broke the clasp. "We need to let your mother know you're safe."

"Does she know about the fight?"

"She knows you were at the dance, Jim. I went to your home first, looking for you. I told them you must be somewhere on the way home."

The interrogation, the condemnation—he saw the hurt in his mother's eyes. The arguments would begin immediately. "I can't talk to her yet; just can't go through that..."

"Then let me tell your mum and brother you are all right and that we want to talk for a while?"

Jim consented and sat silent as she drove back into town, his mind remembering Pearl.

Pearl...the rescuer.

Pearl...the conciliator, the champion of fair play. He recalled her suggesting the softball game called "Scrub" could encourage all to participate by limiting a player's turns at bat, arguing passionately, as it stood, the game was only of interest to those who were good.

Pearl, the student, the creative thinker!

Yes, he won the medal, but only by fractions of a percentage point. He knew Pearl was the more original thinker, the one feeling much more at liberty to question.

"You're constrained by your religious views." She had told him bluntly. "You feel certain things are given, not to be challenged." Poking fun at him, she mimicked, "The Bible says....

"What if Copernicus, Galileo or Newton had felt they couldn't question? We would still be living in a medieval, unscientific world."

"Pearl, do you take the Bible seriously? Do you read it?"

"I believe the Bible has its place. It's stories and theology not science."

"Pearl, where do you get all your ideas?"

"Mainly from my father."

What was my father really like; what would he say to these questions? Was he like Mother? He pushed the thought away quickly, wanting to remember the kind and gentle man.

"I'll only be a minute." Pearl's voice broke into his musing. "I'll explain to your mother it's a tradition on graduation night for grads to watch the sun rise on a new day. She'll agree as long as you remain with me." A smile and she was gone.

Pearl, the Davida. Did she know what she was taking on when she confronted his mother? Yes, indeed, recalling how over the past two years his mother had slowly developed a respect and a fondness for Pearl.

"You are in my care and keeping until one hour after the sun rises," Pearl announced, returning. Jim relaxed as she drove south of town, up onto the plateau, navigating a number of small off roads and finally bringing the car to a halt facing a wire gate. "Can you open that?" her grin teasing.

They proceeded to stop on a treeless knoll providing a view of the town and the valley below. The dozen lights of Kenton broke the darkness. The glow of Valley City washed the more distant sky. The eastern horizon was faintly yellow.

"How did you know about this place?"

"It's known as Lovers Lookout...." Pearl was coy knowing she would gain his interest. "It's a sheep pasture. I've been here before on wiener roasts with our girls' group from the church. The land belongs to a friend of my father."

"How did you know I was at the bridge?"

"Just a guess; I got lucky." She looked at Jim, hesitating to probe. "Jim... were you thinking of...Would you have hurt yourself?"

"No, I was enjoying a little self-pity. Today, for just a few hours I thought Kenton was proud of me. Tonight, I learned I am still the fool, to be used, called names, embarrassed. And what's worse, I've disobeyed my mother." Silence settled, Jim's mind in turmoil. Could he mention the real hurts—Cheri and Ferris? "I got stung good tonight."

"You mean Cheri and Jeb?"

"Yeah, she let on I was...important...someone special, but then I realized she was using me, just waiting for Jeb."

"Are you sure she set you up? She sees qualities in you she doesn't see in Jeb."

"You think?"

"You saw how Jeb treated her tonight. No girl likes to be hurt and put down in front of her friends. Jeb was pretty much out of control there. Maybe you are important to her." Pearl hesitated for a moment. "It's not always easy to break off with old boyfriends."

Pearl, the magnanimous! Silence filled the confines of the car.

Pearl reached out to touch Jim's hand, "You're my friend, Jim. Knowing how hurt you must have felt after Ferris sent you out, I had to speak to you, but when you weren't at home, I got worried. The words then tumbled out of Pearl. "I went home and told my folks, and dad said, 'Take the car and find him.'"

Jim saw the tears swelling in her eyes. Again, a picture from a childhood storybook flashed into his mind – Jesus, the Good Shepherd, holding a little lamb in his arms. "Your father... he must be a good person."

Pearl nodded and found a tissue to wipe her eyes.

"I thought I saw my father calling to me there at the bridge."

"You miss him a lot."

"Yes, I'm not sure what kind of a man he was. Mother has grown so strict since we moved to Kenton…

"My mother says it was a sin for me to be at the dance tonight, but you were there, and you're not plagued with guilt. Your parents give you the car, allow you to be out until after sunrise. I know my mother will be questioning where we were, what we were doing up here on the hill."

"It is a matter of how you define sin, Jim. Life is too…" Pearl hesitated, was pensive… "Maybe we overuse the word sin. We label certain things or actions as sin. To me if I willfully hurt someone or myself, I call that wrong. We could label it sin. Am I hurting myself or someone else while dancing? Is that a moral action against loving your neighbour as yourself?"

Jim frowned. "But look at all the terrible things that happened as a result of me going to the dance. I got into a fight. I'm embarrassed in front of the whole town. I allow Ferris to get the last word. I've hurt my mother terrible."

"We learn from mistakes. Is God going to condemn us for a mistake from which we learn? Graduation is the moment we begin to launch out on our own. Finding ourselves apart from our parents is important. We need to find our own moral ground, don't you think? This was our day! Why can't you celebrate the events of a day with a dance with your friends? Life is to be entered into, not run from!"

"I've tried hard to be a part of our class; thought for a moment I had achieved that today, but look at tonight. Everybody was rooting for Jeb, not me."

"Jeb has always been the king with our class. Girls like him; he's tall, good looking. Boys like him; he's good at sports. It's hard to change allegiance in a day. There are many girls and guys in our class who like you, Jim. Acceptance, you know, works both ways."

The encroaching flame of daylight began pushing back the darkness. The web fencing defining the perimeter of the pasture was now visible. Beyond the tiny hamlet of Kenton, the mountains, hills really, were now discernibly defining the perimeters of the valley.

"Jim, did you know that tonight is Midsummer Night?" Pearl broke their silence.

"Yeah, the summer solstice."

"The Druids had all kinds of ideas about this night. They believed there was a continual struggle between light and darkness, not in a good-evil sense but just a period when light dominates and then a period of dark domination, both good in a sense. Life is kinda' like that isn't it?" She turned to face Jim. "Don't you think we learn and grow from both?"

Jim observed Pearl, her face silhouetted against the growing light of dawn, her auburn hair curled out at her shoulders despite the long day, her petite freckled nose. In the increasing daylight, he could see the enlarged pupils of her green eyes fixed on him. Pretty, Jim thought but she's more than pretty, she's smart. "You're so sure of things. I'm screwed up." Jim hesitated. "When you spoke to Ferris on the dance floor tonight…I thought you were the bravest, the most beautiful thing alive."

"Jim," Pearl reached to squeeze his hand, "When I say I trust you, that includes your honesty."

"Oh, I meant what I said."

"The day after tomorrow I leave for Clear Lake. I have a full-time summer job as camp counsellor. In September I hope to be in residence at St. John's College." She sensed despair settling over Jim. "What's up for you?"

"I'll know better later today. I hope to go to college. First, I'll have to deal with mother…Sure would like to get a job away from Kenton this summer. You won't be here to rescue me. I have an uncle in the city."

They looked out over the buildings defining the town. "Kenton is small," Pearl's voice barely a whisper. "Don't let it destroy you." Jim heard compassion in that soft voice. "My father always says," her voice growing stronger, 'Life is a dance. Sometimes we dance with family, sometimes with friends; sometimes with people we don't even like and sometimes God comes and dances with us.' Dad encourages me to dance strong, imaginatively, with no regrets and with God. Let's promise to meet again, Jim and share a dance." She gripped his hand more tightly. "Promise me you'll take your award and use it in a bigger world."

Jim's emotions slowed his response. "I promise. When you took hold of me there on the bridge, I think God was dancing with us then."

"Will you write to me at Clear Lake, Jim?"

A moment of insight dawned. Pearl, not Cheri, showed genuine interest in him. "I'd love to write." Jim's smile dimpled his cheek. Time for them in Kenton had run out but they could stay connected, and maybe meet in Winnipeg.

The morning wisps of clouds had turned a bright pink fanning into the sky like giant flames. Jim studied the pattern of the clouds for a moment. "Do you see the horses pulling the chariot?" Pearl nodded, affirming the image. "Elijah's horses and chariot escaping death," Jim offered.

"Apollo beginning a new day's journey," Pearl countered.

Jim felt a surge of hopefulness. He was going to leave Kenton, find his own moral compass and keep in touch with Pearl.

A brilliant golden crescent broke from behind the distant hills – sunrise.

By the tender mercies of our God
The dawn from on high will break upon us
To give light to those in darkness and the shadow of death.
Luke 1:78-79

REFLECTIONS ON THE DANCE

1. Were you able to relate to this story? Was it through the setting, the conflict, theme or one of the three main characters?

2. Which of the three main characters, Jim, Cheri or Pearl, best describes someone you know?

3. Jim was struggling with a moral question of his time and family. Was Pearl's counsel to Jim good? How might yours have differed?

4. In the 1950s the specifics of this struggle were very real. What does the moral struggle look like today? What popular practices in our current world would you discourage participation by young people?

CONTRARY WINDS

Wally Johnson didn't notice the contrary movement of the white clouds racing beneath the slow, east drift of dark gray billows above, nor did he sense the threat of a coming storm. The sting of brisk northeast winds bit into his jacket as he trudged from his father's car to the front doors of Centennial High School. He stopped outside the glass doors and fumbled in his jacket pocket to extract a cigarette and lighter. Shoulders hunched, cupping his hands to protect the tiny flame, he lit his cigarette. With the first drag, he felt the satisfying penetration of smoke drift into his lungs. Initial craving satisfied, he let the cigarette smolder between his gloved fingers. With several more repeated drags he felt the gradual release of tension. Then dropping the white butt, he touched it with his shoe just before the wind tumbled it across the concrete to gather with an old drink straw and gum wrappers along the sidewalk edge.

Scenes from Cutforth's math class the day before tumbled through his mind. The needling, always the needling as Wally stood, looking at the equation on the chalkboard...

"If you're such a big fellow, why can't you get this simple question?" Cutforth's voice was always acidic when directed at Wally.

"Since when does size have anything to do with understanding math?" He'd looked defiantly at Cutforth.

No... he only wished he had. Instead, he reddened and looked down at his hands.

Standing awkwardly at the chalkboard, shifting from foot to foot, his ignorance displayed for all to see, he came up with an answer of his own.

I don't know how to solve the mystery of the equation.

Another attempt: someone giggled; Cutforth coughed. He erased it before it could be seen by others.

He used to be good at math, but math like life had suddenly changed – gotten much harder.

Confused, he moved toward his desk to sit down, recognizing the futility of this situation. Cutforth barked, "If you're too proud to be helped, you'd better leave!"

He hadn't planned to slam the door, but he was angry, his muscles tense. The sound of the breaking glass and Cutforth's shouts to halt didn't stop him. He kept walking.

His father's anger upon hearing of the episode was intense, threatening. It was the reaction of a man who had lost control. His son too big to punish physically, too distant to help.

Wally zipped his jacket a little higher to fend off the sharp wind. He lit another cigarette. This meeting could mean trouble. Yesterday's episode had not been the first occasion this fall he had angered a teacher., He sensed Mr. Knox, the new vice-principal, didn't like him. His only hope was Bowering.

Wally took two more deep drags on his cigarette then plunged it into the sand bucket. The warm air of the school swept around him like a mother's embrace as he opened the door. He hadn't been hugged by his mother for some time.

He dropped his books, sat on the floor with shoulders propped against the heat radiator on the wall. As the heat warmed his body, he watched the wind beyond the glass doors toss scraps of paper, tumbling some into the shelter of the school wall, while sending others across the street to shift restlessly with other litter. Wally shut his eyes; the warmth penetrated his body.

Harvey Knox approached the building conscious of the debris tumbling with the wind, collecting in hedge and lee. The mess aggravated him. He was prepared to declare smoking and loitering off limits on the front campus, but Cliff Bowering, the principal, would not support him – just another personally disturbing issue.

He didn't accept that high school students could not be given rules. He had run a taut ship as principal of the neighbouring elementary school. The building had been immaculate, the grounds like a park and there were rules the students knew and obeyed.

He was appalled at the casualness of the teachers and students in Centennial High. Rules and changes were needed. Surely, his appointment here as vice-principal was to provide more law and order.

Two students huddled outside the school doors. Their appearance reminded him of sparrows, feathers fluffed, perching on a branch in the dead of winter. *What these teenagers will suffer in order to smoke!* He walked by them without a further glance.

Inside the building he caught sight of Johnson, his legs sprawled into the foyer. Knox held the door open for a few seconds as he surveyed the lengthy frame and the broad shoulders. A blanket of cold air layered the floor where Johnson sat. Still, he did not move. Mr. Knox moved toward Johnson and nudged the side of his leg with the toe of his shoe. Johnson retracted his legs and looked up slowly. "Good morning, Sir," he drawled.

"Johnson, I don't appreciate you cluttering the hallways of the school." Knox shifted his gaze to the books dropped on the floor and then back to Johnson. Wally's eyes moved up slowly to meet the cold gray of Knox's stare. He dropped his eyes quickly, his focus suddenly centered on his own feet. How big they were looked at from this horizontal position. Embarrassment flushed his neck and cheeks.

"I'm talking to you, Johnson. Get up. You can sit in the main office until Mr. Bowering and I are ready to meet you." Knox moved quickly down the hall to his office door, turned to see Johnson moving slowly toward him. *What the military could do for a guy like that.* Knox was remembering his youth.

Unlocking his office door, he removed his coat and hat and glanced at the memo pad centered on his well-ordered desk. Before settling down to review the day's agenda, he opened one door of the cupboard beside his desk and glanced into the mirror fastened on the inside. Pulling a comb from the inside of his jacket, he ran it through his graying hair, cut short in military fashion. He drew the comb through a neatly trimmed full mustache and then ran his hand down his angular, strong jaw as if to check the thoroughness of his morning shave.

Glancing again at his desk, he noted the conference with Johnson topped the list on his memo pad. That was in ten minutes. He picked up the telephone and dialed the caretaker's number.

"Pete, Harvey Knox here. Can you get those papers and cigarettes picked up from the front of the building this morning?" He listened for a moment. "Ok. Do your best."

Don't be too demanding of the caretakers, he warned himself as he replaced the receiver. He knew he could get them on his side because caretakers liked law and order. It made their job much easier.

He had noticed an indifference to classes beginning punctually. Just yesterday he saw Mr. Schultz talking to a clutch of students in the hallway while inside his classroom students were engaged in a maelstrom of chatter. He also noticed the common practice of teachers carrying coffee mugs into their classrooms. That he wanted to stop. It did not set the proper tone for learning – far too casual.

The door of the general office opened and Mrs. Thomas entered carrying a plant wrapped carefully with newspaper. "Good morning, Mr. Knox. Thought we needed something to brighten up the office on such a chilly day," she bubbled as she unwrapped the plant. Having centered it on her desk, the rich green foliage punctuated by buds revealing hints of yellow, she continued. "Probably foolish to bring it today; I've learned this plant's deceptive. It looks sturdy but one breath of cold air and its leaves wilt for a week."

"Dorothy", Knox interjected her tumble of words. "Would you bring me a coffee and then take a memo I want sent out to the teachers this morning."

When the memo was finished, Knox glanced at his watch – 8:41. Mr. Bowering was late for his conference. Knox would have liked to call Johnson in and settle this matter on his own. However, last evening Bowering had been quite emphatic about being at the conference with Johnson.

Knox looked out his window to see Bowering walking spritely up the front walk. Perhaps the tardiness he had noticed among the staff was bred from the top? It was Bowering who had set the 8:30 meeting with Johnson.

Bowering waved to several groups of students now lining the front walk and smiled infectiously as he approached the building. At the front door he chatted briefly with the two students still huddled close to the school. When Bowering swept into the office, his presence filled the room like a rush of warm wind.

"Good morning, everyone," his voice rang out, "good to see you all made it!" His smile recessed the wrinkles about his eyes brightening their soft blue colour. He stuck his head into Knox's office door. "Good morning, Harvey. Sorry I'm a bit late. I stopped to help a lady who won't be at work on time this morning either – car trouble!" He ran his fingers through his rather long hair. "I dropped her off at the corner service station. Dot, is the coffee ready?" He looked back to her desk.

"Sure is, Mr. Bowering! Can I get you a cup?"

"Thanks, Dot, I'll pick one up for myself in just a moment. Is Wally Johnson here? Oh, there you are Wally!" Bowering just then saw him sitting at the side of the office door entrance, his huge frame somewhat slumped, his sandy hair looking unkempt, long over his ears, a boyish face on a man's body. "Come into my office and sit down, Wally. I'll be back just as soon as I grab a coffee." He poked his head into Knox's office. "Say, we'll get this meeting with the Johnson boy going in five minutes. I want to grab a coffee and catch a couple of people before they're off to classes.

Knox sat for a moment feeling as if he had lost all effective control of his morning. "I might just as well make a check around the school while I wait," he sighed to himself.

On the third floor Knox met Cutforth still furious at Johnson who had defied him blatantly. Knox listened to Cutforth's demands for some stern action. There were some on the staff who appreciated strong administrative authority.

Returning to the office, he met Schultz, coffee cup in hand just heading for his classroom. "Mr. Schultz, were you not able to finish your breakfast at home this morning?"

Schultz scanned Knox's face for a trace of a smile but found none. "Yes", he replied innocently.

"Why the coffee cup in hand now then?"

"Just my usual practice to have a second cup; didn't have a chance to drink one earlier in the staff room."

"I would like the practice of coffee in the classroom stopped. It fosters the wrong image of a professional keen on his work. I assume you have a nine o'clock class?" Schultz slyly looked at his watch. It was five past nine.

"I would like my teachers in their classrooms fifteen minutes before morning class. Carry on, Mr. Schultz."

As Knox turned to enter the office, he glimpsed the look of puzzlement on Schultz's face. He will figure it out soon enough, Knox thought. Schultz was a good one to confront like this first. He is too quiet a man to question me head on, but he will not be caught carrying coffee to class again. Best of all, he'll talk to others and the message will get around fast.

Knox picked up a folder from his desk and crossed over to Bowering's office. Johnson and Bowering were sitting beside each other in two chairs. Knox sat down in Mr. Bowering's chair behind the desk.

"I've just been questioning Wally about his classes, Harvey. Seems as if he is a little behind,"

"I think, Johnson, you are quite a way behind!" Knox's voice was firm. "Waving a folder and then opening it, I have reports here from all the teachers. "English, Science, Math – frequent absence and bad attitude; a similar story in other subjects with the exception of Art; seems art you are attending regularly."

"I don't get hassled there," Johnson muttered.

"Johnson in the past two weeks I have had three reports of you not completing major assignments. Yesterday you slammed a door, broke a window and then blatantly ignored a teacher. Your October Report was nothing to be proud of. I think it is time for a tough fellow like you to meet the real world – the world of work. We could suspend you on this basis of past conduct, but I would like to suggest a voluntary withdrawal."

Wally, elbows on his knees and chin resting on his hands, didn't look up or indicate in any way he had even heard the last comments. Bowering studied the broad shoulders of the young man.

Knox looked from Johnson to Bowering proud of the direction he had given this meeting. He stood and leaned over the desk as if to deliver an ultimatum.

Bowering spoke first. "Wally, what happened yesterday that set you off in Mr. Cutforth's room. Slamming a door and breaking a window is not behavior we can condone. What happened there that made you angry?"

Wally shuffled his feet, continuing to study them. He was hesitant to explain his feelings. "I just got so angry."

"But why, Wally? What was happening there in class?"

Wally bit his bottom lip gently, hesitant, then it came out uncensored. "I'm having difficulty with math right now and sending me to the board to display my ignorance in front of everybody and hearing Cutforth insinuate I'm dumb, I just couldn't take it anymore. I didn't mean to slam the door so hard, but when the window broke, I just couldn't go back to face that."

Bowering pondered the explanation wishing Mr. Cutforth had been aware of Wally's present circumstances. "Things haven't been going well with you lately, Wally." He reached over and gently touched Johnson's shoulder.

The gentle touch of the hand on Wally's shoulder reminded him of the way his father used to touch him. The quiet sincerity of Bowering's voice combined with his own exhaustion from a lack of sleep the previous night brought emotion welling up in him. He fought the tears he felt stinging his eyes.

Bowering's voice continued quietly. "This is your final year, Wally. I think you want to be in that group of graduates, don't you?" Bowering's arm tightened around Johnson's shoulder.

Johnson could fight the emotion no longer. He covered his face with his hands to hide the tears on his cheeks. "That's just it, Sir," he sobbed. "Nobody is really interested in me graduating. What's there to graduate for?"

The two men remained quiet while Wally struggled to gain emotional control. His search for a tissue in his pocket was futile, but he wiped his cheeks with his sleeve and swallowed the tears in his nose with a bit of a snort.

"You sound hurt and angry, Wally. Is that what's causing you to strike out at the teachers lately?" Bowering's question hung for a moment.

"I suppose so, Sir;" came the weak reply.

"We can't have you continuing to behave that way, Wally, but we don't want you dropping out of school either." Bowering withdrew his arm from Wally's shoulder. "We need more time to talk this through, but right now I want you to get a hold of yourself. I'll get Mrs. Thomas to call Mr. Friesen's office and arrange for you to talk to the counsellor. I'm sure we can work things out and get you back into class."

"Yes, Sir," Wally whispered.

Bowering and Wally walked out of the office. Mr. Bowering spoke to Mrs. Thomas then he stepped back into his office.

Knox turned from facing the window. "Well, that was some mighty good drama!"

"Do you think so, Harvey? Bowering's blue eyes held Knox's steeled gaze. "That young man has gone through a bad month. I talked to Mr. Schultz about Wally just before we met with him this morning. I thought he might be aware of some things. I was right. Good man, Schultz; gets close to the students, solid academic teacher and very personable besides."

Knox dropped his gaze to the floor for a moment. Why didn't Schultz say something about Bowering keeping him, he wondered?

"Wally, it seems," Bowering continued, "walked in on his mother in bed with another man sometime late this summer when the father was on a business trip. Wally stayed with a friend until his father returned, and it seems the mother has moved out now. Schultz says Wally was cut from the football team in early October. He just hasn't put his heart into anything lately."

"Well, he's not the first young person to have problems," Knox replied. "He should learn he can't use such experiences as an excuse for any kind of behaviour."

"No, it certainly doesn't excuse his behaviour, but he doesn't need rejection or being publicly put down by anyone right now and that's why I refuse to turf him out, Harvey."

Knox sat frustrated. He was convinced you learn more by facing the consequences of your actions. Besides, a teacher had been insulted by this kid and many students had witnessed his behaviour. Now was his chance to stand up for this teacher and rally his support. "Johnson's conduct," Knox pressed on, "has been far too public for us to not make a visible punishment. That's why I'm advocating for his withdrawal or an expulsion. We cannot run a tight ship if we let this kind of behaviour go undisciplined."

Concern deepened the wrinkles about Bowering's eyes. "There's a point, Harvey. This isn't a ship we're running. I believe in teaching young people how to cope with these emotional crises. Does kicking Wally out of school succeed in helping him? That's why we sent Wally to the counsellor. Let's help Wally get through what's a very difficult moment for him. Let's talk later Harvey. I need to talk to Sandy Cutforth. He smiled and was gone.

Knox stood quietly beside his desk pondering the discussion. Did he envy Bowering's quiet way of dealing with people? That quality is good if you're their counsellor or social worker, but a school principal? Administrators need backbone, decisiveness, strength to punish when it's called for. The Board, he thought, appointed me to this school to provide the necessary law and order. If so, I had better not be swayed over by Bowering's humanitarian appeals. He recalled Johnson's emotional sobs earlier. "Self-pity," he muttered, drumming his fingers on the desk.

He turned to the window. Pete was struggling to pick the papers out of the hedges against the fury of that strong wind. Knox smiled. An occasional snowflake appeared out of the grey sky, swirled in the wind and dropped to the ground.

Bowering sorted through several piles of papers strewn on his desk before locating the one he wanted. He sat down and took from a drawer a well-thumbed national magazine displaying a colour photo of Centennial High on its cover. In bold print superimposed against the light limestone walls of the school ran the caption, *Celebrated Student-Centered High School.* Bowering thumbed through three pages of script interspersed with pictures of groups of students with teachers in different parts of the building. His gaze lingered for a moment on a picture of him sitting with a group of students around a table in the cafeteria.

His brow wrinkled and he contemplated the recent growing criticism of the school, most dramatically evidenced in last year's election of two new militant board members. He skimmed through the notes on the paper and then penciled in a title for the report he was preparing to give the Board tomorrow: *Celebrated Student-Centered High School Still Celebrated.* This was a priority to have done today.

The banter and laughter suddenly stopped when Knox walked into the staffroom shortly after noon for a cup of coffee. Schultz, sandwich in hand, sat central to several groups of teachers eating their lunch. The bridge group, lunch already devoured, clustered at one end of a table, cards extending fan-like from their fingers. Betty Lawson laid on the couch seemingly asleep while Betsie Turner in a chair close by worked busily with knitting needles fashioning a scarf.

Knox moved toward the coffee pot where Cutforth stood sprinkling powdered milk into his coffee. Knox nursed a little sugar into his coffee watching it saturate and sink into the brown liquid. He stirred methodically for a moment, noticing a more muted hum of conversation in the lunchroom had resumed.

Cutforth, glancing sideways toward Knox, spoke quietly. "What's the story on Johnson?"

"He's seeing the counsellor, and then we will take it from there." *Obviously, Bowering hadn't talked to Sandy yet?* Knox felt uncomfortable. He wished he could be more emphatic. Cutforth knew he could be one of his crew.

"What happened to the suspension or voluntary withdrawal," Cutforth queried?

Mr. Bowering won't support that, Knox glanced around at the activity in the room.

I want an apology in front of my class, from Johnson, before he gets admitted back to my math class. Cutforth was emphatic.

"Yes, I'll press for that." Knox met Cutforth's eyes, turned and walked back to his office. The laughter and dialogue flowed freely in the staffroom again.

Johnson emerged from the counsellor's office smiling, to bump into Mr. Bowering hurrying to the cafeteria for a quick lunch.

"Everything worked out, Wally?" Bowering swept Johnson along with his hand on Johnson's back.

"I think so, Sir." Johnson felt awkward walking so quickly.

"Then you're back to classes this afternoon?"

"As soon as I have a bit to eat, Sir; didn't have time for breakfast."

The door to Mr. Bowering's office was closed when Mr. Friesen entered the office. "Mr. "Bowering out, Dorothy?

"He's in, but he did say he needed a bit of time to finish some work." Noting the look of concern on Mr. Friesen's face, "Something urgent Jim?"

Just then Mr. Knox walked into the office. "It's ok, Dorothy, I'll speak with Mr. Knox." Peeking his head into the VP office he asked, "Got a minute?"

"Just wanted to let you know, I've had some time with Wally Johnson."

"Yeah, and…"

Wally's not in good shape. In fact, I've already contacted social work. We need some family contact here to get at this problem." Mr. Friesen reached and closed the door completely. "There's a lot of buildup anger in that boy, so until we get some connection with the parents Wally's behavior could be volatile."

"And that's exactly why I'm pushing to have him removed from the school. We don't need a walking time bomb."

"Social worker says he'll try to meet the father tonight. With this storm that may be difficult. Jim put his hand on the door to leave. "I'm going to speak to Mr. Cutforth, ask for a little slack until we get this resolved."

"Let me do that. I'm going up that way."

"Well, Mr. Cutforth is sometimes… what can I say… set. He may need a little persuading, so I'll go."

Johnson approached the door to his math class five minutes late. He noticed the window had been repaired. The door was locked. Another late comer arrived and waited for a response to the knock Johnson had just made. When the door opened, Cutforth blocked the door. His glance took in the two students. He stepped out into the hallway toward Johnson. The other student slipped into the classroom.

"And what do you want?" Cutforth's tone was acid.

"Sir, I need to get back into my math class."

"After yesterday's escapade, I demand an apology. Cutforth's voice was ragged, his neck red above the collar.

"I'm sorry, Sir," Johnson's voice was quiet. "I've had some problems. I haven't been behaving well lately. Things will be goin' better now."

"Your performance yesterday was witnessed by the class, Johnson. I expect the same with that apology." Cutforth's glare at Johnson was as icy as the tone of his voice.

Wally Johnson felt the rush of blood into his cheeks and ears. Self-consciously he sensed his size, his weight and his embarrassment all made him stand out. He glimpsed the class intently watching him, their smiles and giggles restrained at the moment by the presence of a gloating Cutforth. Johnson's glance shifted from the floor to Cutforth's face. "I don't think I can do that, Sir."

"It looks like we've got a real snowstorm, Dot," Bowering said as he emerged from his office. "We may have more trouble getting home than we had coming here," he laughed.

He tapped lightly on Knox's door and promptly opened it a little. Seeing Harvey sitting alone at his desk, he moved in and squeezed the door gently shut behind him. "Harvey, I think we've got the Johnson boy back on track. I had a brief talk with him over lunch. He's ready to work hard; seems as if he now has a vision of wanting to graduate this year. Big guy but mellow really when you get below the hurt. This thing about his mother really bothers him. I'd like to see him back in his math class now.

"Cutforth is demanding an apology in front of his class," Knox faced Bowering.

"Let's not encourage that pound of flesh mentality, Harvey. It's rather important to young people they not lose face entirely in front of their peers. Johnson feels embarrassed knowing many of his peers are aware of his mother's affair. I think Mr. Friesen is on it, but I'll talk to Sandy in just a moment. I need to place this phone call first."

"I'm concerned the teachers have lost some face in these escapades of Johnson's?" Knox was aware of the growing tension in his voice. "Didn't Cutforth lose some face yesterday?"

Bowering continued, "I think it's important, Harvey, that we don't lose sight of significant goals in an effort to protect egos." Bowering leaned back against the cupboard. "I encouraged Wally to get back to his classes as quickly as possible. He's missed enough."

Knox stood and leaned back against his desk caressing his tie with thumb and fingers before he spoke. "This kind of treatment is indulgent, perhaps self-indulgent. Tough decisions aren't always easy, but they must be made. What's Johnson learning by smashing a window, insulting a teacher, and being coddled the next day?" The question hung in a moment of silence. Knox stood and leaned slightly toward Bowering before answering his own question. "That he can get away with it! What will he do next?" His voice had risen again, and his words were clipped.

Bowering breathed deeply. He had wanted to be as patient with Harvey as he would have been with a student, but the comment about hard decisions angered him. For three months he had watched this man operate on his tic-tac-toe principles – his primary concerns being clean hallways, rigid punctuality and a demand for severe discipline. He silently cursed the Board for lack of vision. The years he had worked to build the reputation of this school were not going to be threatened by some fifth column. Now was no time to remain silent. He could have reached out and touched Knox, but he stepped back and his blue eyes, without their usual trace of a smile, held Knox's. His voice was firm.

"Harvey, you talk about tough decisions as if I've chosen the easy road. Believe me, for every ten people out there, seven would have chosen the penalty you advocated. Discipline is not unpopular particularly in these circumstances. Who would question our right to suspend or recommend Wally be expelled for yesterday's demeanor? Few, if any! It's easy to see Wally as big and tough and to treat him that way. It's more difficult to see Wally as frightened and lost. I'm taking a chance on Wally. He may explode again any minute. There's a lot of anger inside that fellow. Who knows what he may break next? I'm taking a risk that isn't easy. Bowering stepped toward Knox. "If he's going to make it, he'll need more help than I can give alone. Perhaps we can meet all his teachers after classes today to give them a word of explanation. They deserve that."

Knox was conscious of Cutforth's demand for an apology in front of the class and wondered how Jim Friesen made out. I'll go speak to Cutforth now. Tell him about the meeting."

Moving quickly down the hallway and up the stairs, Knox mulled over Bowering's last comments. He has more grit than I had expected, he mused. He knew he had backed down again after saying he would support Cutforth's ultimatum.

His abrupt and misinformed confrontation with Schultz this morning, and his lack of concern for Wally, the person, gave Knox a moment of pause. His call for discipline and order had its place, but high school students were a different breed than those elementary students. He and Bowering could make a good pair. The school could indeed be tightened up but he himself needed to loosen up. *I'll have to work on that.* He smiled at the insight. That's when he noticed Friesen coming up the stairs behind him.

The reverberation of loud voices in the hallway reached Knox before he got to the top of the stairs. He heard the tension in Cutforth's strident voice. Knox pushed open the door to the third-floor hall. Johnson, red faced, towered above Cutforth.

"I've apologized to you, Sir. I just can't do it in front of the class. I'd like to go into my math class."

"Your math class! This happens to be my math class," Cutforth snarled.

"Mr. Bowering and Mr. Friesen said I should get back into my classes." Johnson's voice remained calm but determined. He made a step as if to go in through the door.

"And I told Mr. Friesen, I am in charge of my class, not he."

"Johnson!" Knox's voice boomed like a crash of thunder.

Students watching in the classroom and those drawn instinctively to the location of tension and combat, froze in their locations at the sound of Knox's voice. In three quick strides he had reached Johnson and pulled his bulk back from the door. The sight of Johnson towering defiantly over Cutforth, the mocking calmness of his voice, his insolent move toward the door had spelled insult and insubordination. Knox's resolve to be more compassionate a moment earlier was lost to his instinctive military command. The pent-up anger and frustration he had felt toward Johnson all day focused and burst. "So, the sobbing boy of this morning has become the he-man by mid-afternoon. Has your mother not had time to teach you proper manners?" Knox regretted his comments and innuendo as soon as they were voiced. It was as if a dam had burst.

Shocked by the suddenness of Knox's fury, Johnson stood pillar straight. He had resented Knox's digs this morning. He knew he could expect no empathy from this man, but the reference to his mother relit something deeper.

Knox's head exploded with pain and lights.

Bowering finally finished the last details of his report. The events of the afternoon had spiraled so quickly they had postponed and complicated the writing of his report. His desk tidied, lights off, he glanced out his office window. Awareness of the full fury of the winter storm assailing the city by late afternoon suddenly dawned. Snow swirled and drifted with such intensity he could not see across the street.

He let the car warm for a moment drumming his fingers on the steering wheel as he thought back over the afternoon.

Sensing the philosophical values of student-centered learning for his school were being eroded and needed defense, he put writing a convincing report to his Board front and center that afternoon. In so doing he had failed on the most elemental task – keeping Sandy Cutforth informed immediately about Wally Johnson.

The ten years it took to build the reputation of this school could be undone by a Wally in ten seconds; or is it a Harvey Knox who can undo it so quickly?

Wally had made little effort to defend himself about what had happened, and Knox chose not to speak. Cutforth had laid the blame for an unprovoked assault entirely on Wally. Bowering was sure something must have triggered Wally to such an outburst. But with Harvey being taken away for medical attention and Cutforth demanding the incident be reported to the police, Bowering knew he had no alternative but to suspend Wally.

"The important principles I have been working to uphold all day – poof, gone," Bowering muttered as he started to drive off. But another thought bothered him as he fought to make his way home through snow and the storm. With the attitude of the new Board members urging a return to more structure and discipline, Harvey Knox just might have won the day.

Harvey Knox sat in the waiting area of the dentist's office. He wondered if he would lose some teeth. But, he reasoned begrudgingly; he might have gained some insight. His remark to Wally was out of order for a principal. When the final report of the afternoon was written and his remark recorded, it would certainly influence future decisions on his leadership. Perhaps the Board had placed him in Centennial high to learn from Bowering.

Wally Johnson had sat in the school office waiting for the police to arrive. Finally, they had called saying they were tied up in storm issues; they would meet him and his parents at his home. Now he sat alone at a table in the local coffee shop eating a doughnut he didn't really need. Neither of his parents could be reached by telephone when Mr. Bowering attempted to call. The new beginnings he had anticipated just hours earlier were as lost as he. *I thought things were workin' out for me today but whatever...* He shrugged his shoulders.

A gust of wind rattled the door near Wally, driving snow against the glass and chilling the air. A glance out the window revealed a white screen of driven snow. He butted his cigarette into the ashtray, zippered his jacket, pulled up the hood and began the inevitable trudge toward his father's house. The bulk of his huge frame was soon lost from sight in the storm.

> *"Every kingdom divided against itself will be ruined,*
> *and every city or household divided against itself will not stand."*
> *Matthew 12:22*

REFLECTIONS ON CONTRARY WINDS

1. How does the backdrop of the weather parallel the story?

2. Have you known a person like Mr. Bowering, Mr. Knox, Mr. Schultz, and Mr. Cutforth in your education? Share a memory from your own experience that relates to an aspect of the story.

3. What "mistakes" did each student, teacher, principal make in the story? What were the consequences?

4. What might each of the principal characters in the story have said or done that could have led to a more favourable resolution to the predicament?

5. What points do you think Bowering made in his report to the School Board? How might the happenings of the day affect the Board's reaction to the report?

6. What significance does the last sentence have for Wally?

THE RIVER

Charm is deceitful, and beauty is vain…
Proverbs 31:30

Chad glanced and nodded toward Butch, signaling his intent. As he passed Emma, his shoe bumped her foot, toppling her forward. Her books scattered as they struck the floor. He trumpeted, "Hey, Big Bird, watch where you're stepping." A burst of student laughter erupted as Emma lay sprawled on the floor. Her face turned crimson as she viewed an assortment of shoes and legs. Rising slowly to her knees, Emma reached out to collect her books. She hesitated when she saw Keara crouching in front as if to help. To her dismay, Keara only whispered, "You know, you're not my friend anymore."

Later, Emma sat hunched on the river bench, her dark hoodie drawn over her head like a monk's cowl. Giant jagged puzzle pieces of ice moved steadily around the bend of the river as April's cold north wind swept across the ice. Pushing her hands deeper into her hoodie's sleeves, Emma pressed them against her stomach to suppress her shivers. Closing her eyes, she was oblivious to all but the pain, the shame and her despair.

Eventually Emma looked up. She watched the ice chunks in the river jockeying, as if to avoid being pushed onto the bank, there to lie powerless to move. One block was pushed up, stranded on the far bank.

That's me.

Memories of Keara now flooded Emma's mind. Opposites in every way, they had found in each other the friendship they both needed. Together they had engineered tree houses and snow forts, and thrilled to the adventure of sledding down the riverbank on cardboard pieces. Their friendship had helped Keara experience outdoor life she would never have dared to attempt on her own. Sensing someone approaching, Emma sat motionless, hoping to be ignored.

"Hey, Emy, missed you at Math class."

Emma recognized the voice. "Miss anything?" Lethargy seeped from her voice.

"Yeah, I got an assignment sheet. I can go over the stuff with you." His voice rose a little at the end making it a question. Freddy moved a little closer to Emma. "You havin' a hard time again?"

Emma turned to look at Freddy, conscious of how small he appeared beside her, his brown eyes behind the black framed glasses large and inquisitive. She had seen him regularly, scurrying along the outer edges of the school hallways, backpack slung over a shoulder. Known in the school as Bugs, he was Emma's one friend.

"Chad tripped me. His guys and girls stood around me waving their arms and cackling like hens while I sprawled on the floor totally embarrassed. It's just too damn much, Freddy! Her voice cracked with emotion. "Just too damn much! Every day! Every single day! I think I'll quit school,"

"Sorry. Chad's a mean one."

"Totally! Popular guy, school jock, so why does he have to be nasty?" Emma's comment was more a plea rather than a question.

"Don't know, Emy; some psychological need." Freddy chuckled at his comment, not being into social sciences. "Chad has his group of followers he has to impress. Keara one of the girls?"

"Yeah."

"Don't give up, Emy. I'll pop over tonight and help you with math."

"Ok."

He slid off the bench, picked up his bike, and rode away leaving Emma to sort through the morning's incident once again. She had stood up to Chad once. The consequences were his abuse and the loss of Keara's friendship.

Emma's world, like the spring river ice, had begun breaking up when she was twelve. She lost her mother to cancer, Keara to another city, and her childhood to a turbulent adolescence. By the ninth grade, Emma could not fit into a regular school desk, so she was shunted to the back of the room. Sitting at a table on an ordinary chair only emphasized she didn't fit in. Her voice had deepened, puberty had reshaped her body and her cascade of blond hair, perpetually in disarray, lacked a mother's touch.

Keara's return to Emma's high school during their eleventh grade had brought hope of renewing their former friendship. But too much had changed.

All the girls envied Keara's long black hair and hazel eyes – a legacy from her black Irish heritage, her classic nose and pouty lips on slender, fine-boned face. Her trim figure, blossoming into womanhood, made her the attraction and fantasy of every boy. Keara and Emma, both physically and socially, now belonged in two different worlds. "If Keara was my friend," Emma sighed, I wouldn't be such an outcast." But at that moment, Emma knew such a wish was nothing but a dream.

"Mattie will need some company now she's moved to River View Seniors Residence," Emma's father commented while they were tidying away the supper dishes. "She wasn't happy about the move to the city but her daughter, Tory, insisted. She's lonely. Loaded with money, so get to know her," he had added with a chuckle.

"Where did she get her money, Dad?"

"She and her husband owned several sections of good farmland. When he passed, she sold the farms. Land is expensive."

Emma craved maternal affection, having gone five years without a mother's care. Visiting an Auntie was a welcome suggestion. Wishing to avoid school, with a bouquet of flowers in hand, Emma dropped by Mattie's. She had imagined a small frail woman. That Mattie was not.

"You say you're family; just how do you and I connect?" Mattie's voice had a bit of an edge as she arranged the flowers in a vase and placed them on the windowsill.

"My father is your brother's son."

"So that makes me…?"

"Well, my great Aunt, but may I call you Auntie?"

"Sure."

Tory, Mattie's daughter, had Mattie placed in an upscale personal care home. The large window of Mattie's room looked out onto the curve of the nearby Assiniboine River. She now stood at that window watching the slow movement of brown water. Emma moved to stand beside her. Without speaking, they watched the occasional ice sheet move slowly down the dark expanse of the river. Other large pieces of ice, pushed up on the far shore, now waited for the sun's warmth to release them back into the flow.

Emma glanced at Auntie. She was as large and tall as Emma. Her hair, a blend of steel and lighter shades of grey, thanks to the skilled work of a beautician, looked good in classic pageboy style. Her blue eyes penetrated from

behind round, black-framed glasses. The natty navy and white outfit, together
with a coordinating shrug spoke quietly of elegance. A contemporary design
necklace of gold squares added a finishing touch. Emma was impressed. "You
look lovely, Auntie."

Auntie turned from the window to Emma, estimating her momentarily.
Emma blushed, conscious of the scrutiny. Like Mattie's, her shoulders, waist
and hips were equally dimensioned. Emma's abundance of hair, well below her
shoulders hung disheveled like wind-blown, yellow grass. Emma knew why
she was nicknamed Big Bird.

"You look a lot like my younger self," Mattie's tone was somewhat deferen-
tial. She adjusted her glasses as if to take a closer look. "Your thin nose, blue eyes
and full lips are so similar to mine." She reached up to touch Emma's hair. "I
never had my hair as long as yours. She let her eyes appraise Emma's attire. Why
do young people have to wear jeans with rips at the knees and along the thigh?"

Emma smiled at Auntie's candor. Emma didn't mind comments about her
face as long as it wasn't her body being criticized. Moving closer to Auntie, she
put an arm over her shoulder in an effort to bring her closer.

"Well, it was nice of you to drop by." Mattie reached up to touch Emma's
hand. "I spend so much time here at my window watching the river; waiting
for Godot I guess."

"Who's Godot, Auntie? What do you mean?"

"It's an expression." She gave a low throaty chuckle. "For me it means
waiting for something to happen, or maybe a purpose." She sighed deeply and
remained silent as they both watched another large piece of ice slide past.

"Daddy says you're lonely here, Auntie." Mattie moved to return to her
chair; Emma followed.

"I am…I had a nice place and friends where I lived, but my daughter
thought I couldn't look after myself and dumped me here, closer to her, I
guess… It's a nice place but…"

"No new friends here?"

"It's not easy; they all have their table of friends. I'm the newcomer, the
intruder it feels like."

Emma knew the feeling and sat down in the chair beside Auntie. "I'm so
sorry."

"I could go down to the lounge; play the piano some – I remember all
the songs from way back – remember plunking out tunes on the old family

piano before going to school." Her face brightened at the memory. The smile revealed white dentures; her glasses now sat lightly on the bridge of her nose. "School dances and church, that's where I played."

A soft knock on the door interrupted. "Dinner has started, Mattie; time to come down." A nameless head poked around the door and issued the summons. Emma took her cue to leave.

A week later – again wishing to avoid school – Emma entered Mattie's room, this time carrying a box of chocolates. She placed them on the table, then took the chair next to Mattie. "You're crying, Auntie." Moving closer, she put her arm around Mattie's shoulder and placed a light kiss on the top of her head.

"I am happy you dropped by today. A cup of tea, Emma?" She rose to pour a cup from a china teapot resting on the small kitchen counter. "I spend too much time alone just watching the river." Mattie fished for a handkerchief to wipe her eyes.

"What happened? Thinking about something sad?"

"Just having a hard time fitting in here." She glanced toward Emma.

"I'm so sorry. What can we do to get you some friends?"

For the first time, Mattie noticed the shadows under Emma's eyes, her cheeks sunken and pale. "Gal, you don't look well. Here I am all wrapped up in me. You ok?"

Emma had spent three days at home not feeling well. She was very anxious, truthfully, a bundle of nerves following days of hazing and embarrassment at school. Chad seemed so determined to make her cry publicly or to throw a tantrum. She was determined not to. *Is this the moment to share?* Emma's mind screamed, *No, I'm not ok. I'm ugly, nobody likes me; I'm made fun of constantly.* Instead, she replied, "I'm missing too many classes. I might not graduate."

"Oh, Emma, be sure to graduate."

Auntie's concern brought a touch of warmth. "I'll try. Did you have problems in school?"

"Oh, indeed!"

"What kind of problems?"

"All kinds. I was shy, awkward and vulnerable." Mattie took a moment to sip her tea. "Without Marty and our little band, I would have been nobody – I had a hard time meeting others. It was my music and Marty that got me out. He played the trumpet; I played the piano at dances and two other fellows –

can't remember their names – made up our little group. It was my music that saved me."

Emma looked admiringly now at Mattie. She wore some wrinkles of age but her blue eyes, and the smile that hovered around her mouth gave an attractive radiance. Emma wanted to share her story; her hands clenched her cup and her mind whirled with indecision.

Mattie, observing Emma's hands, the nails bitten back, declared, "Emma, girl, why are you here? What's keeping you out of school?"

The dam burst and like the water rushing out so did Emma's story. "Jeez, Auntie, I'm the laughingstock at school. I'm so big, my voice is low, and the way I dress and walk makes me stand out. There are days I just want to end the pain." Emma's words ran out to be replaced by sobs.

Mattie set her cup aside, took Emma's hand, and gently stroked her hair. "My child, your auntie knows a thing or two about trouble! Tell me what's happening at school?"

Between sobs, Emma shared. "They call me Big Bird, because of my size and blond hair I suppose. I can't walk down the hall without this one guy, Chad, shouting out 'Big Bird.' Then students in the hallway start clucking like chickens and flapping their arms. It's so embarrassing."

"Oh dear, that's so mean! Does your daddy know?"

"Yes, Daddy knows but what can he do? I did tell my principal and she called Chad in but it's kinda' gone underground. They're subtle and whisper 'Big Bird' at me as I pass and then go "Cluck, cluck." I get text messages with chickens flapping their wings. I can't seem to escape the ridicule." Emma turned to look directly at Mattie. "Honestly, Auntie, some people come so beautifully packaged, right size, perfect features, lovely hair, and then there's me— too big, too tall, too clumsy, my voice too deep— and because of all that they make fun of me." She turned to gaze out the window. "There are days I just want to disappear; just jump into the river or something."

"Emma, you mustn't talk that way! Promise me you won't do that!" Mattie stood to take Emma's arm.

"Oh, I won't, but at times I feel like it." Emma's cell phone vibrated. She pulled it from her back pocket. It was Freddy sending a text, saying he wanted her to come over.

"Emy…" Freddy sat crossed legged on his chair, twirling a pencil in his fingers. "I got to thinking about Chad and the kids picking on you."

"Yeah?" A skeptical tone laced Emma's response. "Got some ideas to get even?"

"I'm a misfit too, you know."

"Not really. You can sneak along the side of the hallway. I don't have that luxury."

"They call me Bugs – that's not flattering. Someone always gives me a hip check. I'm told to 'Get out of the way.' Some say, 'Big Guy; others, Small Fry.'"

For the most part Freddy went unnoticed. His size and his brown eyes, like two dark olives, did make him a butt of jokes, but he did have something going for him. When no one else knew the answer, he did, offering it meekly. He spent his spare time in the computer lab or in the library on a computer. When students needed help, they sought out Freddy. Even Keara sought him out when in a crisis.

"Yeah, what am I exceptional at?" Emma wanted to know.

"You got a great voice. I've heard you sing. Sing at the school talent show coming up. Knock 'em dead, Emy."

"You're kidding? You think this big lug should get up in front of the whole school and sing?"

"Yeah, exactly! You heard of Susan Boyle, the Scottish woman who blew the British judges away on that talent show?"

"Yeah, I kinda' remember."

"That's you, Emy."

"As soon as I start waddling up to the mic, they would be hollering, 'Big Bird' and making clucking noises."

"Maybe…but then you start to sing and wait for the applause."

"Hardly likely, I'm not going to get popular in a month."

"Yeah, but some, maybe many, will remember you differently."

"Thanks anyway, Freddy."

"Auntie, you've been looking for an excuse to play the piano in the lounge." It was a Saturday visit. Auntie had encouraged Emma not to skip classes. "Freddy thinks I should sing at the school talent show. Would you hear me sing; tell me what you think?" Emma had struggled with Freddy's suggestion all week. She knew she had a good voice, but would she gain approval or more ridicule by singing at the Talent Show?

Auntie shuffled through some books retrieving sheet music of songs she loved. "I know these aren't your songs but let's try some."

Clusters of people were scattered throughout the lounge; some at round tables playing cards, others watched a large TV monitor, a few sat in high wing-back chairs looking at magazines while others dozed in front of a gas fireplace. No one paid heed to Mattie and Emma. "Try this one. Here, you take the music I don't need it."

Heads turned, card games stopped, magazines went down, and eyes opened when the strings of the baby grand began to vibrate under Auntie's touch. Emma listened to the melody once and then began hesitantly, the words invoking memories of a sentimental journey. Her voice was rich. Just learning the melody, Emma proceeded cautiously.

By the time Emma had finished the third and fourth verses, a dozen seniors were gathered around the piano. Mattie looked up at the group. "Oh, sorry to disturb you, we're just doing a little practice…"

A chorus of overlapping voices broke in.

"Please keep on."

"That was beautiful, young lady."

"Just delightful! I love that song!"

"Can you sing another song for us?"

"Emma, try this one," Mattie suggested, handing Emma sheet music; she launched into the Tennessee Waltz.

Emma looked up from the words to see four couples dancing. Mattie continued to play. Her skill at the piano, her improvising on the melody sent reverberations and excitement throughout the room. Soon more responded to the invitation as they left their chairs to dance.

A staff member rushed to the cluster at the piano, "Mattie, you play the piano so beautifully! You must come down more often to play. Would you play at our Sunday service?"

Back in Mattie's room, Emma gave Auntie a hug. "I think you may have found some friends."

"You have a remarkably beautiful voice, Emma. You must sing at your school talent show."

"Would you play for me if I sing?"

Keara lounged in a cushioned chair on their sundeck, looking out to the river. She fingered a drop earring and on her long, sun-tanned legs lay a folio of papers. A party boat made its way up current, the deck crowded with well-dressed summer party goers. She and Chad would be on that boat the night of their graduation just a few weeks away. Graduation and Prom, what a party! She could hardly wait. Reaching for her cosmetic bag on a side table, she withdrew a small mirror. A moment of careful observation, finger-brushing her hair, and she felt confident of her appearance.

Shutting her eyes, her thoughts went to Chad – he was a bit ruthless, but attractive and popular – captain of the basketball team, and the hockey team. A smile brightened her eyes and drew the corners of her lips upward from the memory of Chad dumping his girlfriend, Tiffany, of two years to choose her, Keara, when she arrived at Riverbend High. He had been her instant nexus into the socially prominent crowd giving her the status she enjoyed at Riverbend High School. Surrounded by a group of admiring friends, she was experiencing the attention and repute of privilege.

Now, Emma's application to sing in the Talent Show lay on Keara's lap. As chair of the Social and Activity Committee at R.H.S., she and two others processed and approved the entries to the show. A thought crossed Keara's mind. *Chad would love it if I engineered this embarrassing moment.* But Bugs had said to her that afternoon when he was tutoring her with some math, "You should be helping Emy. She was your friend; she's even had thoughts about dropping out of school. Let her perform in the Talent Show."

So…denying her request to sing, I'll offend Freddy, but to approve her request could see Emma badly humiliated.

The party boat disappeared out of sight. Keara faced the river without seeing it. She recalled relying on Emma's adventuresome spirit as a child. Memories of hurrying her piano practice on a Saturday morning to run to Emma's home for adventure brought another smile. But recalling the more recent morning Emma came to her door to welcome her back after her years of absence brought a tad of embarrassment. Shocked at Emma's physical change – an Emma hardly recognizable – she did not invite her in. She had talked to her distractedly for a few minutes, and with the excuse of helping mom and needing to get back, had left her standing on the step.

To befriend Emma threatened her position in the group. She hadn't engaged in any hazing until just a few weeks back, and then Emma's look of devastation and disbelief that her closest childhood friend would make fun of her had prompted Keara to defend her action. Frown lines creased her forehead and distorted the smooth skin around her lips.

The Spring Talent Show at River Bend High School was the last student body social activity for the school year. Every seat in the performing arts theater was taken. Emma and Auntie sat in one of the front rows with the other performers. Emma, her hair trimmed and highlighted, thanks to Auntie, looked much more polished. She still fidgeted and nibbled at her fingernails.

Keara had debated whether to include Emma but when Chad heard about her application, he had rubbed his hands gleefully. Now, as emcee, Keara announced, "Our final performer today is Emma Hughes."

At first there was a hush, prompted by disbelief when Emma and an equally large elderly woman stepped onto the stage. Someone gasped and then snickers sounded sporadically.

Emma hesitated. "I can't do it," she whispered to Auntie.

Auntie's hand was firm on Emma's elbow; her mind determined. "Yes. we will!"

Auntie proceeded to the mic before going to the piano. Silence fell as students waited and watched. Mattie, at that moment, stood even taller than Emma by two inches in her wedge-heeled black shoes. Nicely tailored black slacks and white top with a grey shawl, a double strand of pearls around her neck, and her highlighted gray hair just at chin length gave her a striking and commanding appearance. She placed her hand on the mic.

"Hello everyone, I'm Mattie, Emma's aunt. Her voice was firm, command-ing attention. "This is my first visit to your lovely school, and I'm impressed. What talented people you have here! I loved all your performances. Now we have one more. Please let us present it to you this afternoon."

The theater remained quiet. Mattie sat down at the piano and began the music, her hands moving effortlessly across the keyboard. Emma began qui-etly, her voice a little uncertain but rich with feeling. She had purposely chosen to sing the song "Yesterday" as it recalled days when things were better, less trouble.

A ripple of laughter spread throughout the theater as students recognized Emma's situation in the words. Emma's voice strengthened, becoming more secure on the next two lines referring to a loss of a special friend.

Keara, sitting not far from Emma, sensed the connection of the words and felt a rebuke in her heart.

The last line recalling how things had been better, Emma pronounced each word slowly, quietly and with feeling.

Students listened riveted. Many of them tried to wrap their minds around the realization that the student some of them had mocked was the one with the beautiful rich tone, the one who was able to project so much feeling as she sang.

A moment of quiet reverence hung in the air while Mattie completed the performance with a short outro. Emma stood at the mic; head bowed.

Keara stood and began the applause; the audience followed. Then there was a shout, "Hey, Big Bird, sing another one." But the clapping for an encore soon was replaced by a scatter of cackles. Mattie and Emma left the stage.

"Well, we didn't exactly win them over," Emma said as they walked back to Auntie's room.

"They did listen very attentively, Honey. You sang beautifully. You know you don't win every battle on the first try."

But Emma continued to hear the cackling.

Emma awoke the next morning in a cold sweat prompted by a night of unsettling dreams. By singing she had surely exposed herself to more ridicule.

Students hurried along the hallway, all focused on a destination; locker doors clanged, books fell to the floor and shouts of greeting rose about the commotion. Emma stood half hidden by her locker door attempting to be invisible, knowing it was impossible. Feeling a touch on her back, she turned cautiously to see a student from another grade. "I loved your song. I'm a Beatles' fan," she enthused. "You have a beautiful voice."

"Thank you." The compliment brought a tiny thrill of acceptance. Just then another student rushed over, "Hey, Sara, there you are." Then, as if seeing Emma for the first time, "Hi, really liked your song." And then both rushed off. Emma turned to her locker feeling a blush of pride.

She gathered her books, turned, then wanted to duck, to hide, but there was no escape. Chad, Keara and their entourage approached. Pausing beside her, Chad began in a falsetto, "Yesterday, oh yesterday all my troubles seemed so far away..." and then the group broke into a spasm of laughter as they continued down the hallway. Keara's smile devastated Emma.

"It's not easy to befriend an outcast without becoming an outcast," Freddy commented that evening.

"Just hang in there, Sweetie," Aunt Mattie encouraged. A river doesn't make its way through rock by strength but by persistence."

"She was once my best friend!"

"My mother used to tell me, 'Be a friend to make a friend.'"

"Yeah, I wish it was that easy."

"Oh, Emma, I feel so badly but you mustn't think so poorly of yourself. God makes us in all different shapes and colours. We are all beautiful creatures of God."

"Auntie, I'm not beautiful! I'm a friggin freak!" Emma's voice broke into sobs.

"Beauty is packaged in different ways, Emma. Your childhood friend, Keara, has physical beauty and that's one kind. I had to find attractiveness in something other than my physical shape. It wasn't easy. Everyone has beauty, but it shines in different ways. You need to find your gift."

The warmth of late afternoon June sun caressed Emma's face. Summer was about to begin. She was just a few weeks away from graduating from R.H.S thus ending Chad's harassment. At her doctor's suggestion, Emma had taken to regular walking. She paused; certain it was Keara she saw just ahead. Someone sat there, hunched over, a yellow sun hat shadowing her face. Curiosity drew Emma to the river bench.

"Emma, what are you doing here?" Keara snapped.

"I live nearby and walk here regularly, but you're further from home. What brings you here?"

"None of your damn business!" Keara returned her gaze down to her pink and grey running shoes. "Can't I walk down by the river?"

"Totally...You don't look very happy." Emma turned to leave.

"Damn right, I'm not happy!"

Emma hesitated. "Once, we would have shared our problems," her voice expressing concern.

"You mean, a long time ago." Keara refused to look at Emma.

Emma observed Keara's face, furrowed with worry, devoid of its usual smile. "Have you broken up with Chad?"

"No."

"Are you not well, Keara?"

Keara turned to Emma. "What makes you so curious?"

"You seem so sad, so...down."

Keara remained quiet for several minutes. She was sad, alone, so frightened; she wanted to share...but... "You're the last person I should tell... You'll just gloat."

Emma didn't speak. Only the quiet gurgle of river water, as it circled rocks on the riverbed, filled the silence. She waited.

"I know you hate me."

"No, I don't. I have reason to hate you and your pretty friends, but my Aunt Mattie told me hate drives people away. I don't have that luxury. If I can help…" Emma sat beside Keara.

"I'm pregnant."

A gasp of air-filled Emma's lungs and then left in a whoosh. Her mind whirled as she tried to grasp what Keara just said – Keara pregnant! "Yikes, Keara, I'm sorry. Are you sure? It could be just stress; exams, prom, all those things you get involved in."

"No… I bought the test; I'm definitely pregnant."

"Have you told your parents, the fellow?"

Small lines creasing Keara's forehead deepened, her mouth turned down and eyes glistening with tears, her cheeks streaked by shedding mascara, she rose from the bench. "I don't know how this happened. I'm on the Pill. It's not fair!" She stamped her foot, turned back to face Emma, "I mean, this is ridiculous. I've got to get an abortion."

Not knowing how to respond, but trying to imagine the terrifying, life changing feeling Keara was experiencing, Emma struggled for some words. "What's stopping you?"

"Oh, I don't know. It's frightening. I haven't told my parents; Daddy will go ballistic.

"Have you talked to your friends, Koko, Breeze or Madison?"

"Oh. God no! I don't really trust them. They'll be delighted to think I messed up. They'd love to blab to everyone."

"Wow, that sucks…! But you told me."

"And who are you going to tell?"

Emma ignored the insult. "You should tell your mum and dad. They'll be upset but they'll be there to help you."

"Maybe." Keara twisted the hair that fell over her left shoulder.

"Talk to your mum. She'll help you." Emma got up. Keara waved her away.

Emma and her father were finishing supper dishes when the doorbell rang. Emma observed the carryon luggage, the coat Keara held over her arm and then her face.

"Keara, what's up?"

"May I come in?" Keara's black hair, always so carefully groomed, now in disarray hung partially over her face; her posture so customarily straight now bent forward, penitential; her eyes brimmed with tears.

"Come in. Come to my bedroom." Emma led the way and sat down on her bed. "What happened, Keara?"

Keara, her body shaking, proceeded between sobs and shivers, "I told mum and dad like you said. Daddy went ballistic, just as I thought. He wouldn't quit yelling at me, telling me I've ruined my life, I've committed a mortal sin. He's a deacon in the church, how can he and mother show their faces in church or to their friends with an unwed, pregnant daughter! How could I possibly have committed this sin? Then he just yelled at me, 'Pack up and leave.' Mother was crying and pleading with him to settle down. He grabbed my arm, pushed me to my room and said 'Get packed and get out!' So here I am. Emma. I know…I know please… Can I stay until I work something out?" Her look at Emma was contrite, pleading.

About to hang up Keara's coat, Emma paused. *Beautiful – probably the prettiest girl in the school – pleading for my help. She's using me. I'm not good enough to be her friend in school but if she needs a hiding place then I'm ok.* Angry and hurt, she nevertheless began cautiously, "Keara, your boyfriend, Chad – the name came out explosively – "and his friends have been very mean to me."

"I know...I'm sorry."

"So have you! You and your friends have been mean, Keara. You all have caused me so much pain."

A flash of hurt, then anger crossed Keara's face. Retrieving her jacket, she lifted the handle of her carryon, "Sorry, I had no right to ask."

"Where will you go?"

"I'll figure something out." She turned.

"Keara wait…." But she was gone.

Emma returned to her bed and cried – for Keara, for the anger she felt, and for the lost friendship. The past years had been so difficult. Bitterness was stronger at the moment than forgiveness. But in Keara's penitent look, Emma recognized fragility.

"She just came to our door wanting to spend the night, but I reminded her how she treated me and she took off. I feel bad, Auntie, but she was using me, totally." Emma had made a quick visit to Mattie's.

"Yes, she was about to use you. But she did remember how kind a friend you once were," Mattie reflected.

"She's desperate and thinks I'm desperate to have her back, so she can now use me. Says she doesn't trust her skinny girlfriends."

"You're right, she is desperate, and desperation helps us realize who real friends are. Remember this Sweetie, 'Hatred stirs up conflict, but love covers all wrongs.' You once told me you really wanted one good girlfriend. Be a friend to make a friend."

Emma found Keara sitting on the river bench. The June sun having set behind the buildings on the far side of the river offered a touch of relief to the June heat. She put her arm around Keara's sagging shoulders. "I'm sorry for being angry a while back. I was thinking of my hurt rather than yours. I really want you to stay with Dad and me. I'm not pretty like your friends. My goodness, my thigh is just about as big as your waist – she gave Keara a playful hug – but I want to be your friend, a good friend, not a used friend."

Keara's smile was brief but accepting. "Thanks."

"But I have one request?"

"Yeah…what's that?"

"Tell Chad and his friends to stop making fun of me." Emma spoke more emphatically than she thought she could. "I've had enough!" *I never could have said that had it not been for Aunt Mattie's encouragement to think better of myself.*

"Ok, I'll try, but Chad's Chad."

They stood and embraced; one large body pressed against a much thinner frame. "Call your mum. Let her know where you are. Then I want you to talk to my Aunt Mattie. She sure has helped me. I know she'll listen." Emma was taking charge just as she did when they were little girls.

With a soft tap at the door, Emma and Keara entered Mattie's room a day later. "Hello, Aunt Mattie." I brought a friend to visit."

"Come here, let me see her," she ordered while sitting looking out her window towards the river.

"This is Keara, Auntie."

"Oh!" Mattie gave Keara an appraising look detecting a rigid, defiant posture. "Yes, you're the young lady we met at the Talent Show. You did a nice job of introducing everyone.

"Emma, please bring another chair. I probably spend too much time watching this river, Keara." Mattie patted the chair beside her. "But I love the way rivers change. In the spring they flood swooshing as they rush between narrow banks, dirty brown from runoff water, sometimes flooding, and causing havoc; but in the summer and fall, crystal clear, gurgling pleasantly as they pass over rocks. People can change very much like that." Auntie reached over to touch Keara's hand. Keara withdrew the hand abruptly.

"Mattie," Emma interjected. "Keara has a problem she'd like to tell you."

"Oh, Keara, I'm so sorry. I get rambling on about things. Yes, of course. What is it dear?"

Keara told her story and then added, "I just want to go on with my life. I have a scholarship for the University; I've had an audition for modeling. I mean, what's going to happen now? Daddy's not going to pay for my university for sure. Chad's not going to marry me pregnant. He wants me to have an abortion. How can I care for a baby? Oh God, I'm so screwed!"

Emma raised her eyebrows and smiled at the irony. "Keara, if you're so upset about this pregnancy and how having the baby will change your life, why have you not had the abortion?"

"Well, I've grown up in a religious home. Daddy has repeatedly said, ``It's a big sin."

"Keara, what you and your boyfriend did was irresponsible since neither of you is prepared nor seemingly want to look after a baby. That was wrong. Mattie reached over to take Keara's hand again.

"I was on the Pill. I was trying to be responsible!"

"The baby created wasn't a sin. That child is just as much one of God's creations had you been married." Mattie smiled and stroked the back of Keara's hand.

"Being pregnant will cost you friends but it will gain you other real friends. The course of your life will change, but there are some wonderful people who will step in to help, especially your parents. Believe me, I know they will."

"But my father has kicked me out." Keara withdrew her hand from Mattie's. "He doesn't want me pregnant and I know he wouldn't want me to abort. Where's the love?"

"True, and that's unfortunate. He was shocked and disappointed but give your father some time he might just surprise you. God has a purpose for us all. He doesn't want us to toss aside his creations even if conceived under problematic circumstances. I've had a lesson or two to learn Keara. Your pregnancy is not God's punishment for something you may think you did wrong. Be sure of that."

Mattie rose and went to her window. "Keara, Emma, please come here." Her voice took on a thoughtful tone. "Rivers don't run in straight lines to get to their destinations, do they? When they come up against a resistance what do they do?" She looked at the two young women who remained quiet. "They move around it, making their way across miles of country moving this way and that way but growing bigger and stronger every day. Their determination to reach their goal is what always brings them to the sea." She reached out to take the hand of each girl. "What can you do to work around the problem?"

"Chad's angry at me!" Keara entered Emma's house a week later with a slam of the door. She kicked off her shoes. "He dumped me; insisted on an abortion by the weekend and when I didn't do it invited his former girlfriend as his prom date."

Emma placed her arm around Keara. "Yikes! How can Chad do that? Doesn't he accept any responsibility?"

"Blames me! Says I must have missed a pill or didn't take them right. I mean, why is it always the girl's responsibility?" Keara dropped her books on a chair with a bang. "Oh, he's so selfish" – she stamped her foot – "thinks only about himself!"

"After all the work you have done for grad. Who are you going with?"

"Maybe I won't go…but I did have two different guys invite me to prom once they heard Chad dumped me." A smile brightened her previously glum face.

"So why aren't you going?"

Keara spun to face Emma. "To watch Chad dance with Tiffany all night. I mean, that's what he wants. I'm not doing that! Oh, Prom's not going to be the party I anticipated just weeks ago." Keara paced the hallway, flinging her arms erratically.

Emma, tasting the bitter bile she felt toward Chad, saw a comeback. "Keara, you have to go. This is your big night. Dance with your date and all the boys who will now feel free to ask you. Make Chad jealous."

Keara stopped her pacing; a sinister smile etched her face and her head nodded affirming a developing idea. He'll regret dumping me."

Saturday, three days before grad and prom and after an afternoon singing at two different senior's residences accompanied by Auntie, Emma returned to discover Keara in her room. She lay stretched out on the bed, both hands behind her head, her unblinking gaze toward the ceiling. "What's up, Keara?"

Keara slid over on the bed, "Come sit. You won't believe this story. Mother called me this afternoon and asked me to come over."

"Ok, so they're letting you come back home?"

Keara sat up, repositioned the pillow behind her back, "When Mother and Daddy were engaged to be married, about six weeks before their wedding, Mother met up with an earlier boyfriend who was on his way to the Alberta oil patch the next day. Well, while remembering former good times, before the evening was over, they had sex. Can you believe that?"

"Yikes! Keara…! Wow…! Your mom…? She told you that? A month before her wedding? This is hard to believe."

"Well, a little more than a month. I felt sick. I looked at my mother and despised her. 'How could you do that to my father?' I shouted. She was crying Emma. Said she did a wicked thing but how could she tell husband to be?" Keara changed her voice to represent her mother's – "'it was a premarital indiscretion. I love your daddy.' Anyway, a week before their wedding she knew she was pregnant."

"Oh my God…! What did she do?"

"Embarrassed, she was too frightened to tell Daddy or anyone."

"So, what happened?"

"They were married. After one month, Mum told Dad she was pregnant. Daddy just believed it was his child." Keara swung her legs off the bed, stood and faced Emma. "Do you see? I'm an illegitimate accident!" She screwed up her pretty face into an ugly scowl. "I'm a bastard, only legitimate by my mother's deception…! I mean, I don't even know who my biological father is…!'" Can you believe that? With each sentence, Keara's voice was rising like a musical crescendo as she now paced back and forth.

"Wow! Oh, Keara, I don't know what to say." Emma put her hand out to take Keara's. "I guess your mother is kinda' like you and me. You just never know another person's life, do you? How can we behave so irrationally at times? But had it not happened, there would be no you. You're so beautiful, so intelligent, I'm so glad it happened, illegitimate or not. Aren't you?" Emma stood to give Keara a hug and kissed her on her forehead.

Keara broke from the hug. "Now, let me finish. Well…when I told them I was pregnant and Daddy kicked me out, Mother couldn't live with her deception any longer. She told Daddy the truth.

"And…?"

"Daddy was furious; wouldn't sleep with her. He has moved out. Daddy's very dogmatic and has his principles.

"So just like that, he and your mum are separated?"

"Yup!"

"I told Mother I'm going to use the Abortion Pill. She's adamant; does not want me to abort. She told me –I'm not sure I believe this –it says somewhere in the Bible God gives us a name while we are still in the womb. She wants me to come live with her and she'll help care for the baby."

"Well, that's good. Ok, so you're moving in with your mum."

"I'm not sure."

"You're keeping the baby then?"

"I mean, it's not right for mother to take care of my problem." Keara's pacing stopped. "A few pills and it's over; just a blip on the radar looking back in ten years, a bad month.

"The option – instead of all the things I dreamed about, I'll be a mother at nineteen years of age. Keara pacing began, then spinning around on the sole of one foot, "I'll be an angry mother resentful of the child for changing my life." Walking to the wall she stood facing it for a moment, then back to Emma, "I accused Chad of being selfish" – she fixed a strand of hair behind her ear – "I'm selfish too. I'll be a mother filled with regret rather than love." She approached Emma." "Now, you see why I have to abort?"

"What about adoption?"

"I'm still left looking like a stuffed balloon for how many months…With my build…I'm going to look so… pregnant."

"You will still be beautiful," Emma took Keara's hands.

Keara jerked them away. "Can you imagine me with this big a stomach? She mimed a big mound in front of her. I'll look terrible."

"You'll have a bump for sure." Emma chuckled. "I could hide a pregnancy for eight months, maybe nine.

"Ok, but your mother just broke up her marriage so you would have a place to live and help to raise the baby!"

"I mean, that's Mother's decision. Her income is nothing to Dad's. I'll be a burden."

"Chad is legally required to help support, isn't he?

Keara uttered a snort of contempt. "Chad will support my aborting, that's it. He's too selfish to think beyond his nose."

Emma took Keara into her arms again. They hung onto each other silently for a moment. "I will miss you if you decide to leave."

Mindful of Emma's kindness and friendship, Keara placed her cheek against Emma's. "I'm sorry for the way I've treated you. I can't believe you let me stay here."

"Believe me, I thought twice about it," Emma's voice choked with emotion.

"Emma, you're compassionate. I don't think I've ever felt compassion."

Keara couldn't hold it together any longer. With wrenching sobs, she choked out, "It's going to be too hard. I'll never be free again…but then I keep thinking what if mother had aborted me?"

"Oh, I'm so glad you came to visit," Mattie exclaimed as Emma entered her room. "Come I have a surprise for you."

"What is it, Auntie"?

Mattie went to her table, returned, handing an envelope to Emma.

The pleasure of a young child opening a birthday gift lit up Emma's face. She withdrew an official looking document. "What is this?"

"I've set up a trust fund for you, Sweetie. I want you to study vocal music at the University. You have such a great voice."

"Oh, I don't know what to say!"

"Emma, you have been my Godot!" Mattie moved to take both Emma's hands in hers. "Your visits have been such a pleasure. You have helped me make friends here. I'm playing the piano again." Shaking Emma's hands up and down she stated emphatically, "you've given me a purpose to live."

"Oh, Auntie, thank you. You've saved my life too, you know, given me purpose, more confidence, helped me find my voice, perhaps my beauty." They came together in an embrace. Emma placed her kiss on Mattie's forehead.

"Hi, why the urgent text?

The warmth of a July evening embraced Emma and Keara as they relaxed on the river bench.

"Daddy's back…"

"Oh, wow that's good?"

"I think so…You know that interview I had for modeling… got a job for the summer."

"Yikes, Keara, that's so cool. You look so happy!"

"Chad and I are back together. I'm going to abort the baby."

"What...oh Keara why? I thought you decided to keep it?"

"Chad came over. He says he loves me. I should be thinking about myself. We're only young for a short period of time. There's lots of time to have babies later."

"Ok, but shouldn't it be your decision, Keara, not Chad's?"

"I think it's mine...I've been regretting all I would be giving up."

Emma sat down, placed her arm around Keara. "This has been a very difficult decision for you, hasn't it?"

A surge of anger gripped Emma. All the meanness she had suffered from Chad, the name calling, physical abuse, congregating his friends to be just as mean. Now he was bullying and manipulating Keara. This was no longer revenge. Chad was history. This was love for a friend.

Rising from the bench to face Keara, "Ok, why are you doing this? Chad dumped you at graduation because you wouldn't do what he wanted. Now he's back saying he loves you. Can you believe that? He's selfish, manipulating, untrustworthy and mean. His interest in you is very...self-serving."

"Woo, slow down, Emma. Why do you say that?"

"Because of the way he treated me. I stood up to him once and he has hated me since. Because of my size he found it easy to ridicule me. Ok, when you didn't jump to his demand for an abortion, he dumped you – remember that! But because you're beautiful, he wants you back; you attract attention to him. He's no good, Keara! He's absolutely no good!"

Each word Emma spoke made Keara more visually angry, but each word carried a grain of truth. She liked Emma's friendship, her kindness, but she was so confronting.

Keara's silence prompted Emma to continue. "You're having second thoughts about aborting. You wouldn't have asked to see me here if you didn't. You'd have had the abortion by now." Emma raised her eyebrows.

"I wanted to tell you I am back with Chad, and I've made my final decision. I didn't expect a lecture."

Emma undeterred pressed on. "Well, it's your decision, Keara, but I think you should dump Chad. He's no good! Then make the decision – your decision." Emma sat down again and took several deep breaths, turned on the bench to look at Keara now sitting pensive, her look defensive. *She is beautiful, so vulnerable, and unsure at this moment...* "It has to be your decision, Keara. But you now have the support of your mother, father, and my support too." Auntie wants to talk to you too."

Keara straightened her sitting position, raised a determined chin. "Chad wants this, and Mother wants that. You're telling me what to do." Emma, I need some time to think. Please, please just leave me alone."

"Will you be alright? Safe?" Keara nodded. Emma walked away but just out of sight to stand vigil. Keara began a slow pace between the bench and the riverbank.

Chad's black Dodge Charger roared to a stop beside the bench. "Ah, there you are," he shouted as he strutted towards her. "Your mother said you had gone for a walk."

Keara faced Chad observing him carefully for a moment until he started to fidget.

"What's the problem?"

"Have you told any of your friends I'm pregnant?"

Chad remained still, measuring his response… "No…"

Keara's gaze remained directly on his eyes as he shifted weight from one foot to the other, looking down at the grass then back up to see Keara watching him carefully. "Are you sure?"

"Well…I guess I told Bo and Butch I knocked you up. Why do you ask?"

"Well, for one, you promised you wouldn't tell anyone…and I'm questioning your concern for me or your baby you want aborted.

"Yeah…but I told you why you have to do it," his voice became loud, forceful.

Keara turned her back to Chad, stood quietly, her head bowed. "It's over Chad…You and I are done…" Her tone was quiet, mournful. Turning to face him; her voice becoming firmer and controlled, "Get lost! Do you hear me? We're done! If you couldn't keep one promise or tell me the truth now, how can I ever trust you? And, if I keep the baby, I now have the names of witnesses to confirm you said you're the father. My father will be in touch with you with the details of your financial assistance in raising this child."

Chad remained motionless, a statue, for a moment and then shot back in defense, "My friends will deny I told them!"

"Don't forget, DNA doesn't deny, Chad."

He grabbed Keara by both arms. "You don't mean it! You don't want to break up with me," he pleaded.

"Yes, I do, Chad. We're through. Go!"

"You bitch! You deceiving little bitch!" His hands released her, tightened into fists. He spun to walk to the car. "I hate you! I hate you!" he shouted back. There was the screech of rubber on asphalt as the Charger leapt forward to disappear.

Keara returned to the bench, her body trembling, tears flooding her eyes; she sat down and cried. At that moment she felt so alienated from everyone: Chad, his crowd, the girl friends, her parents; she had even sent Emma away.

The warmth of the summer day evaporated to an evening chill. Restlessly Keara wandered back and forth to the river's bank and bench until hit by a wave of exhaustion. Evening twilight had given way to darkness. Pinpoints of light from across the river touched the water revealing its movement; a gentle murmur confirmed its constant flow. Oblivious to risks, she stretched out on the bench, using her leather handbag for a pillow.

Keara's past pressed up against the present; conflict and fear crowded her mind. Like Jacob of old, her sleep was troubled by a dream – not a ladder but what seemed like a raft. She struggled to push it up the river away from rapids but with each stroke of her broken paddle a gust of wind, whispering a jumble of justifications and then judgements, pushed her back. She dug in the paddle pushing forward. *I've been led astray by Mattie's simple philosophies…* Another thrust forward… *Chad was right – I am too young; it is too inconvenient.* She pushed the raft forward again… *I was born beautiful, a gift to present to others, a model to be admired, emulated.* She was making headway battling the current… *I should not suffer the agony of motherhood, the loss of goals for what I carry in my womb still ill-formed, unborn.* Thrust and push… *This thing was not conceived as it should be out of love, but accidentally as two people sought erotic pleasure…*

The wind caught her raft, spun it around, and knocked her into the water. She grabbed onto a floating log and hoisted herself up. *I was conceived unintentionally in an unwed mother's womb and allowed to live…* The water was moving faster now… *my mother suffered the agony of deception to provide home and love.* The log struck a rock and almost threw her off… *what I carry in my womb is not important enough to upset my goals. Should a moment of indiscretion be held against me for a lifetime…* The log hit another rock, spun her around as the river took her down-toward the rapids… *My mother took the brunt of shame to confess to my father in order to stand by me…* The river's current now so strong she knew she would be thrown into the water. *My father has returned home humbled and accepting…* The water covered her head.

Jacob emerged from his dream crippled, humbled, renamed, a changed person. Keara awoke gasping for breath, heart racing and her body cold from sweat. She was conscious of the night's stillness. Only the continued murmur of the river intruded on the silence. She bent forward to rest her head on her knees. *I hate what it has done to me and then I feel sorry because I hate…* She wept.

Fastening her bag over her shoulder, she rose to begin her walk home.

Emma, having stood sentinel nearby, now emerged.

"Emma, you're still here!"

"Keara, excuse me but… I just wanted to be sure you were safe."

Keara took Emma's arm. "Friend, please walk with me." Arm in arm they proceeded, neither asking nor telling the other anything.

As they neared Emma's home, Keara released Emma's arm. "Thanks, I'll be ok." Emma watched until Keara disappeared into the darkness and until the sound of her shoes, clicking on the pathway, faded into silence.

"Oh, Keara I'm so delighted you came," Mattie commented when Keara entered her room two weeks later.

"Emma said you wanted to see me."

Mattie observed the young woman in front of her – eyebrows carefully shaped, eyelids shaded, and lips glossed in a soft coral to match the top she wore over a white tee shirt and body-hugging blue jeans appropriately frayed on thigh and knee. But something was different. That defiant, brittle look Keara previously projected was not there. Her face and stance presented an open humbler appearance "Keara, you look so different."

"Oh, I just came from a modeling appointment. I have work for a month."

"How lovely... but, your face looks so...what's the word I want…gentle?

"Oh, Mattie, thank you. I want to tell you, late one night last week I decided to put another life ahead of mine regardless of the struggles I'll face. I think it's the first, very difficult step I've ever taken."

"Oh, Keara, I am delighted to hear. I'm proud of you.

"It wasn't easy…. I still have misgivings."

"Come, I have a surprise for you." Opening a drawer, Mattie retrieved an envelope, and handed it to Keara watching her excitedly as she opened and read. Seeing Keara's face wrinkle with puzzlement, Mattie asked, "Is something wrong, Keara?"

"Mattie, I don't understand. Why?"

"It's just a little gift to help you go to college since you're keeping the baby."

"Thank you, but I can't accept your gift. You hardly know me, Mattie. Why would you do this?"

Mattie's eyes glistened with tears. "Keara, I'm so happy with your decision. You see, when I was your age and unmarried just like you, I had a baby. It was taken from me immediately after I gave birth, and before I could even see it. I have never known the beauty of that child."

REFLECTIONS ON THE RIVER

1. What societal, moral, religious issues surface in the story that specifically affects girls/women? Boys/men?

2. What options are available to girls/women when confronted with unwanted pregnancies?

3. What are your reactions to Keara's decision? Were you surprised by her decision? Why or why not?

4. Identify pieces of each character's struggle that fit Mattie's comparison of the river to life.

5. Emma, Keara and Mattie each experience character development in the story. Who and what influences that growth in each?

6. Have you had a Mattie in your life?

THE MARATHON

The weather had changed dramatically in one week. The soft regular thump of Garrett's shoes on the concrete street contrasting sharply to last week's crunch on ice or snow patch. The above-normal temperatures of the past three days had erased the last traces of winter. Winnipeggers poured outside in shorts, shirt sleeves, halter-tops to soak up sun and begin summer tans. Tonight, as Max Garrett jogged his regular suburban route, he heard the voices of children at play, the whisper of the occasional lawn sprinkler set to work to urge dry grass back to life, knots of people on front lawns talking and laughing as they became reacquainted after months of isolation behind the walls of their homes. These were to him the music of spring. As Garrett turned onto Kilkenny Drive, the distant choir of croaking frogs in the water pools near the river replaced those earlier sounds of suburbia. His running had gone well; he felt strong.

His thoughts kept coming back to Clare. She had left for England two weeks earlier with her parents to connect with family. His mention of the European trip he had been planning for the following summer to mark their twentieth wedding anniversary did not deter Clare for a moment. "This opportunity to travel with mum and dad may never come again," she had stated bluntly. Max accepted this reasoning, but it hurt. Clare's call saying her parents were coming home, but she wanted to visit continental Europe while there, sent a shiver of foreboding. Her explanation of an unexpired Euro rail pass and making the most of the cost of her flight over and back didn't assuage his premonition.

The past five years of their marriage had not been ideal. With the children in their teens, Clare had gone back to college and then to work with Max's support and encouragement. Excited at finding a job, and thrilled by a new challenge, she was developing a new personality. It had been exciting for him to watch her enthusiasm and confidence grow. That was before the social activities of her job became so important.

An unfamiliar landmark made Max realize he had passed his usual turn off for his five-kilometer route. He still felt strong. *Go for a few more kilometers and suffer tomorrow.*

A group of teenagers bantered not far ahead. A shrill female voice pierced the evening air with a strident vulgarity.

Clare's language of late had changed too. She had always been quiet, reserved but lately he noticed a more aggressive tone sprinkled with occasional vulgarities. The last two years had obviously given her a new sense of self.

Glancing up at the street sign just to be aware of his location, he turned the corner moving from the sidewalk to the dried grass on the boulevard. Memories from Clare's office Christmas dinner and dance played in his mind. It was the memory of her dancing with Wes Lawson that persisted. Their actions and eyes revealed the enjoyment each was sharing in those moments. When the music stopped, Max had noticed their hands lingering together while they moved toward the vacant chairs. Later, when Clare returned to his table, he said, trying to be jovial, "Let's make this number our last dance."

"Max let's go home now. I think I've had enough for tonight." Clare had tilted her head slightly away from him to adjust her earring. He noticed Wes and his wife, Nancy, were leaving the room just then.

How much longer would she stay away? Loneliness engulfed him for a moment; anger quickly followed. Expressions of affection from Clare had been minimal of late, his mind reviewing recent events.

A guilty thought robbed him of his anger; cold shivers momentarily tighten his muscles. The memory of that traumatic weekend when he had broken his entanglement with Lois wanted to surface. He pushed it back.

Mind and body seemed separate now, his mind distant, caught up in another time and place. Garrett's feet led him instinctively from street to street, bringing him closer to home.

Turning onto his street, Garrett slackened his pace, finally walking the last half block. He stopped momentarily to remove his shoes at the back step. Straightening, he looked at the outline of a new moon. The thin crescent was tipped down – a wet moon his mother had called it.

Later, showered and sitting by a fire he had lit to take off the cool evening air, Garrett tried to work his way through a badly written student essay. The ringing of the telephone made him automatically look at his watch – ten-thirty. That would be early morning in most western European cities. He caught the phone on the second ring.

"Hello."

"Hi, Max."

Garrett felt his heart beating faster than it had on his run. "Clare, where are you?"

"Copenhagen. I'm boarding an Air Canada flight to Winnipeg in an hour."

"I'll be there to meet you," Max replied.

"Good!"

Max didn't want the conversation to end just there. He had to say something. "What are all the places you've been?"

"Max, how are the kids?" Avoidance, Max thought.

"Max, are you still there?"

"Yes...the kids...? Oh... the kids are fine."

"Good. I'll see you in a few hours. Bye"

He stood motionless for a moment after replacing the receiver. Turning on the FM tuner, he walked slowly to the fireplace and gazed at the red glow of the dying embers. A blue spurt of flame sprung up as a pocket of gas was released from the coals. *Do we have the desire and energy to rekindle our relationship?* He felt a soreness in the back of his legs; his left knee hurt. He knew now he had gone beyond his limits.

On an impulse, he picked up the telephone and placed the call. "Nancy, I'm sorry, I know it's late, but may I speak to Wes?" He listened but intuitively knew the answer. "Wes has been in Europe on business the past couple of weeks. He will be returning home late tomorrow afternoon."

Max snapped off the lights and the tuner and walked slowly to his bedroom. Hurt by her betrayal, angry at her deceit, guilt ridden with self-condemnation, sleep would not come.

He found the wedding album in the closet. Each picture brought back memories of that happy day. Clare looked beautiful. They had planned that day with much devotion to each other and a growing sense they shared so many values and ideas. He sat back in his chair, tightened his robe around him a little more and closed his eyes. *Oh God, I am so terribly sorry. How do I, maybe it's we, rescue this once so beautiful union from the destructive fire of infidelity?*

His remorse turned to pain, the pain of rejection. If she and Wes have been over there together, surely, they have been sleeping together. Now it was adultery. Had he not walked that ring of fire? But, he hadn't physically...*What was the difference? Hadn't Jesus said something to the effect that to lust after another woman was adultery?* There was a big difference he thought in self-defense, a really big difference; there is temptation and there is submission.

Guilt gave her a sharp pain of panic as she stood there in that small cubicle. The romantic pleasures of the past few days had been intensified by its subversive nature; but now moments from meeting Max she wondered, *where do I go from here?* Clare brushed her hair at the small mirror in the airplane washroom and practiced a smile. A touch of perfume on each wrist would be an excellent ploy. Their plan was to be totally discrete; neither wished to disrupt their families' lives.

As she descended on the escalator, he could not help but admire. Her hair coiffured beautifully in spite of a night on the plane; a new coat distinctively European cut and style, poised and serene; she portrayed not a tinge of guilt. At that moment he resolved, *no matter what it takes, I will not lose this woman. Please help me God.*

Smiling, she waved to him and threw a kiss. He waved back but his mind recalled Hamlet's desperate cry: "O most pernicious woman! O villain…that one may smile and smile and be a villain." He struggled for a moment; could he maintain his resolve from a moment ago?

Clare's kiss was passionate, their embrace warm and prolonged. She gripped his arm firmly drawing him close as they walked to the carousel. She asked about the children, about how he had managed, what he had been up to.

"I'm thinking of running in the Marathon come June," he told her. She was delighted and encouraging.

But suspicion, like fog, obscures reality. Every action can be viewed as guilt. Clare's declaration the next day that she suffered too much jet lag to accompany Max on a walk seemed plausible, until her sudden hanging up the phone when he returned, seemed too abrupt. Her casual "Just catching up with friends" did little to alleviate his doubts.

Clare was stretched out on the couch. Her long lashes covered her brown wide-set eyes; her round face framed by her abundant, mahogany coloured hair. She presented a look of innocence. She was not beautiful in the classic sense, but she had prettiness about her that when combined with her energy and laughter created attraction. He recounted the good times: sitting together sharing dreams, planning family trips, reading books out loud to each other, skiing with the children, trips to the lake. What happened to bring about the

dissidence in a once happy relationship? Like a cancer it starts small, unde-
tected, benign, and then morphs into a carcinogen taking hold of mind and
body.

Clare turned slightly on the couch, both hands tucked beneath her cheek,
her breathing through her slender pointed nose deep and regular. Max rose
from the chair to walk to the window. He gazed out at the dry grass, the leaf-
less trees, their buds swelling in anticipation of new leaves. *Does the weight of
deceit and neglect accumulate like ice in an ice storm?* Just weeks earlier he had watched
the ice gradually thicken on the tiny branches and limbs until one could bear
no more and snapped. Remorse draped his body like a heavy coat.

This evening's run was proving difficult. Max seemed to stumble unnec-
essarily and find himself winded. His plan to run the marathon had been
impulsive. It was a good idea, but could he be ready? Each time he ran he
expanded his distance. His route, now over ten kilometers, at one point passed
the building in which Clare worked. At this moment the Dyke Road behind the
University was desolate, the river to his right and experimental fields to his left;
no streetlights here to illuminate his path. Recessed thoughts surfaced like tiny
bubbles from a sinking bottle. If Clare was having an affair, was he to blame?

There had been steps forward. Mother's Day had been a triumph. They
had prepared and presented a decorative and surprise breakfast for Clare in
bed. Gifts had followed from all of them. Clare, he knew, loved her three
children. This overt affection could only bind her to them. But it was one step
forward and then several steps back it seemed. Her initial gush of affection
at the airport would wane considerably and then reappear as if by a sudden
determination.

At times she seemed to freeze at his touch. He thought her eyes had lost
their sparkle; her smile seemed contrived flashing on and off rather than
spreading from lips to eyes as it once did. He had come up behind her and
put his arms around her waist as she stood at the kitchen counter. Startled, she
pulled his hands away, shouted, "Don't do that!" and walked away. Turning
then, she said, "The gang at the office like to go out for a bite and a drink on
Friday and they have invited me to join them."

"How late might you be?"

"Did I ever ask you that question when you did your Friday night thing or
any other night for that matter?"

He merged onto University Crescent. His feet now determined his steps; up and over curbs, around this obstacle or that individual, his mind busy attempting to reunite their affection once again. Can it ever be the same? Their love making had been tepid of late. He smiled as he thought of the term "making love." Can you by some action make love, some formula or strategy produce love?

What actions, what appeal brought him and Clare together in the first instance and how could he replicate those qualities now? God knows he was trying; helping her with reports, bringing coffee and a sweet while she was working, really being the parent to the children at this moment, those hugs, which seem to backfire this morning. He had been hurt and silenced.

He hated to admit the many nights he had stayed late talking to his fellow teachers, chit-chat really, nothing necessary. In those days Clare had looked forward to his early arrival home to help with the children.

Clare leaned back in her office chair, her hands cradling her head. The events of this morning had upset her day. She had not intended to be so harsh and abrupt with Max. *He has been good of late; helpful, taking charge of the kids with homework and sports, preparing meals when I'm late. He is a good husband.* Thoughts of what she was doing trouble her.

She had been a prisoner to her home, a custodian to children for so long that this new freedom was exhilarating. She had told herself, it's time for me now. Were all affairs, she thought, so intoxicating?

But extra marital relations are also exhausting…the price is guilt and constant anxiety; an inner sense of turmoil threatening my poise, my self-image… brought up in a Christian family where marriage vows were considered sacred, how did this happen? The transition from friendly office help to passionate relationship has progressed so innocently, so quickly. Have she and Max been the perfect couple? Neither of us is what you would call good looking, but we are intelligent, stimulating, adventuresome, sharing a lot in common; the list goes on. Where did the bonding begin to fray…children occupying most of her time, household chores creating walls of isolation…Max, is preoccupied by his teaching and all the extra things he takes on at school or in the community…we aren't partners anymore. Do I suspect Max of looking outside the relationship during those extracurricular activities at school? Not really…Max is pretty doctrinaire and dependable although there are times when his family does not seem to come first.

She remembered that frightening evening. *I panicked, wanted Max, wondered why he wasn't home…I have never quite forgiven him for that. Somewhere in those years we began living together without the romance or mutual regard we once had…getting back to work outside the home has been a release, a call to engage in office challenges and social interaction…it is like premarital days when I explored ideas, met people, accepted who I was and made decisions on my own…And then Wes – instrumental in getting me this job, surprising me with his attention, complimenting me about work and appearance…I have felt that sensation again…I am someone worth noticing. Our meeting in London gave opportunity for sex. What a complexity of pleasure and guilt!*

Firm hands touched her shoulders and began to massage the tension gently. "Ready to join us?" It was Wes. "The others have long gone." She turned to look up at him. He bent down and kissed her lips.

"Wes, this charade is difficult. I'm certain Max has suspicions. Some of his questions, the way he looks at me?"

"Play it cool, my lovely or blow the whole party." Wes held out her coat.

This is so wrong, so wrong, she thought.

What can take possession of a forty-some mother and wife to try and navigate a double life…I have three teenage children for whom I should be setting an example and counselling in their years of puberty…a husband, although not perfect, has provided home and security for many years…he deserves better. I try not to give a hint of my life apart from the one at her home, but love making…I am an imposter feigning orgasmic pleasure to assure no suspicion…my thoughts often elsewhere…stress leads to tension and tension to unplanned, explosive comments…Wednesday night's need to catch up at the office has become a regular affair and Friday evenings with the gang becoming later and later especially when Wes and I return to his office…Max's questions this morning had been pointed…I exploded reminding him of how scared and hurt I had been the Friday night he didn't show up and we had almost lost Ashley. 'Where were you when I needed you? Now it's my turn to enjoy my friends.' His quiet reply, 'Friends or friend,' provoked an instant alarm but my silent stare implying, don't accuse me of anything you can't prove, seemingly worked…he walked away and left me to finish breakfast on my own.

The Marathon was approaching quickly. Max knew he wasn't ready. *Should have started training a lot sooner.* He was now running twenty kilometers once a week. *I'm a long way from the thirty-two recommended before doing a marathon.* Tonight, he was pushing himself as pent-up anger fueled this burst of energy.

Fragments of Max's relationship with Lois surfaced: snippets of conversation between classes and after school, shared stories of successes and failures of the day; then longer chats, gradually moving more and more to talk about their own lives and finally the day he realized his feelings for Lois were much deeper than friendship. She had come into his classroom after the last class to share a funny story, but it was the fresh scent of perfume, the inviting smile and the casual touch that had moved him deeply. In that meeting they had recognized their mutual appeal. Gradually they had become caught in a vortex of increasing intimacies, drawing them closer and closer.

The bar had been crowded but their group had managed to find a table in the corner, and they all pressed in around it. They sat next to each other as the group shared jokes and stories of the week. TGIF. He sensed the faint intrigue of her perfume, the caress of her hair or the brush of her breast against him as she leaned to talk or listen to someone else across the table, the thrill of her hand on his leg. The conversation which at first had been shared with the group became localized because of the noise. They became absorbed in each other; their eyes sharing unspoken urges.

Then some of the group began to leave; he became aware of the time. It was nearing seven and he had not called Clare to tell her where he was or that he'd be late.

They walked slowly together to the parking lot, unwilling it seemed to break the spell of intimacy. "It doesn't seem right to be going to separate homes," he had said quietly as they walked between their cars.

The touch of her hand taking his, her eyes as she turned to face him, her reply, "I know," soft, compelling, had suggested an invitation. He felt the swirl and tug of the narrowing vortex of desire. His reply was inappropriate.

"I didn't even tell Clare I'd be late this evening." At the mention of her name the spell had been broken. They had touched lips briefly and each entered the empty haven of their cars.

Max felt a sharp pain in his leg and then a cramp brought him to a standstill. He massaged the calf to work out the knot.

Arriving at home prepared to answer an onslaught of questions, instead the shock of an empty house, signs of a supper meal half eaten and evidence of a hasty retreat. Finally, he found the note. Children at the neighbours; Ashley and I are at the hospital. Fear and guilt had combined to create a moment of crippling panic.

He had rushed straight to the hospital, not daring to betray his guilt to next door neighbours. Then came relief; Clare, Ashley, OK. The questions were all his; the explanations Clare's: A small bone in her throat. She had been struggling to breath but thank God the hospital was nearby.

And then the carefully prepared story: a beer with the gang…time got away. Clare had not questioned further, but he sensed that through his deceit and betrayal a wall of separation had begun.

During the remaining hours of that weekend, he had privately made his choice. Silently and alone, he had asked God for forgiveness, help and pledged to himself and God he'd put Clare and family first. But he never confessed to Clare.

Now the tables were turned. Clare was engaged in a choice, and the consequences of her choice affected him and the family systemically. He felt helpless. *I am like Hamlet, burdened with suspicion, analyzing the nuance of every action but unable to act. Should I set a trap? Should I confront her directly? What would be the outcome, an admission, denial, clarification to their situation? But what if it led to separation? I do not want that. I am determined to reclaim her affection. Like a therapist I will continue to practice my "making love" in the holistic sense of small daily actions to let her know I value her and care. I think I'm making progress. Any action that might drive her out would be wrong.*

Her cell phone sang its song for attention. The screen showed Wes's number. Conversations or covert touching were not enough, but like two magnets they were drawn together. She could already feel the heat rise in her body in anticipation as he spoke. "I'm coming over." This was no longer intoxication; it had become an opioid, the physical magnetism so compelling. *This will be my undoing!* Clare soothed her wrists with a touch of perfume.

Max had circled back retracing part of his route. His leg was sore; he did not dare push it or risk further injury. The light was on in Clare's office. I'll catch a ride home with her and spare my leg.

Her office was empty. Wes's name marked the door from which came sounds of two people seemingly engaged in a struggle. The curtain on the glass panel beside the door, slightly open, invited a peek. A naked Clare aggressively taking the lead in a tango of love, when suddenly her back arched, her head lifted high she erupted in a primal squeal of attainment before collapsing on Wes. Max stood frozen as if struck by a blinding light, his eyes closed. Suspicions were confirmed in that paralyzing flash. The knowledge that such abandonment, such screams of attainment were unknown to him created a feeling of apoplexy. Angry, heartbroken and frustrated he kicked the door, hard, before hurrying away.

Never had walking been so painful! His leg ached, his mind a torrent of thoughts and incriminations, cramps twisted the muscles of his stomach. He stumbled along at best, occasionally stopping to rub his leg. A pathway bench provided a moment of reprieve. Moonlight set sparkling diamonds of light glistening off the dark waters of the river. The haunting "woo, woo" of a nearby owl broke through the distant noise of traffic. These distractions could not block the image of Clare astride Wes. "O Clare, Clare", he raged, beating his fist into the palm of his hand, "O Clare how can I ever trust you? God, O God that I should see this! How can I forget?" Witnessing her death would have been less hurtful he thought. Death did not bring humiliation, shame and thoughts of utter repudiation. He could no longer feign ignorance.

Normally tall, broad of shoulder and strong, at that moment Max bent over, hunchbacked, with hands clasping his face, looking like a twisted cripple. He cried with loud agonizing shuddering gasps. Devastated and broken, his determination to forgive, to love and to reclaim seemed impossible? A cauldron of disdain boiled within. In that glimpse, that one moment, life had been sucked out of him.

Looking up, he noticed the moon beckoning on the dark waters. Somehow, he made his way to the river's edge. The brown water drifted silently along; small white collections of foam circled in eddies by the shore. The current set the trunk of a long ago fallen tree bobbing up and down as if keeping time to an inaudible melody. Max straddled the log and sat mesmerized. Despair and pain prompted a paralysis, but his mind was alive. Trust, communication, everything had been broken. She had betrayed the deepest of their intimacies. To meet her eyes, to touch her would be repulsive. In what way was she now his wife?

His eyes focused on the brown water and the contrasting white foam. He recalled a moment in his childhood when he thought he was drowning. He had taken a bad fall while water skiing, bumping his head on the ski as he nose-dived into the water. Disorientated and stunned he could not resolve how to get up to the surface. Panic set in. He needed to breathe; his lungs ached. Then rescuing hands from below pushed him to the surface. He could remember taking that reviving gulp of air. Now he thought of his three children. Slowly he took three deep breaths, turned and hobbled toward home.

He lay in a hot tub of water, his mind numbed by the excesses of adrenalin; his leg tender from strain, his mind vacillated between an angry resolve to kick her out and more sober reflection. He slept in the spare bedroom.

Guilt can promote renewed expressions of commitment. In the following days, Clare acted more energetic, talkative, and available to the kids than she had been. Max, on the other hand, rose early, came home late, and proceeded as in a stupor, mechanically going from task to task, a robot, moving without feeling.

Running became his outlet. He pushed himself, punished himself until exhausted he fell to lie for some time before rising to walk slowly home. He released anger but never despair. Why had he not confronted her on her arrival home from Europe? His turmoil raged; to confront her now would prompt her leaving; to dissemble, prolonged the agony. His sense of shame hindered disclosure to colleagues. He was alone.

Stopping to rest at a park bench one afternoon during a grueling run, Max was joined by another runner – a stranger. Impulsively, looking straight ahead, Max declared, "My wife is having an affair. I saw her having sex with another man. It's driving me crazy!"

"Ditch the bitch. She's making a fool of you. You deserve better. That's what I did when I found my wife whoring." He spoke impassionedly, his eyes focused on a distant point.

"Your wife had an affair too!"

"There's quite a few of us cuckolded buggers. Don't think you are alone." He rose, ran on the spot for a moment and then shouted back as he took off, "Meet her at the door tonight with her suitcase. That's what I did." That's exactly what he wanted to do, total repudiation. But his children were still innocently unaware; to toss her out would destroy his family.

The moment Clare stepped into his office; she knew something was amiss. He slouched in his chair, his gaze unfocused. There was no greeting, no attempt to rise and embrace. Alarmed, Clare questioned, "What's wrong, Wes?"

"Nancy knows! I don't know how." Clare sat down across from him. "And…she says she has pictures. She's calling Max. Nancy will get the children and the house. Max will claim the same, I'm sure." The blood drained from Clare's face; her stomach tightening in a knot. *Exposed! I am like the Emperor wearing no clothes.* A flush of shame reddened her cheeks.

"What's to happen to us?"

"We were having a good time, Clare; we were having a good time, that's all. I am not willing to lose my house and family."

For days she didn't go to work feigning sickness. Paranoia crippled her confidence. Suspicion, she assumed, etched the faces of anyone she met. Someone had kicked the door. Someone had informed Nancy. Someone had taken pictures. To see Wes would invite rebuke and reinforce his loss of interest. Worst of all she did not know how to tell Max. He had stood behind her in her wish to work, had applauded her successes and carried the household chores; he did not deserve an adulterous wife. But her children, how she agonized for her children! A beautiful teenage daughter struggling she was sure with the ups and down of puberty hormones. To find out her mother was having an affair. And her sons to whom she should be setting an example of a virtuous woman, what were they to think?

Marathon day arrived, canopied with blue sky and caressed with gentle breeze – a day promising heat. He started strong, out pacing the pack; too strong he concluded later. Shouts of support all along the route were background noises to his concentration and focus. His children relayed beside the race route. Some of his students offered bottles of water and shouts of encouragement. If Clare was there, he never saw her. At kilometer 30 his legs ached; he feared another disabling cramp; his pace was slowing; his vision blurring from time to time. He fixated on a point, a corner, a building ahead, breaking up the remaining kilometers into attainable segments. Through the pain and laboured breathing, he pushed to attain the next point. He was almost there.

Five kilometers from the finish line he collapsed. Medics were by his side carrying him to a nearby shelter, recording his vitals, offering him water as he lay on a gurney, devastated. He had failed to complete the marathon. Jeb, Joel and Ashley were suddenly beside him inquiring, consoling. He closed his eyes, comforted in their presence and let his body relax. He felt the kiss, opened his eyes to see Clare leaning over him.

A renewed hope – a powerful motivator – revived his lost expectation of romancing Clare back to earlier days of love. He had felt that emptiness in his teaching, his family and now his running. But this touch of her lips on his was prolonged and warm; tears pooling at the corner of her eyes.

Pride kept Max from confiding his dilemma to his colleagues or clergy. Awkwardly he managed a muddled relationship with Clare. It was a delicate dance to maintain appearances and to protect the kids from the truth. He barely touched her. He slept in a separate room now on the pretense he got a better rest. His survival was to run and so he set out a training procedure for next year's marathon.

He had passed this church – new, beautiful in design and inviting – on several occasions. Today, on an impulse, he jogged up the sidewalk to the front doors. They were unlocked. Feeling like an intruder, nevertheless, he entered the narthex and removed his ball cap. The nave was empty, silent. Afternoon sunlight shone through the upper windows. Proceeding toward the chancel, he sensed a subtle aroma of incense. Behind the altar, a modern rendition of a broken Jesus, a crucifix, dominated the wall. Such large iconic images were foreign to his religious tradition, but there was Jesus hanging twisted, arms and legs pinioned to the posts, a broken person.

To trash Clare before God was not an option. After all he had been just one step removed from her actions. Just one step. Fragmented memories from his own church experiences came to his mind. He recalled Jesus' declaration to the woman caught in adultery, *"Neither do I condemn you. Go and sin no more."* Easy for him to say, Max reasoned, he wasn't married to her.

A dark-skinned man stood beside him, dressed in black except for a white clerical collar. "Don't let me interrupt your prayer, but…"

"Not praying. Perhaps I should be…"

"If I can help, let me know." He began to walk away.

"Please," Max requested, "I have a question."

The question turned out to be a full confession. A confession revealing what he had seen, how he had neglected his family, and how, some years back, he had almost done with another woman, what Clare was doing. He had loved Clare but now revolted by what he had seen he had no idea how to restore love or his family…Here he was with yet another stranger asking for direction.

The priest sat beside him. "We humans are all given to frailties. Those are the stories of Adam and Eve, Cain and Abel, Joseph and his brothers, David and Bathsheba, Jesus and Judas. The Bible is full of sin stories. He spoke with a lilting accent. "Don't blame yourself for your wife's infidelity." This was your wife's choosing not yours. We are not given excuses to break sacred vows just because things are not going well. That is not a solution. As you can see, it has created a bigger problem. You say you loved her."

"Yes, but that scene with her and her boss has destroyed that love."

"To love can be difficult; that's why we have this crucifix here in front of us to remind us of the cost of loving and forgiving. Your love for her calls you to do that. Be patient. Stop blaming yourself; get out there and win her back, man. Don't give up. God never gave up on us!" Max left the sanctuary with new resolve but with undetermined direction.

She walked to work now to claim a few minutes of aloneness and thought. The walk home this evening was slow. Questions, thoughts and anxieties bubbled up and cluttered her mind like hot lava: *did those at the office know...surely Max knew...when would the children find out...who had kicked the door...?* Like frost slowly dissolving from a window providing clarity of vision, Clare was gaining a clearer picture of her situation. In her reckless abandonment of morals to satiate pleasure, her willful intoxication with new experiences, her needless exploiting of her husband's congeniality, she had disregarded all restraints. Now her marriage, her children, her home all were on the line. She was on her own. The excited, hardworking, newly gregarious woman suddenly felt fatigued, ashamed and insular. *Like Icarus I have flown too high, but like Hercules I will take responsibility.* The decision she had just made came from weeks of agony. It would have been easier had Nancy called Max, which seemingly hadn't happened. Max had been distant and distracted of late, but, Clare reasoned, his focus on the marathon was to blame. His disappointment in not finishing his first race had been intense. Now to hear his wife confess to adultery...?

She had arranged for them to go out for supper. She had considered canceling, but resolve had held the day. *Confess tonight and learn the consequences.* As she circled the block before stopping at the restaurant, panic gripped her determination again. She circled the block a second time, then seeing Max's car, she parked.

Sitting at a table in the back corner, awkward, like bashful teenagers on a first date, their tongues seemed bridled. Max knew of her affair and wanted to say so but was afraid of the consequences. Clare, humiliated, knowing her affair was now going public wanted to confess, but was embarrassed and fearful. They groped for conversation settling on the kids, then the marathon and Max's resolve to try again. "Max..." Clare hesitated unsure, "I have something..." but looking at Max she saw the lines of anxiety etched across his forehead. She braced herself for Max's response.

"Clare, I know."

Clare was silent a moment parsing his comment. "Nancy told you?"

"Yes and no. Nancy told me Wes was over in Europe when you prolonged your stay. I drew a conclusion. That's all Nancy has ever told me. But your Wednesday and Friday nights confirmed that...well I found out it was more than catching up with work."

Suddenly, as if wronged, "When were you going to let me know?

"Tonight."

One truth was now expressed. Simply, with few words, the infidelity had been exposed. But the truth uncovered is not a matter reconciled. Max could have more easily dealt with a sobbing, broken Clare than one who suddenly seemed more estranged and hurt by his failure to confront her. He reached over to take her hand; she pulled it away.

"Do you and Wes have plans?"

"No! Wes and Nancy are dealing with it. He does not want to lose his family."

"Do you?" The question was little more than a whisper.

Emotions swelled up in Clare. She wiped a tear away and scanned the other patrons. "Let's go outside," she suggested. Clare insisted on paying the bill. It had been her invite. It was raining lightly when they stepped outside. She invited Max to her car. They had sat side by side many times before in a car; at times to hold hands and kiss before going their separate ways, at other times to join in song as they travelled. But tonight, Clare was in the driver's seat, Max, the passenger.

Clare sat silent for some time. Max's revelation had derailed her plan of confession. The pretenses of the past weeks angered her. Her hands gripped the steering wheel. Tears pooled in her large eyes and began their flow down her cheeks. Her emotional constraints burst. Her head fell forward onto the wheel as if in exhaustion; quiet sobs, then loud and wrenching, shook her body. Max reached over to place his arm on her shoulder. She shook it off defiantly with a "Don't touch me!"

Silence overlaid by sobbing delayed the answer to his question. Determined to push on, but not wishing to seek a pound of flesh, he wanted a sense of her regret. His questions were rapid, her response slow. "Clare, how did this happen? What went wrong? Are you in love with Wes? Is it just about sex? I need to know."

Confusion eroded her confidence, but defiance provided an outlet for survival. "What difference does it make? As far as you are concerned, with your puritan upbringing, I am a soiled and sinful woman. Why drag out all the dirty details when it's over, Max. It's over!"

"Clare, I don't want it to be over!"

Clare's interjection was caustic. "Get real! I'm not proud of what I have done or become but to think we can play, Let's Pretend It Never Happened, is unreal. We were both taught marriage vows are sacred. I've broken that vow.

No matter what you say, you'll never see beyond what I have done!"

Hesitant, wanting to share his own mental adultery, Max proceeded. "During the past several weeks of knowing you had found more pleasure with someone else, I have been in despair, humiliated, angry, and at times dysfunctional. I have been jealous and afraid. I didn't say anything earlier out of fear of losing you; that you would walk out and go to Wes. I want you."

"So, you are ready to forgive me, then?" the question laced with cynicism.

"Yes, I want to."

"Ok, Max, you forgive but you'll never forget. I'm on the up end of the teeter-totter with my feet off the ground. As such, I will always be subject to some control, pressure or…You'll never trust me again. How can we ever have a normal, congenial, healthy relationship with you carrying that grudge?"

"I want you as my wife, mother to our children, my companion at their graduations, marriages, and the birth of grandchildren. Don't you want that?" A renewed burst of sobs broke the stillness in the car.

Yes, she did. But as hard as she tried, the thought of what she had done, how she had been the plaything of Wes, had broken fidelity with her husband and brought shame to her children overwhelmed her. The atrocity of her behaviour was like heavy rubble burying her as in an earthquake. How could she ever be restored? "I'll leave tonight."

"No. Don't do that. We already sleep separately. You need to live with the children and me in order to work this out without the kids knowing."

"Not too likely, "Clare spoke between sobs. "The story is out there. It's only a matter of time for them to hear about it; better from us right now."

Silence filled that tiny space. The sobbing ended, eyes wiped, Clare turned to face Max. "When was the last time we felt real affection for each other. Growing into years of marriage is like wearing old clothes. Comfortable yes, but their attractiveness gone, they become faded and worn. I have my routine of responsibilities and you had all those commitments. Am I off the mark? So, what is love at our age, Max?"

"So, you wanted something new, something a little more attractive?" The scene in Wes' office came to his mind. "Is that what you are saying? What we had, grew stale, unexciting? You're right. Expressions of love change. I know I missed you when you were away. I know I am proud of our children, each of whom has expressions of you in their features and personality. I am proud of your accomplishments, Clare. I still admire you physically. I believe that is part of being in love with you."

"I am asking that question because I know in the last few months I have been rejuvenated, felt valued and…"

"Loved?" Max filled in the hesitation.

Clare studied Max's face. If she had felt loved by Wes in a certain way, perhaps superficially, it disappeared when he chose wife and home. Certainly, she was not about to rush back to where she had been with Max. She was too proud for that. "I'll pack some clothes and take a room tonight."

"How long since Wes said Nancy knew?"

"A couple of weeks."

"I have a suspicion," Max ventured. "I think this has been a ruse. Wes wanted this to end before Nancy found out, so he told you that story to break it off. Nancy doesn't know or she would have called me. Neither does anyone else except Wes, you and I."

Clare straightened up from her slouch over the steering wheel. Max's idea had merit but, "somebody kicked the door," she muttered.

"What do you mean? Max was intrigued.

"We thought someone may have been watching us at the office." But her thoughts continued. I will confront Wes tomorrow. This knowledge might be very limited. Somewhat relieved, she agreed to come home.

But she didn't. Max waited up long past midnight. Anticipating the sound of her car, his sleep had been shallow. He rose early. What should he tell the children? He wasn't about to lie to them. Ashley was first to question, "Where's mum?"

A good question, Max thought. He took Ashley into his arms. "Your mother and I are having some problems now. She needs a little time to think. Let's give her some space," he whispered.

"Are you planning to divorce?" Ashley's voice had grown thin from anxiety.

"No! I am not planning to divorce your mother."

Ashley's concern continued, "Where is she staying?"

Max didn't know the answer but provided a calculated guess. "I think she's with her parents." She had work. She didn't have extra clothes. Where else? She would be back, he was sure.

Clare decided she could not go home. Regardless of Max's knowledge of her affair and for all his declaration of forgiving, she was damaged goods. How could she expect to be his wife knowing what he did? She needed some time to think in her own space. Max's car turned the corner and disappeared.

Making a quick U turn, she drove until she reasoned she was far enough from home. She turned in at the Paradise Motel.

She had done wrong. To leave Max was one thing but her children? A mother doesn't abandon her children! By morning she had a plan. By evening she had clothes and a determination to return to work. A quick call to Wes to explain her absence from work, to share what had gone down between her and Max the night before, and to ask him whether Nancy really knew. He insisted he was not free to talk of such on his telephone, but they needed to talk. Could he come over?

A light tap on her room door a little later, a peek to confirm Wes was on the other side and she let him in.

The parking lot at the Paradise Motel was crowded but Max found a space at the far end. He would walk past the front desk as Ashley was able to get her room number earlier with a little conniving. Then he spotted Wes' car since the license plate carried his name. Vanity plates indeed! But tonight, this was devastating in its confirmation. O my God, he thought! All that crying last night was about the breakup with Wes, not what she had done to her family. Just then Wes came out of the door of the motel.

Max went directly to room 613. She would come to the door because she might be expecting Wes to return. A rattle of the chain and the door opened.

"Oh my God," Clare exclaimed! "Does everybody know where I am?"

"Some of us care about you", Max stepped inside.

Tonight, he was determined to take charge. *This will be tough love in action.* "Clare, pack your bags; you're coming home with me. Your children are beside themselves worrying about you. Ashley tracked you down. How can you walk out and leave three kids who love you when I know you love them?"

"I was going to keep in touch, "Clare offered weakly.

Clare was a strong woman; not one to be pushed around easily but tonight she actually welcomed Max's direction. She mourned for what she was doing to her children.

Preparations for the June marathon included a regular routine of physical fitness. Weekly Max arrived at the fitness center to exercise both body and mind. This Saturday morning after a vigorous workout, he entered the sauna. His relentless question, "what would you do if you caught your wife cheating?" was to an elderly man sitting hunched over on the sauna bench directly across from him. His weathered face looked strong. Judging from his full head of gray hair and accompanying short gray beard Max figured he must have life experience.

Max rose from his seat and ladled water onto the hot rocks. Steam rose providing a mist and hiss filling the small space almost obscuring the other man. Securing his towel about his waist he returned to his seat. He ventured his question.

"You talkin' for yourself son or is this a general question," the ghostlike figure with the gravelly voice requested?

Max hesitated a moment and then ventured, "For me."

"Tell me your story. What's your name?"

"Max."

"OK, Max."

In that tiny sauna, amidst the steam and heat, Max retold his story, every detail and then waited.

"Do you love this woman or just stickin' with her for the – nice thing to do?"

"Yes, I love her. She has been a wonderful wife for twenty years."

"Do you go to church Max?"

"Not lately. I've been ashamed, maybe embarrassed"

"Max, there is a book in the Bible called Hosea. Have you heard of it?"

"Yeah, he was a prophet, right?"

"You're right there, Max. Did you know his wife, her name was Gomer, was a prostitute?"

"A prostitute?"

"Hosea loved that woman and stayed with her begging her to leave her prostitution. It's a story of how God reaches out to all of us no matter the circumstances and is persistent in his love."

Max was speechless. Are you a preacher? What's your name?"

"Don't matter what my name is. Call me Bob. Yes, I am a preacher down at the Cowboy Church but I'm sayin' this not as a preacher. Your story is my story, but in spite of my loving Jenny, until I got to the bottom of things with the lady, we weren't goin' nowhere. Sometimes to love takes a lot of patience.

Max had a lot of homework. They hadn't shared details nor had Clare said, "I'm sorry." Saying, "Sorry" is a difficult thing at the best of times, Max mused? It requires a certain amount of self-confidence. It's an admission to making a mistake and perhaps the need to take responsibility for that mistake. Max knew after his years with her that Clare didn't say "sorry" easily. He started to the showers.

"Come visit us at the Cowboy Church, Max," Bob called. "You'll find us on Facebook. "Oh, don't go on an ego trip."

Max paused. "What do you mean an ego trip?"

Easy to think you're the good guy because you're so big to forgive. Remember bein' forgiven isn't easy to accept. Just try to accept her as a different person. She's not the same lady you first fell in love with."

With the warm waters spilling over his body washing away the salt, sweat and oil, he felt a sense of determination. Two people who had loved each other passionately, conceived children together, shared joys, dreams and exclusive privileges were now estranged. Two things he pledged to complete. He would do well in the next marathon. He would reclaim Clare's affection and devotion.

They sat in silence. Finally, hesitantly she asks, "What do we do?" It was her birthday. They had risked another dinner out. Perhaps leveling the playing field would help Clare share some details, Max reasoned, and finally shared his story about Lois and the night Ashley choked. Instead, it did the opposite. Clare erupted like a volcano long thought dormant; a cork from a champagne bottle hitting the ceiling. "You've made me feel like dirt for all these weeks and now you're telling me you were dallying with that Lois woman while Ashley was choking to death. That's as good as manslaughter! And you're asking me for an apology!

"I am sorry. I've told myself and God many times that I was sorry."

"But you didn't say it to me and now it is a bit too late, Max. Let's face it, you and I are finished. This living together as two solitudes is ridiculous. You go, get a new life and I'll do the same. I'll stay in touch with the kids and if you tell them about Wes and me, don't forget to tell them your little story about Lois and Ashley nearly dying." With that she was gone.

April returned with the promise of new life. Dark days had given way to the longer daylight of spring. Winter snow had melted, and the frogs croaked again in the ponds. Then came May, Max's favorite month when trees blossomed, and the world was fresh with the greens of early summer. His runs this past week had been infused with the scents of blooming lilacs, their lush blue flowers bordering the streets and the white tongues of chokecherry flowers bordering the trails. It was a beautiful world except for one thing.

He was into his final weeks of preparing for the marathon. Tonight, he had postponed his run until late evening to catch the benefits of the coolness. Just as victims of serious accidents find returning to the scene evokes the sounds, odors and emotional trauma that accompanied that impact, Max had changed his jogging route to avoid going by the building where he had witnessed the violence to his marriage. This is like a Post Traumatic Syndrome he thought his mind feathering through the details as he jogged inadvertently by her office. Why did I do this? He cursed himself at the memory. Like a callus on a hand, he had hardened himself to thoughts involving Clare and Wes.

Clare's arrival at her parent's home that birthday evening was a surprise. Her mother's persistent questions about what was wrong, her father's accusatory silence was annoying and invasive. She needed a place of her own. But when she found a condo of a colleague on sabbatical and out of town, the privacy brought the return of Wes. A sordid chapter, Clare concluded on reflecting back on the past few months. She had resolved many times to set new goals without Max or Wes. But to wish was one thing, to abstain another.

A promotion at the office came with more involvement and travel with Wes. She hadn't questioned why he seemingly lost his fear of losing home and family. She clung to his affection, attention and his help. That his affection was contingent upon expected benefits was mentally abhorrent, but nonetheless she complied. Tonight, a flush of shame, like a beginning fever, gave her a shiver.

They were in Toronto for meetings. She was ready for bed when the expected light tap came on the door. "Just want to say goodnight and go over the details for tomorrow morning's meeting." Wes came in dressed in PJ's and gown. He sat down on the chair beside the bed. Clare had been on the bed propped up with pillows doing some review herself.

Business quickly dealt with; the talk became personal. Wes' eyes betrayed his real goal. Her earlier thoughts of remorse prompted Clare to counter directly, "You orchestrated a break in our relationship some months ago. You were afraid of losing Nancy, your home and your children. How has that changed?"

"Well…, Nancy now knows the truth about you and me. How she found out I'd like to know."

"Remember, Wes, someone kicked the door."

"The fat is in the pan. She's not leaving the house or kids and she's tacitly given me the liberty to fool around but it must not hurt the kids. She claims the same options whenever she wishes. I guess that's what has changed."

The words, "Just fooling around", aggravated Clare. Max would never agree to such an arrangement, she reasoned silently.

"So," Wes continued, rising from his chair to sit next to her on the bed. "That danger is over. You and Max are living separately. That's why our relationship is good." He placed his hand on her leg.

She felt the warmth of the hand, the usual quickening of her heart and the adjustment to her breathing. She placed her hand over his and held it for a moment. Tonight, she would act differently. She removed his hand from her leg and slid off the bed. "No, Wes, not tonight; let's keep this strictly business." She walked to the door. "Good night, I'll see you at breakfast."

Wes left, but the look of resentment, if not anger, as he passed her at the door promised a reckoning.

Surprised at how emotionally upset and how quickly her body always responded to Wes' touch, her hands trembled as she picked up her notebook. She closed her eyes and took a few deep breaths. "Thank you, God! Could that be step one." she voiced audibly. A smile edged the corners of her mouth at the irony. It had been a long time since she thought about God except to sense he or she would not be happy with her. Perhaps I need to ask for a little more divine help in this journey. How long, she wondered, could she maintain this new resolve. But she didn't offer a prayer, just closed her book and pulled the blankets up to sleep.

Business did not wrap up as planned Friday evening; Wes left Clare, intending to return Monday, as soon as the details were all in place. A weekend in downtown Toronto all to herself! Saturday shopping was exhausting but cathartic. Sunday threatened boredom. She woke up to a sense of great loneliness. Rebuking Wes had strengthened her resolve but introduced tension. Was her job at risk? Estranged from her husband, separated from her children and now in contention with her boss, this morning she was experiencing a feeling of despair. Forcing herself out of bed she drew back the drapery. Dark heavy clouds obscured her view of the skyline. Water in serpentine rivulets slithered down the window obliterating the street below. The tall buildings outside were wrapped in dark mist.

Donning her raincoat and picking up the umbrella, she stepped out onto the street. This was wind and rain. She struggled to maintain the umbrella upright. Determined, she pushed on eager to shake her mood. Rain soaked her legs; her shoes became wet; her walking slowed. Faint sounds of music filtered through the discord of wind and rain. The doors of a large gothic style church stood open offering respite. She stepped inside; the music, now distinct, came from within. Wet, but curious, she proceeded. A tall, buxom, woman with a bright smile approached. "Please, let me hang your wet coat. The women's washroom is to your right." She pointed with a somewhat gnarled arthritic finger. "Go dry yourself. I'll be right here."

Emerging minutes later, she saw her helper assisting another late comer some distance away. Curious, she cautiously opened the doors to the sanctuary. Large columns rose upward fluting out to support the high ceiling. Stain glass windows surrounded the interior. She had never before entered such a large, elevated and beautiful space. Clutches of people sat randomly throughout.

She took a back seat. A man handed her a leaflet of papers and pointed to a specific page. On a cue, unknown to Clare, the congregation slid from their sitting position to kneeling. She noticed the small folding step that was pulled down on which they knelt. She remained seated. The people began reciting together the words of the prayer printed on her paper.

God of healing,
God of wholeness,
we bring our brokenness,
our sinfulness,
our fears
and despair,
and lay them at your feet.

God of healing,
God of wholeness,
we hold our hearts and hands,
minds and souls
to feel your touch,
and know the peace
that only you can bring.

God of healing,
God of wholeness,
this precious moment
in your presence and power

grant us faith and confidence
that here broken lives
are made whole.

Clare had prayed: table graces, the Lord's Prayer, nighttime prayer verses with her young children. This prayer was succinct and how appropriately the words applied to her. She was broken. She had no thought for Nancy when engaged with Wes in their affair. Nancy had been her friend and neighbour. She had skillfully rationalized her infidelity to Max as a need for new experiences and now as a means of prospering her job.

Clare's thoughts returned to the service. A woman was speaking. The story was familiar to Clare: The Prodigal Son. What about the prodigal daughter, Clare thought? Her parents had been upset by her living separately from Max. She had refused to entertain the full implications of the word adultery. Her thoughts returned to the woman speaking.

We know the details of the young brother. He asked for and got his portion of the estate only to leave home, leave his faith community and squander his money in "riotous living" We could assume prostitutes, gambling, lots of eating out, the whole nightclub type of activity."

Clare was watching the woman intensely. She was of medium height, dark shoulder length hair. She wore a white gown with a sash or stole in green over her shoulders. It stretched to her knees. A rope-like belt snugged up the gown around a narrow waist. She focused again on what the woman was saying.

"Older brother was the good guy. He stayed at home and did his work – faithfully, dutifully, without prodding. But he too was the focus of this story. His conduct was to be equally condemned."

Was that me, thought Clare when I stayed home, looked after the kids, washed the clothes, saw to my husband's needs – the faithful wife?

Clare carefully lowered the kneeling bench and placed her wet feet on it pushing herself back against the pew, her thoughts reviewing her life. Then she refocused on the speaker.

"Now the punch line," declared the pretty, gowned-clad speaker. Younger brother, living in total debauchery, recognizes his wrong and returns to father begging forgiveness. Forgiveness granted. The father represents God. The young brother represents the out and out recognizable sinner."

That's me I guess, thought Clare.

"He's welcomed, restored and partied because he recognized his wrong and asked for forgiveness. Older brother is the self-righteous one, striving all his life by his work and faithfulness to be recognized by dad. But he didn't even get a small party. Go figure, the speaker challenges! Do we achieve God's acceptance by the good things we do? Or is it our request for forgiveness from whatever wrongs, however scandalous. It is our God who is prodigal, lavish in his love and eager to accept the repentant." She sat down.

Wonder if it's still raining; I need to get out now. Clare slipped out, collected her coat and moved to the door. The rain had ended. The clouds were breaking. The sun peaked through as Clare arrived at the door of her hotel.

Max was at the Investor's Field starting line early, rested and strong along with what appeared to be 12,000 others. This marathon was his to achieve. By his calculations he should finish in time to qualify for the Boston. Yes, the Boston! His year of training had put him in good physical shape. He had found joy in running. Why not the Boston?

Jeb, Joel and Ashley were all prepared to follow his progress today, provide water and encouragement, Ashley on her bicycle; the boys had the car. His one regret was Clare. Ashley had encouraged mum to come watch dad at the finish, but she had not made a commitment.

He positioned himself midway in the starting pack. His bib carried a chip keeping track of his time as he went along. No need to panic at the beginning. He had studied the map, was well aware of his route. Assiniboine Park marked Km 20. He was almost halfway there. Groups of spectators lined the route more densely at some points than others. He was somewhat aware of their shouts of encouragement: "You're looking good." "Way to go!" "Keep it up." Jeb, Joel and Ashely appeared regularly offering a bottle of water, some chocolate and always encouragement. At Km 27 he touched Pembina Highway briefly and then veered left toward the river. He was tiring. Fifteen more kilometers to go! Fortunately, this was a flat course; no big inclines to deal with.

Jed was at Km 38. "Your time is great, Dad. You're almost there."

He was coming down Crescent Dr. approaching Pembina Highway again when he noticed a frantic Jeb waving his arms and beckoning him to the curb. He veered to the side. "Ashley's been hurt, Dad. Badly! She was knocked off her bicycle by a car." Jeb had been running alongside as he conveyed the message. "Joel went with her in the ambulance. They took her to Victoria General."

The only words that seemed to register with Max were "Badly" and "Victoria Hospital."

He left the race. Jeb had the car just a block away. "I'll run there, Jed." With adrenal surging Max dashed past cars and over curbs. The Vic wasn't far away. Ashley had left triage and had been hurried off for x-rays. Both legs had been broken. Some fractured ribs, but a head injury the severity of which they still had to ascertain.

She had lost a lot of blood – a rare type. None at the hospital at the moment. Sending out for some. Does a member of your family have the same? Do you know?

"Her mother has that type too," Max said.

"This is critical. We have sent a request to another hospital but if she's available let's get her here.

He tried to call Clare again. "She's not answering her phone." Another call went immediately to voicemail. "Ashley has been seriously hurt, unconscious. It appears as if she has a concussion. She needs a blood transfusion – your type. Please call."

Clare sat in the restaurant nursing her second cup of coffee. Wes was meeting her for breakfast. He had been particularly abrupt and distant with her this past week. But it was he who said, "We need to talk. Let's do breakfast Sunday morning."

Soul searching had been her homework this past week. She had made a private commitment to go celibate. Was last week's experience in the church fortuitous or planned? The rain, her mood, the welcome at the door, the beauty of the building – God was not a part of her life lately, or was He? She had been captivated by the speaker, but the story resonated so aptly with Clare Garnett.

Wes arrived all smiles. He hugged her lightly before sitting down. Talk was casual – the marathon. Clare remembered then she had half promised Ashley she would be at the finish line to see Max finish.

"He's so pumped, Mum," Ashley had said. "If there are no hitches he could qualify for the Boston. He sends his love." She always added that phrase or "Dad says to say 'Hi.'" Ashley had been their communication nexus.

Breakfast came. They ate quietly for some time. Wes, congenial, shared some details of office matters. *He's taking a gentle approach. Win me over with kindness and hope to bed me again.* As if on cue, Wes placed his hand over hers. "Clare, I miss what we have between us. Let's enjoy it." Clare tried to remove her hand, but he held it fast. "Tell me honestly, Clare, you miss it too" His voice was quiet, seductive, his eyes compelling and his grasp on her hand firm. "We work well together. We share interests…"

"If you feel that way Wes, leave your wife," Clare interrupted.

"I don't have a marriage, but I have a home and children. You're in the same boat, Clare. So let's accept that and enjoy each other. We can't rectify what's broken in our marriages can we."

I may have children, but I don't have a home, thought Clare. "I need some time outside of a relationship, Wes. I'm asking for that." With a tug she withdrew her hand. Reaching for her phone in her purse to check the time she placed it on the table. She realized then it was turned off.

Wes immediately picked it up. "I don't want us interrupted by phone calls. We need to talk this out."

"Don't bully me!"

"Clare, you and I are in love. Let's take what goes with that."

"Are we in love? Please give me my phone." Reluctantly he complied. Once it sputtered into action, several messages appeared of missed phone calls from Max. *Why Max? Has he finished the race already?* Just then the phone rang again. She listened as horror spread across her face. "I'll be right there." Grabbing her bag, she called back to Wes, "Ashley's been in an accident."

Clare flew through the door into the waiting room. Max's only words were, "It's critical. They need your blood."

She watched the bag slowly fill with her blood. Tears moistened her cheeks. Blood – life giving, special in type, passed on to her daughter in conception and now needed to renew that life again. *Oh, God, please may I have arrived in time?* Clare closed her eyes. *There is nothing like an accident to sharpen your focus on values in life — I have been caught up in a spree, an orgy perhaps — self-indulgent, pleasure filled, an attempt to revitalize my life, a mid-aged crisis perhaps — I have lost my husband of 20 years, my moral values and self-respect —Am I depending on a compromising relationship with my boss to gain promotion? Am I now about to lose my daughter?*

Ashley's life hung in a tenuous balance for three days, Neither Max nor did Clare leave the hospital. One or the other kept vigil in her room. The bib with his race number hung on the back of his chair testament to his unfinished marathon. When I finally turn it in, he mused, I will have recorded the longest running time possible.

Day four Ashley's breathing grew shallow prompting a flurry of activity. The neurologist was called in to perform another surgery to relieve pressure on the brain. There was no need for words when the doctor entered their waiting room. "We tried our best. I am so sorry."

Clare's response was uncontainable grief. At first, she sat down with her head between her knees, her agony expressed in intense wails bursting and subsiding like huge waves. Max tried to embrace her but she pushed him away. "Look what I have done, look what I have done," came in raspy whispers between shuddering sobs. "I should have been here sooner. I should have been with Ashley." She stood up and approached the doctor. "She needed my blood. I wasn't here."

The doctor placed a hand on her arm. "Blood was important, but it was the severe blow to her brain."

Clare turned to Max. "She wanted me to be with her. It would never have happened."

"Clare, it is not your fault. I could say I should not have run this marathon. It is not your fault!"

Grief like a drug dulls the senses, suspends time and place, and blocks reality. Somehow Clare emerged from the funeral uncertain as to how those previous days had passed. She did not want to be alone. She would not return to Max and the boys. She agreed to her mother being with her at nights and to visits from Max and the boys during the day. She wept until she thought there was no more moisture for tears.

Finally, the crying stopped. Grief and guilt settled like a smothering blanket. She lay quietly wrapped in thought. The loss of her daughter was inconceivable. That she may have contributed was unforgivable. Assurances from the doctor and Max that brain damage was more consequential than blood loss, seemed of little balm. She had been with Wes, holding hands, talking about being together with him when Ashley had wanted so much to be with her. She heard Ashley's sweet voice over and over, "Dad is so pumped! He'll want us to be there when he crosses the finish line." But he never made it to the finish line nor did Ashley. Her beautiful fourteen-year-old daughter's life was over before it scarcely started. Grief clutched her again like some huge monster squeezing out her life.

Mother sat beside Clare's bed holding a limp hand while listening to the mantra of her lament. Never one to mince words, Mother spoke. "No, you can never go back to what it was before, Clare darling. Your family has lost Ashley, you do not have a history of fidelity to your husband, but you do have two wonderful sons and a husband that wants you back."

"Max can never forgive me now, mother. I'm an adulterer, a hypocrite, a runaway mother for the past year. I walked out on Max in anger accusing him of potential manslaughter when he told me the story of Lois. Now I am more guilty of neglecting Ashely than he is."

"Max has forgiven you; I know and so will God. Do you remember that beautiful verse from the prophet Isaiah? 'Though your sins are like scarlet, they shall be as white as snow; though they be red like crimson, they shall be as wool.' That's a powerful image, darling of how God can clean up our lives and make us whole again."

"Don't talk to me about God right now mother; just give me one of my sleeping pills please." Days stretched into weeks while Clare kept closeted in her room.

Then one afternoon when Max arrived, she was dressed and looking somewhat cheerful. "Take me for a walk, Max. I want to walk down by the river.

Clare had laced her arm through his pressing her body close. They strolled in silence for some time. "Max," Clare's voice was weak, "the trees are so beautiful, so green this time of the year, so full of life." The path sloped down toward the river at one point. Clare stopped to watch the water move slowly by brown circling eddies from miles of prairie travel. Max observed her stance, her mood. She's so pensive, so compliant, he thought. Not her usual feisty self yet.

"You must hate me, Max," she continued to watch the water and spoke in the same quiet voice.

"No, Clare. I don't hate you!" Max was emphatic!

"Look, what I have done to our family. Oh, you must be angry."

"Clare, the boys and I love you very much"

"Can you still forgive me?" She looked up now to focus on his face.

"Yes darling, I can. I have."

She turned toward him and clutched both his arms. "Max, I'm sorry, I'm really sorry. May I come home?"

"Absolutely, we are all waiting for you."

"It won't be easy, Max. You know that don't you?" Her eyes glistened, tears pooling in the corners as she studied his face. "You'll have to learn to trust me again. You'll have to look for ways to love me again. It's going to take time. Do you have that time, that patience, Max?"

Max took her hands and lifting them to his face kissed each one. "Clare, I'm sorry too. I'm sorry our love unraveled like this. I've waited this long for you to come home. I'll have the patience to help you back to good health. I really will.

"But what if I can't forget?" Clare tucked her face against his chest and Max pulled her close.

"Neither of us will ever forget, but we can put it in the past." He spoke into her hair kissing it as he continued. "We make mistakes, darling and then we have to move on and learn from what we have done wrong. I'll help you; you help me, and we'll need God's help. We'll need extra help."

"I'll come home tomorrow. Come take me home tomorrow."

"Why not right now?"

"Oh, Max, I'm so tired. I want to pack up some things. I'll be ready tomorrow. Come for me tomorrow." They continued their walk; a feeling of contentment having settled over both. Occasionally, Clare commented on a touch of beauty she observed along the trail.

I'll remember this walk for the rest of my life, Max thought.

But Clare never came home.

Max found her the next day stretched out on her bed in the same clothes she had walked in the day before. Her eyes were closed; her skin was cold to the touch and pallid in death. Her one arm hung beside the bed and an empty sleeping pill bottle laid on the floor. In her other hand between her thumb and fingers was a paper. Max took it away carefully. It was a church bulletin and on it were the words of a prayer. Max read the simple prayer and fell on his knees beside Clare. "Oh, Clare, Clare, if you could accept God's forgiveness why, could you not trust mine?"

Outrage and disappointment struck like sharp chest pains.

The memory of yesterday's walk, the satisfaction of Clare's wistfulness, her longing to come home and now the magnitude of defeat, emptiness, despair. "Yesterday I thought I had won you back. But I didn't make it to the finish, Clare. We didn't make it to the finish."

He hugged her still, cold body and wept.

The steadfast love of the Lord never ceases;
his mercies never come to an end;
they are new every morning.
Lamentations 3:22-23 (NRSV)

REFLECTIONS ON THE MARATHON

1. Did Max make the problem worse by postponing a confrontation with Clare?

2. What gave rise to Clare's infidelity? What causes infidelity in marriages?

3. Was it possible for Max and Clare to regain wholeness in the relationship?

4. How did each person Max talked to about his situation influence him to strengthen his resolve to not give up on Clare?

5. Can one understand Clare's suicide given her circumstances?

REQUIEM FOR A SUMMER HOLIDAY

B ob Harrison couldn't remember the last time he really enjoyed a summer vacation. He did not look forward to this one either. *How does an intelligent person explain the strange and illogical behavior of vacationers?* Bob ran his fingers through his greying, abundant hair. A flickering smile wrinkled the corners of his eyes. He recalled having similar feelings as a child at the end of school vacation – the exciting exit from the school doors, shouting, throwing books into the air that last day in June. But, six weeks later that excitement faded into dreary leisure and summer chores. As a child, he eagerly anticipated school opening, but never admitted it.

The past winter, Jan had been willed the family cottage. So excited, she talked about it constantly for weeks, telling the children about things she'd enjoyed there as a girl and what they could do at a cottage. Bob listened but had lingering fears.

He paused in tidying his desk to reflect on that conversation.

"I've heard about cottage life," Bob declared to Jan that winter evening as they enjoyed the warmth of the fireplace. "You just trade your place in the city for another, where you are faced with a year's maintenance to be done in two weeks. If you're lucky you might end up beside a lake."

"Oh, Bob, it's not that bad." Jan reached over to touch his arm, her voice cheery. "Sure, there are little things that need fixing, but there's also time to enjoy the beauty of nature, to relax and be with the children."

"Why do hundreds of people torture themselves yearly in the name of a vacation?"

"What do you mean, torture?" Jan's voice betrayed a touch of irritation. "Is that what you think about our holidays?"

Bob had glanced toward Jan, his blue eyes intense. "Remember the vacation we spent in a small tent while it rained for a week and you and I tried to keep two small children happy as we watched all our clothes and bedding get wet?" Jan's dark eyes softened as she smiled.

"Remember the year we travelled a few thousand kilometers in three weeks in a car without air conditioning and returned home suffering from heat rash, leg cramps and exhaustion?" Bob had delivered his complaints staccato-fashion.

Jan reached over and clasped his arm. "We saw a lot of beautiful countryside. Remember Tower Falls? We were both so impressed. How are we to see the beauty of God's creation without some travel? We were younger then. Live and learn! Now that we have the cottage we'll relax.

Bob resumed clearing his desk of the last nagging odds and ends before leaving. He was anticipating supper at home and a chance to pull himself together before leaving for the cottage the next morning. But, upon coming home, he was surprised to find Jan expected to leave as soon as he arrived. "Jan," Bob barked, "I was hoping for a little relaxing time here this evening!"

"The kids are so looking forward to it. I have things packed and a snack ready to eat in the car. We'll get there, have an evening swim and then have something more to eat later. That's the way Daddy and Mother used to do it." Her brown eyes shone as she kissed him briefly on the lips.

He got into his cut-offs and began loading the canoe. Placing his prized thermos coffee mug on the roof of the car, he fastened a tie-strap to one of the roof mounts. While standing on the edge of the car door opening, he reached to snug the strap on the mount and his hand slipped. He made a desperate grab with the other hand but, unbalanced as he was, he fell backward, clown-like at a circus. He sent the mug spinning as if part of the juggler's act; it clipped the top of the car door. Now it lay on the driveway. "Damn!" he roared in an outburst of pent-up rage.

Neighbours, preparing for their own weekend exodus, turned to stare. Jan rushed from the house. "What happened, Hon? Are you all right?"

Bob reached down to retrieve his dented, cherished cup. "Look!"

Jan broke into peals of laughter. "Come, I'll help you lift that canoe onto the racks." Bob's anger was spent, but somehow, he knew he was off to a poor start.

After a cooling swim and a snack, he and Jan sat out on the dock to watch the sun's crimson retreat behind the forest canopy. The children, chilled by their evening swim, were happy to be inside. These were delightful moments as Bob and Jan watched darkness gradually block out their vision of the lake. Stars emerged slowly and finally the swath of the Milky Way spread above them. Jan whispered, "'the heavens declare the glory of God...'"

"You seem to always have a Bible verse to quote." He reached over to place his hand on the arm of her chair.

"It's so true though, isn't it?" She placed her hand on top of his, her gaze fixed on the stars. "The beauty of that sunset over the water a while back, the sound of the waves lapping up against the dock are so … Here's another verse for you Bob, 'God has given all good things to enjoy.'"

He crawled into bed exhausted that first night.

The twitter of tree sparrows and then the chatter of a nearby squirrel called him from sleep late the next morning. Minutes later, the aroma of frying bacon and brewing coffee drifted down to the dock where Bob stood poised, hesitant to break the mirror-smooth surface of the lake. A school of minnows glided from beneath the dock into the sunlight that penetrated to the bottom of the still water, revealing every detail of the lake floor. Bob entered the enchantment of the water in a clean dive and propelled himself with smooth powerful strokes beneath the surface. When he reappeared, the face of the lake was wrinkled by ripples from his dive and a fresh morning breeze.

His heart quickened by the cool water and the exercise pumped energy into his muscles. He felt good. This could be a pleasant holiday after all.

At breakfast Jan placed her hand lovingly on his shoulder while pouring his second cup of coffee. "Hon, I think we will go pick some blueberries this morning before it gets too hot."

Bob's heart sank. "Jan let's sun and read on the dock this morning. Those blueberries will be there tomorrow."

"Not necessarily. I know how the McLeod family brings all their relatives out to pick. If we wait until they pick, there won't be many left. It may rain tomorrow. You know how we all love blueberries," her soft voice pleaded. "If we have a good morning, we'll have berries for desserts and pancakes for the rest of our stay," her smile compelling as she bent down and kissed his forehead.

"Jan, you and the kids go, I'll stay and read." As soon as he said it, he knew it was not a good option. They needed help securing the boat on shore at the end of the lake. They might meet up with a bear. But he had made up his mind. This was his vacation too.

He watched from the window as the three, dressed in long pants and long-sleeved shirts as protection from insects, took off in the boat.

Bob slathered himself in sunscreen, arranged a lounge chair on the dock and settled in to read. Two hours later he heard the sound of the boat approaching. He watched Bobby and Carolyn scramble onto the dock and lift out three pails. Jan secured the boat. Carolyn's knee was bandaged with Jan's bandana. "What happened to your leg, Honey?"

As if suddenly remembering the trauma of the event, Carolyn broke into tears. "I fell on the rock and hurt my leg. I spilled my bucket, so I only have half a pail. Mummy and Bobby got full pails."

Bobby couldn't contain his excitement. "Dad, the patch was sooo good. Just blueee with berries." Then on a more somber note, "I sat on an ant hill. Got some real nasty bites. Had to take my pants off to get all the ants out. Mummy helped." Then both he and Carolyn were off on the run to the cottage.

"Sounds as if you had a little drama," Bob said as they walked up to the cottage carrying the pails.

"We did. It was hot up there and the bugs were bad, but Bobby and Carolyn had so much fun climbing the rocks until they found a hollow covered with the low blueberry bushes. They picked and chatted happily."

"I had sweat running down my nose and back, flies buzzed around my face, mosquitoes bit the sweaty back of my hands, the air was stifling, without even a momentary cooling from a flutter of breeze; the sun was relentless." She looked at Bob to see if she had provoked a response. His face portrayed dismay. Then she continued, "But all around us shone the soft blue haze of blueberries."

"Why do you do it, Jan? What would it cost to buy this amount of berries?" He asked while placing the pails of berries on the counter.

"About forty-five dollars."

"I'll give you forty-five dollars next year."

For the first time since they arrived, Jan's voice took on a tone of irritation. "Bob, it's not about money. It's about the experience. In spite of a couple of mishaps, it was worth it! Didn't you hear the excitement in their voices just now as they talked about their morning? You didn't see the delight they expressed in seeing their pails fill or hear Carolyn's agony at losing some of hers? This is the beauty of vacationing with family." She stopped at that and started preparing lunch. Bob walked away, quiet.

The smooth rhythm of rain against the windows and the grey shadows of light held the family in sleep long beyond their regular waking hour that second morning. Bob stretched lazily and threw his arm over Jan. The clean, lemon smell of her freshly washed hair stirred him. Finding his hand, she snuggled a little closer. No sun tanning today, he thought, but none of Jan's missions either. He kissed her cheek gently.

After a relaxing breakfast, Bob settled himself into an easy chair to read, coffee cup close at hand; Jan and the kids were busy working on a puzzle. A day of promised rest, he concluded.

At first, he denied what he felt. But after several drops hit his neck and began to run down his back, a feeling of despair struck. Raising his eyes slowly to the ceiling he watched three large drops of water hang tenuously side by side. One rolled sideways, joined the other and fell toward his face. He sprang forward, banged the chair back against the wall and saw the droplet hit the floor.

"What's wrong, Darling?" Jan called from the table.

"Wrong? Only that the roof is leaking!" He now noticed water droplets hanging from a number of places.

Jan joined him in his observation. "Daddy was saying a year or so ago the roof at the cottage would need shingling soon."

Instead of a day of reading it was spent on a trip to the nearby town to purchase shingles and arrange for delivery. "Exactly what I thought about cottage life," Bob said, "work, work, always something to repair."

Sunshine returned the following day. Jan organized the children to help in rolling out felt paper and laying down shingles in preparation for the nailing. "A good learning experience," she cited several times. Bobby and Carolyn were delighted to be allowed on the low sloping roof.

Three days later, his back aching from bending and carrying bundles up the ladder onto the roof, his knuckles raw from the rough gravel on the shingles, one finger slightly bleeding from a cut received while finishing the chimney flashing, Bob climbed down exhausted to announce the roofing job was completed.

"Oh Honey, Daddy would have been so happy! He had been talking about shingling the roof for years!" Jan's lilting voice sang jubilantly as she planted a kiss on his cheek.

The following day was heavenly. Bob swam and lounged on the dock. Jan brought him cold drinks and rubbed his back with sunscreen without suggesting a project of any kind. Carolyn and Bobby played with neighbouring children. It was a perfectly relaxing day.

That evening, Bobby and Carolyn tucked into bed, Jan and he settled comfortably in their chairs. She, knowing there would be opposition suggesting a canoe trip into several of the neighbouring lakes the following day, added quickly, "Daddy promised to take the kids on such a trip for several summers, but it never happened," attempting to justify her suggestion.

Bob's generosity to her suggestions was over. "What's with you, Jan? You look at these two weeks as one exhausting adventure after another. Can't I have two days in a row to read?" His voice had risen higher and louder than he intended.

Jan folded her arms in front of her and rose from her chair, her eyes devoid of any sympathy. "Robert, you and I seem to have a very different idea of family vacation! Correct me if I'm wrong. For me, it is an opportunity to be together, to engage in some different experiences, allow the children to see and do things they can't do back in the city. That's what I am trying to create.

"Bob." Her voice took on a softer tone. "I know you enjoy your reading time. The children and I try to give you that in the evenings while we play games. You also get to do that in the evenings back in the city. Can you be with me here in creating some adventures for our children?" Now her eyes were moist, her arms relaxed as she sat down in her chair.

Bob, feeling somewhat chastised, tried at a rebuttal. "Maybe it's my turn to quote scripture. I recall from somewhere the verse 'The Sabbath was made for humans, not humans for the Sabbath.'" He then reopened his book at the place he had marked, sure the argument was settled.

"I believe the verse you quoted was Jesus claiming the Sabbath could be used for the benefit of humans, not just a legal day of rest," was Jan's rebuttal.

So, with a lunch box and paddles, life jackets, fishing rods and camera, they paddled down to the end of the lake to begin the first portage. Carolyn and Bobby managed all the loose items. He and Jan hoisted the canoe onto their shoulders for the first of three portages.

With the canoe stretched out over seventeen feet between them, they started the climb to the next lake; first up a steep incline and then down through dense trees for a kilometer. His back, still sore from hauling shingles, felt as if it would break. It was cooler amidst the trees, but the mosquitoes, seeing both hands occupied in carrying the canoe, took advantage to attack. Sweat poured off his nose, but Jan's cheery voice urged him on. "We're almost there, Hon; just around the next corner."

The day on the water was storybook perfect. The pines and spruce interlaced with birch and larch formed a beautiful perimeter framing the blue water.

Bobby and Carolyn howled with delight when they each caught fish. Two tur-tles sunned on a rock and further along two otters slid down a wet rock into the water, playing like children. Bobby spied a long sloping bedrock on which to draw up the canoe and upon which to eat their lunch. Jan had provided a variety of vegetable nibblers, chips, sandwiches and cookies. They arrived home that evening exhausted and full of wonderful memories.

A couple of glorious days, free from "adventures," followed. Then began the agony – the creeping agony of poison ivy itch. Four days it invaded shin and thigh, stomach and neck, hands and arms. "Why me and none of the rest of you?" Bob moaned.

Nurse practitioner, Jan, counselled, "You obviously are the one most aller-gic to poison ivy." She fussed over him and with the combined force of soap, lotions and pills, his itch slowly receded. He had learned how to sleep with the least amount of physical contact on the mattress.

The home bound traffic moved smoothly. Bob sat relaxed; the car was on cruise control. A cardboard sign at the highway shoulder announced, 'Blueber-ries for Sale.' Bob smiled.

The highway widened to four lanes and the traffic spaced itself. Jan sat with head back against the seat and eyes shut. Her dark hair framed the smooth, olive skin of her oval face. Her skin wrinkled slightly at the corners of her eyes. A slight perpetual smile played around her ample mouth, her full lips, glossed in light pink. Bob glanced into the mirror. Carolyn and Bobby were both fast asleep.

Checking his side mirror, he pulled into the left lane passing a truck tow-ing a large travel trailer. As he moved by, he noticed the tension lines etched on the driver's face. He doesn't look particularly happy, Bob thought. I wonder if he's coming home or leaving.

An evening thunder cloud darkened the sky ahead, droplets of water appeared on the windshield. The highway surface took on the shine of wet pavement.

Flashing red and blue lights ahead brought the lanes of home bound traf-fic to a crawl. Jan and the children sat upright, disturbed from their slumber by the sudden slowing. As they proceeded toward the flashing lights, they could see two vehicles down in the wide ditch. One vehicle lay on its side; the other had sustained front-end damages. A camping trailer lay on its side not far away. Clothing, bedding, toys and household items were strewn in the ditch.

A woman stood at the edge of the road, her shoulders hunched, her face buried in her hands. Police and another man were at the overturned car, working, it appeared, to release or help someone out of the vehicle.

Jan was out of the car in an instant with a "You stay with the kids, Bob." Grabbing her medical bag, she was on her way to the overturned car. Bob and the children watched a man and then a woman being lifted from the vehicle. Jan, it seemed, directed their placement on the ground then she bent over them. Bob assumed she was checking vitals, assessing injuries. Meanwhile, the police had taken out a boy and a girl, both carried to blankets spread out in the ditch.

The shrill of an approaching siren could now be heard. A group of people stood at the edge of the highway, observers to the drama below. The ambulance arrived, drove right down into the ditch, and stopped. It blocked Bob's view of the proceedings. More police had arrived and now worked to move traffic along. Bob moved his car onto the shoulder of the road.

Much later, Jan returned, her usually cheerful face now wearing the mask of tragedy. Tears flowed freely.

"What's wrong, Mum?" It was Carolyn's question.

"Oh, Honey," Jan reached back to caress the face of her daughter as if to assure herself Carolyn was there and safe. "The little girl down there is hurt badly." Snatching a tissue from the box on the dash, she dabbed her eyes and turned to caress the faces of both her children again. Leaning over toward Bob, she gently patted his leg.

The sun broke out from behind the retreating storm in a final burst of evening splendor. Miniature droplets of water on the grass beside the road sparkled like jewels; the wet pavement glowed golden in the sunlight. A huge rainbow arched across the western sky forming a common point with the highway where both met the horizon. As far as Bob could see ahead, cars drove toward the rainbow.

Bob Harrison swung his car into parking stall 12A, reached for his backpack and walked to the rear entrance of the office building. His associates, Cooper and Brown, met him as he waited for the elevator.

"Good to see you back!" Cooper greeted him with a slap on Bob's shoulder. "How was the vacation?"

Bob looked into Cooper's eyes remembering the mirror-smooth lake, the lunch on the sloping rock on a wilderness lake, the warm glow of sun on his back, the clean fragrance of his wife's hair, the laughter of the children at play. Then these images were replaced by Carolyn's cry of disappointment from the spilled berries, the irritating itch, the damaged cars in the ditch, the broken trailer and the injured family.

"Well?" Cooper coaxed as Bob remained silent.

Brown asked, "Where did you go?" The elevator doors opened, and the three men moved in.

"Bob here is one of the lucky guys that has a cottage now," Cooper volunteered.

"Better than staying home and painting the house," Brown laughed.

"Why is it we expect so much of a holiday?" Bob's tone was philosophical. "We plan all year for two weeks of supposed superlative experience. We save our money; we plan our summer around that slice of time; we talk about it endlessly and then…"

"You had a bad holiday!" Cooper interjects.

"No, on the contrary, I had a good holiday, but another family I witnessed ended up with their trailer destroyed, in the ditch, their car a write-off. Worse yet, their children were injured. We expect too much from our holidays, maybe of life."

The elevator came to a gentle stop at the second floor and the three men moved out. Cooper and Brown walked away to their desks shaking their heads in bewilderment at Harrison's rant.

Bob sat at his desk, pensive. *Holidays, like life, come with delights, discouragements, and with tragedy. I guess it's left up to us to know how to deal with each.* He booted his computer. Email lists a meter long scrolled down in front of him; a pile of notes, letters and requisitions were neatly stacked in anticipation of his return. The phone rang as if aware he was back.

"Hello, Hon, everything ok?" Bob listened as Jan told him the young girl was going to make it.

"Jan, I'm so happy to hear that. I know you did everything you could to help there yesterday." Bob was trying to imagine the emotions in that family today! "What an end to a summer holiday!" Both Bob and Jan were silent for a moment. Then Bob added, "And Hon, thank you for making our holiday a pleasant one."

"Oh, Bob, are you serious? I'm so happy to hear that. I was so sure you were disappointed…But I have an apology. I was too caught up in trying to recreate a childhood fantasy. Let's do it differently another year."

"Perception makes a difference, doesn't it?" Bob added.

A capable, intelligent and virtuous woman...
She is far more precious than jewels
and her value is far above rubies or pearls. (Proverbs 31:10 NRSV)

REFLECTIONS ON REQUIEM
FOR A SUMMER HOLIDAY

1. How are Bob's and Jan's perceptions of vacation indicative of their personalities?

2. How did Jan meet or not meet the qualifications of a virtuous woman as described in the biblical quotation?

3. How did this summer vacation reshape both Jan's and Bob's characters?

4. How is Bob's comparison of vacations and life accurate? Not accurate?

5. Reflect on memories, positive and negative, of your family vacations that surfaced as you read the story.

Made in the USA
Columbia, SC
23 November 2021